Y0-CVA-715

CIRCUS DIABOLIQUE

Carnival of Souls
Through the Mirror
Lost Souls

Crymsyn Hart

EROTIC ROMANCE

Siren Publishing, Inc.
www.SirenPublishing.com

A SIREN PUBLISHING BOOK
IMPRINT: Erotic Romance

CIRCUS DIABOLIQUE
Carnival of Souls
Through the Mirror
Lost Souls
Copyright © 2010 by Crymsyn Hart

ISBN-10: 1-60601-861-2
ISBN-13: 978-1-60601-861-3

First Printing: May 2010

Cover design by Jinger Heaston
All cover art and logo copyright © 2010 by Siren Publishing, Inc.

ALL RIGHTS RESERVED: This literary work may not be reproduced or transmitted in any form or by any means, including electronic or photographic reproduction, in whole or in part, without express written permission.

All characters and events in this book are fictitious. Any resemblance to actual persons living or dead is strictly coincidental.

Printed in the U.S.A.

PUBLISHER
Siren Publishing, Inc.
www.SirenPublishing.com

SIREN PUBLISHING *Allure*

Crymsyn Hart

CIRCUS
DIABOLIQUE

CARNIVAL OF SOULS

CARNIVAL OF SOULS

CRYMSYN HART
Copyright © 2010

Chapter One

Alexander stared at the double sliding doors that led into the library. A shiver of fear and intrigue moved through him when he thought of the night he and his brother had glimpsed at the demon in the circle of candles. It had been ten long years since that fateful night. He rubbed his neck absently where his father had tried to strangle him. Alexander remembered the power he felt from the monster whispering in his thoughts. He had desired that power for so very long.

Now was the day he and his brother were going to finally learn what their father had been doing all these years with the demon. Alexander gazed at the library floor strewn with books. Each volume was useful to an extent, but the one that held the power was the one their father kept under lock and key. It throbbed with energy, calling to him over all the years. Tonight the demon would be summoned.

"Are you ready, Alexander?"

"Yes, Father."

"Then enter the circle of your own free will." His father was dressed in a hooded ritual black robe. Salt and pepper hair littered his head. His dark green eyes held ages of wisdom. During certain ceremonies his eyes burned with green flames. He was solidly built, broad shouldered, and could still discipline his sons with a hard punch if he wished.

Alexander took in the surroundings of the library. Candles formed two large circles. One for the demon and another for the three men. The symbol on the floor had been freshly drawn. It was three Nordic runes fused together for protection and the other for a doorway. The curtains were open to let in the night air. The energy of the moon pulsated along his spine. His gaze fell on the picture of his mother painted years before they were born. Both brothers favored her. Alexander had her eyes whereas Donavan had their father's. They both had dark hair, but his was longer than his brother's and curled around his ears. Alexander had always liked his mane, allowing it to grow unruly when society dictated for it to be short. But what did he care about society? He was above them all. His family was among the wealthiest in the city.

Alexander gathered his red robe and stepped through the opening in the candles. His gaze swept over the pedestal to his right, which held the book and a large, silver dagger. The blade was the very same one used to draw blood at his initiation. Now he and Donavan were going to go through another phase in the process of becoming magicians.

"Are you ready, Donavan?" His father's voice echoed the question he asked his twin. His brother did not speak at first.

Brother, don't tell me you've backed out? Alexander whispered inside his twin's thoughts. *We made a pact.*

* * * *

Donavan met his eyes. How could he tell Alexander, his other half, he was not ready to give up his soul to a demon when he had dreams of the future? Alexander would think his dreams were only his worries about the initiation, but Donavan always had prophetic dreams even before apprenticing with his father. He had been able to sense ghosts while Alexander's abilities hadn't manifested until their initiation. Their mother was gifted. She used to speak of the phantoms she saw roaming the grounds or the strange lights floating the hallways at the midnight hours. Donavan had always believed it was his mother's unique talents that had spurred his father into the darker side of the occult. After her death, his obsession had driven him even further into the mysteries until he found the passages to summon the demon.

I know we made a pact, Alexander, but this is wrong. Horrible things will come of this if we go through with the ceremony.

You're just afraid. You've always been afraid I'll succeed in something you cannot, his brother retorted.

Donavan sighed. *You know that's not true. I don't want to see you get hurt or worse. Please.*

"Donavan, time is of the essence. Will you enter the circle or won't you? Choose now." Their father stepped away from the door to give his son room.

The eldest twin locked his gaze with his younger brother. Alexander had always been the more adventurous one. He had convinced Donavan joining with their father would be good for them. Donavan had to admit the allure of power was very tempting. It tugged on his insides. He feared his twin would be lost to the demon the way his father had become. Donavan stepped over the threshold of the library. In the pit of his soul, he knew he had sealed his fate.

Mother, forgive me. I do this to protect Alexander. Donavan stared at the picture of their mother and sent a silent prayer to her. Alexander beamed and slapped him on the back. His father proceeded to close the library doors and set three more lit candles onto the floor. Once the last candle connected to the wooden floor, a rush of air blew through the circle.

His father moved around the two of them to the pedestal. The dark power whispered deliciously against Donavan's mind to posses it. The evil in the text was beyond anything either brother had encountered before. He had ignored the pull for so long. Alexander had become intoxicated with it. What would happen once they had faced the demon?

* * * *

Their father caressed each page of the book lovingly.

"Iterim. Nocturne. Libris est mortum. Sine demoumus." Their father's chants echoed around the room. The atmosphere grew heavy and dark. The faint stench of rotten eggs crawled through the library. Each of the three men had gotten used to it with their dealings in the dark arts.

"You summoned me." In the circle, opposite them, appeared the same demon Alexander recalled from his childhood. The fear and intrigue of that fateful night had burned into his memories. Terror paralyzed him for a second when he stared into its red eyes. Then he remembered the demon was not going to escape the circle.

"I have called you from the depths of hell to present my sons to you so that you may grant them your wisdom and power."

The demon's flaming gaze swept over the twins. A devilish smile curled on its face, running ear to ear. Alexander felt its mind sifting through his thoughts, gleaning what he wanted. He did not fight the demon. This was one of the tests father had warned him about. If he was going to work with the beast, then the demon would have access to his most secret desires. The searing pain left him. He saw Donavan wince while the demon scrutinized him. He wondered if his brother would pass the test. Donavan had always been the weak one.

"Do they meet your standards?" their father asked.

The demon turned his gaze on the older man. "They pass, but the older one does not have his heart in it like the younger one. I like him best," the demon hissed.

Alexander's chest puffed up at the praise. He was going to be granted the power he had craved for so long. He stepped forward first and approached the demon.

"Hail, demon—" Alexander began.

"There's no need for the pleasantries of ritual. Even though I love to hear my name praised on mortal tongues, there will be a time for that later. For now, we must get down to business."

Alexander glanced at his father. The magician nodded.

Come to me, Alexander. Open your mind and show me what you wish of me. I can grant you everlasting life and power beyond your wildest dreams. Do you wish this?

The creature's power dipped into his mind. It snaked up his back and entered his loins, caressing him the way a lover would. Phantom lips enclosed his cock. He curled his fists into a ball trying to hold on to his sanity. God, it felt so good. His father had told him the demon would try something, but he never thought it would be so wonderful, so empowering. Already, the energy of the beast seeped into him and strengthened him. Everything came alive around him. Ghostly fingers caressed his buttocks and ran over his body. Did he want what the demon offered? Yes, no matter what the cost, he wanted it.

Very good. I can be there for you always. Pledge yourself to me. Give me your soul and what you feel now, I can give you a hundredfold. Swear to feed me souls and I will grant you eternal life.

The power of the demon pushed Alexander to the brink of orgasm. He managed a look at Donavan and noticed he was in the same state of aggravation, but his brother was not handling it very well.

* * * *

The demon had extended the same offer to Donavan. The power flooding him overwhelmed his senses. He wanted to fuck the first thing he saw with tits. He longed for release. Deep down, he understood that through the ecstatic torture the creature was getting its evil jollies off at the same time. It would have been so easy to slip into the pleasure and ride the waves.

Come now, Donavan. Your brother has accepted my offer. Won't you, too? You can only fight me for so long until you finally give in. Feed me souls and you'll share in the proposal I gave Alexander. Long life, fucking anything you want. I see the lust in your thoughts at all the lovelies you have screwed. You're an insatiable animal. I can be anything you want. I can be your wildest dream of a whore. I know everything there is about carnality.

The elder twin understood that on a logical level the demon was using its sexual hold to manipulate him. A moan escaped Donavan's lips. His hips bucked forward. He fell to his knees on the floor. All at once, his entire body was alight with pleasure. Spiders of ecstasy skittered across and through his flesh, tickling and caressing him all over. His mind screamed for him to give into the offer since he could not comprehend the end of such an experience. With the demon, he could have it whenever he wanted.

"Yes," he moaned.

Good. So very good. Now, Alexander, seal our bargain.

Donavan came to his senses enough to see Alexander holding the ritual dagger. The look on his face reminded him of their father. Crazed and obsessed. His eyes burned with two blue flames. He tried to reach out with his mind but found nothing more than a brick wall. He grabbed his brother's robe, but his brother whipped around and snarled at him. The face was not his brother's but the demon permeating his soul.

What have I done? What have we done? Donavan thought. Before he could do or think anything else, a wave of pleasure seized him, so intense that he convulsed on the floor and the pain of an orgasm overrode his consciousness.

You're both mine now. Watch and see the price for which you became my slaves.

Donavan was released for a split second to see Alexander raise a bloody dagger over his head bringing it down again into his father's back. Donavan cried out when he felt the full extent of the creature's power filter through him. It shattered his soul, remolding it into something so dark and twisted nothing was left of the brothers except being servants to the creature.

Chapter Two

Alexander ran his hands over his face trying to pull himself free from the memory of their initiation only a few months ago. Each day being paired with the demon, he and Donavan were discovering new experiences and treats. It had been a shame to kill their father, but he didn't serve the demon's purpose any longer. He gazed into the mirror before him studying the reflection. His dark brown hair was longer and his blue eyes glowed under heavy lashes. Stubble adorned his cheeks. *I might decide to grow a beard. It would distinguish me more from Donavan. It's getting colder and it's been a while since I've had one.*

They had plans to go to a traveling circus. The demon required souls, and tonight he hoped would satisfy their master. He grabbed his coat and headed out the door to meet Donavan. Together they rode to the outskirts of the city where the circus was set up. At once, the haunting sound of the calliope came to their ears. His twin brother yawned while they perused the sideshow.

"Bored, brother?" Alexander asked.

Donavan glanced at him. "Everyone knows that every carnival is the same. Freaks and sham psychics. I would think even the roars of the animals sound the same. I'm not one for death defying flips by the trapeze artists or how the sideshow freaks can contort this way or that."

"Then what do you like?" He paid their penny to enter the hall of mirrors. Screams of the other inhabitants echoed to them. All at once their images were reflected a dozen fold.

Donavan placed his hand on the glass. Instantly the image of a jester appeared before him. "I like the clowns actually. They watch the happenings all around them, but no one knows what's under their makeup. What are they truly hiding?" Alexander saw the image waiver, but not before it turned and smiled at them.

They made it through the mirror maze and then took their seats for the main event. The ringmaster appeared and announced the acrobats as world-class acts. The brothers watched the show and he feigned interest. The only thing he found exciting was the ring master.

"You spoke about liking the clowns. I like the ring master. He's always in the spotlight."

"Of course you would. You love being the center of attention. Come on. I'm tired of watching this. We have souls to find tonight." Donavan clapped him on the back and walked through the booths looking for someone to feed to their master.

Alexander stood and took in the crowd eying which one he intended to choose when he spied his twin talking to a lovely red head with a cupid face. He joined them. Donavan caressed her cheek and whispered something into her ear so she giggled. His brother gave him a look that only meant one thing.

"This is Sonia. She's one of the acrobats."

He lifted her hand and kissed her fingers until a giggle bubbled over her lips. Her cheeks reddened when he sent a trail of magick along her skin. Her eyes widened and he sensed the desire inside of her growing. He glanced at Donavan.

You mind giving this one up?

Not at all. I have my eye on the other little filly she was with. I'll meet you at the manor later, his twin answered. He winked and mixed in with the crowd.

"An acrobat. Wow, I bet you're very flexible." Alexander ran his hand over the top of her breasts.

"Only if I'm paid well for a private audience."

He laughed. "You'll be paid handsomely."

Alexander caught her mouth with his and plunged his tongue between her lips. He cupped her breast and squeezed the nipple through the thin fabric of her costume. She gasped when he kissed the side of her neck and pinched her ass before withdrawing. The demon stirred at the aroused passion pumping through Alexander now that he had gotten its attention.

"Ladies first." He gestured to the carriage.

They settled in and hurried back to the house. Once inside, Alexander led her into the master suite with its opulent bed. He leaned in and kissed Sonia, cupping the sides of her face while his fingers tangled in her red ringlets. She pressed herself against him so he could feel the contours of her voluptuous curves and round breasts. She tasted of spice and peppermint. Her fingers loosened the tie at his throat and then pulled his shirt from his trousers. Her free hand slid farther down and caressed his dick. Her warm hand hardened his cock, but the pleasure he began to feel from the demon hardened it more.

He pulled away from Sonia and tugged on her costume, hearing it rip. Her breasts broke free from the fabric. Lifting one to his mouth, he ran his tongue over the ridged nipple and bit down. She moaned and buried her hands in his hair. Alexander nipped along her breastbone sending small bolts of energy through her to keep her aroused. He lifted her skirt and pulled down her panties. His dick needed release. The demon demanded he take the girl.

Sonia lay back on the bed while he stripped and took in her pink folds. She gazed at him waiting for him to take her. He gripped her hips and sent a current of magick through her. She cried out and began to thrash on the bed.

"How can you be doing this?" she moaned.

"I can do so much more to you, pretty one," Alexander purred before kissing her.

Their tongues intertwined before he sunk his shaft deep inside her slick depths. Once he did, her pussy gripped him wonderfully. He instantly experienced her pleasure and the demon's. He tightened his hold on her hips and began to pump into her.

She began to writhe. He needed more time to come so he slowed, but only for a moment when a cold zing tumbled down his spine. Slow kisses wandered over his flesh from invisible mouths. He cried out and shivered from the pleasure assailing him. His cock tightened. Once more he plunged into her wet pussy and he came. He rested on top of her for a moment and then locked his lips to hers. Inside of him, the demon rose up and took control. Alexander felt the coldness of the demon's power ripple through him, reach inside the girl, and pull out her soul. After a moment, the demon retreated. He rolled off her and pulled on his pants.

She tasted wonderful, his master purred Sonia's eyes were lifeless and her expression frozen in ecstasy. There was a knock on the door. Donavan entered shirtless wearing a smug smile. Alexander sensed the enjoyment in his twin.

Come to me. The command overrode their thoughts.

The brothers gazed into the mirror at their master. The demon no longer sported wings or horns. The shape of its face had grown more angular over the past few months. Its eyes burned with deep red flames. A quiver of pleasure wound through Alexander that gave him a hard-on and left him poised on the verge of coming. Tickling fingers raced up his body.

I am bored with all of this, and I sense that you are, too.

The twins glanced at one another. It would not be good for them to lose favor. "What would you have us do?" Alexander asked.

We both crave something that will excite us. All the souls you've brought me have made me stronger than I've been in centuries, but I desire more. The more you bring me, the more of my power I can share with you.

The thought of more power made Alexander tingle inside. "What would we have to do?" A surge of power thrust his hips forward, but he did not ejaculate. The demon pulled the strings of his body making sure he was not going to come. He wanted him to suffer. "God. More. Please."

Only if you do one thing for me.

"Anything." Alexander's hips bucked again. He gritted his teeth against the pain in his dick. His cock never felt so engorged. The demon caressed the underside of his shaft with invisible fingers.

Build me a circus like the one we were at tonight. In it, construct a Mirror Maze for the sideshow where I can store the souls I want to feed upon. My domain is based on reflection and shadow. Do this for me, and whatever power you have now will grow tenfold. Will you do this for me?

Both brothers collapsed on the floor as the sensations overrode their brains. Alexander writhed on the carpet clutching the fabric in his fists.

"Yes." Alexander cried while his mind soared into a white space.

"We…will build it." Donavan echoed.

Very good, my pets. Very good. Now come for me. At that moment, the demon released its slaves.

Chapter Three

Countless years had passed since the twins had completed the circus to the demon's specifications. Now, just like every night before, Donavan finished applying the rest of his white makeup and donned his jester outfit. One side of the costume was emerald green and the other was white. His face was pasty white and green diamonds shaped his eyes. His lips were lined with green and his dark hair pulled back into a ponytail. Glancing in the mirror, he saw his reflection waver. For a moment, it wasn't him staring back but what the demon had made him into—a hollow echo of himself with eyes burning with deep green flames and a gaunt face.

It had been his idea to become the jester in the sideshow after they had completed it for their master. He led people through the show, playing tricks on them with magick, and showing them the sights. Alexander was the ringmaster and loved the attention. Donavan was the opposite. He was perfectly happy not being in the spotlight.

Over the years they had traversed the country gathering souls for the demon. Word spread to every town that they were coming and they had gathered a great reputation. No one suspected what the circus was really doing. Gathering souls for the demon. During all the years they'd been crisscrossing the states, Donavan had begun to stray from his demonic master. He didn't want the burden of claiming souls. The trysts he and his twin engaged in held no more thrill. The one thing he truly craved was a normal life away from the magick and the evil that now shared his soul.

His gaze graced the sleeping form of his new bride, Rachel. He had married her in secret on the hallowed ground of a church in front of a minister. So far he had not burst into flame and was able to share his vows with her. *Please, if you do look upon me even after all I've done, watch out for her. She's innocent in all of this. Please keep the demon's evil taint away from her. I don't know what I'd do if anything happened to Rachel.* He didn't dare utter or think the name of the Almighty in case the demon was listening. Rachel was too dear for him to risk anything ever happening to her.

A sense of joy rode through him. Whenever he looked at her, something inside of her tugged on his soul and made him remember his humanity. His brother thought he was having a fling with the new addition to their circus. She had come to them running away from her family. Rachel had chocolate brown hair and dark brown eyes. There was a link between them he could not deny. The way she begged him to stay moved his heart. First Donavan had her selling tickets to the sideshow and warned her to stay away from the maze of mirrors. During the first few months of her being there, he dared not approach her, but fantasized about her from afar. She grew more beautiful to him each day. His heart opened to her and he began to realize what he had been missing in his life. Love. Humanity. A warm human touch. Everything the demon had told him was a sham. He yearned to protect Rachel from the evils of the world, even if it was from himself.

Donavan kept a wall up around his thoughts so the demon and his brother would not catch the depths of his feelings. If there was any sign of defection, the demon would do something horrible to them. A sense of devotion swept over him looking at his new bride. Pride and anticipation of the life they could have together peppered his thoughts. He ran a hand along her soft cheek. She stirred in her sleep and murmured something unintelligible. The fluff of her hair on the pillow was a dark halo reminding him of his tarnished soul. *There has to be some hope for me yet. We married in a church. That must mean my soul is not completely evil. The Almighty must still favor me because he gave me you.* The more he stared at his new wife, the more aroused he got.

He leaned over and kissed the side of her cheek. His wife twitched and brushed her hand across her nose. Sneaking his fingers under the covers, he caressed her full breasts with the palm of his hand. He flicked his thumb over her nipple, which perked up instantly. With his other hand, he peeled away the bed coverings to expose her naked body to the air. His gaze swept her perfect form. Her hips were wide enough to grip, and her belly a little puckered. Her flesh was tinted pink. A deep stirring started in his loins.

Slithering between her legs, he skimmed his tongue along her nether lips, savoring her tangy taste. He loved all of her. Rachel moaned a little, but still slept. He flicked up to her hard node and nibbled. Her body quivered in response to his attention. A low groan escaped her lips. Her breathing intensified from the pleasure. He looked up. Her eyes were still closed, but he could tell by the subtle movement of her body and the power the demon had given him she was awake. To only prove his point more, his tongue slid lower curling around her pussy, tasting all of her. He spread her legs wider to get better access to her well and then plunged his tongue into her. That made her jump. She drew in a ragged breath that she let out in a long moan. Just the sound of that made his dick hard and he wanted to fuck her right there. The urge to ravage her came over him, but that part came from the demon.

The demon craved to use women up. Donavan had fucked countless women, slowly sucking out their souls at the same time. The demon shared his body at these times. Sometimes, with the demon at the helm, they could go for days in endless torture with the women begging for more while they didn't even know what happened to them. Donavan didn't want that for Rachel. He never wanted her to know about his curse, about the guilt that he felt for what he and his brother had been doing all these long years. Rachel was the angel that had come to him and given him the hope for redemption.

"Donavan, what are you doing?" she groaned.

He looked up and saw the wonderful agony on her face. Her expression made his heart skip a few beats. He reinforced the walls on his mind between him and the demon and his brother. "Just trying to wake you up, love. You looked so scrumptious lying there, and I couldn't leave you there until I had a taste."

He slid up her naked form, claiming her mouth with his own, marking his territory so that no one else would even try to possess her. His tongue parted her lips and delved inside so that she moaned into his mouth. Donavan's fingers wiggled deep inside of her wet depths. Rachel tried to arch her back, but his weight on top of her made it impossible. With a little twinge of his power, he made it so all of her flesh began to feel his hands on her in feather-light touches. She squirmed under him until finally he released her mouth. Her fingers wound in his hair and pulled him back down to her. Donavan laughed, feeling his brother pushing on the edges of his mind.

Go away!

Fuck her hard and good, brother. One day you'll have to let me taste her.

Rachel is mine, Alexander. Stay away from her. You've had your paramours, and she is mine.

Fine. Keep the bitch all to yourself. See if I care, but remember he may want her, too, and if that happens then nothing will stop what he will do. Take your time with her brother and fuck her until she drops dead. Use every ounce of her up.

Donavan did not respond, but strengthened the barrier between him and Alexander. It was wrong to stir up his magick. It would only bring the demon. Her moans brought him back to himself and away from any thought of his brother.

"Donavan." Her luminescent gaze filled his. Every time he stared into her eyes he found salvation.

"Shh, love. I'm here with you." He kissed down the side of her neck enjoying the vanilla taste of her flesh. Her hands moved to his shoulders and pushed him away. Concern filled his being. *Has she discovered something?* He could almost hear the echoing laughter of the demon in the back of his mind consuming him. Her gaze told him that there was something on her mind. The way that she took his hand separated his heart in two. "What is it, love? Did I hurt you? Has anyone—"

Rachel placed a hand over his mouth to silence him. "No, no. I'm fine. I wanted to tell you something."

Donavan looked at her quizzically. She blushed, taking her hand away from his mouth and brought it down to her flat stomach. A few heartbeats passed. "What is it, Rachel?"

"We're having a baby."

A bolt of shock went through Donavan. *Is it true? Is it really true? Can I have children? Has the Almighty redeemed me enough to grant me a child?* "Baby? Rachel, are you sure? Honey, but I thought that…"

Tears came to his eyes. He hadn't shed any in decades. A shadow of his cast off humanity overtook him. Emotion choked him up. Donavan gazed at Rachel still not sure of what to say or do. *Can I be a father and not let the demon know? Would he claim the child as a sacrifice?* Looking at his beautiful wife, none of that seemed important. All he could think about was that he was going to be a father and the ultimate joy that brought him.

"Donavan?" she expression darkened. "Do you not want us to have a child? I—"

"What? No. It's wonderful. You're wonderful. I never thought—It's a miracle." He lifted her up and spun her around in the small trailer. Laughter bubbled out of her lips and followed from his. He hugged her to him. Donavan kissed her. His hands ran the length of her, feeling every contour of her body. When his fingers settled on her stomach, he let the joy of the moment overwhelm him. For once the weight of all of his decisions vanished and he was just a normal man expecting a baby.

Chapter Four

Over the next few weeks, Donavan kept his news locked away in the darkest and furthermost point in his mind where his brother or the demon couldn't access. Ever since Rachel had told him the wondrous news, he had looked at her differently. Her beauty was enhanced tenfold. She glowed when she walked. Everyone noticed a change about her and treated her a little differently than they had before. Even Alexander had looked at her twice. With the passage of time, Donavan realized that once her ripening belly began to show the demon would know that Rachel was with child. *I won't let the demon harm my child. I have to find a way to keep them both safe. Even if it means sacrificing myself. If anything ever happens to them I would cease to exist.*

Donavan wracked his brain for all the dark magick that he knew, that he had been taught by the demon and that he and his brother had amassed over the years. He scoured the old texts. All of them were high, dark magick requiring a blood sacrifice. Donavan combined several of the spells and chose a night the demon was occupied with souls and his brother was ringleader of the sideshow.

Rachel was asleep. The moon was full. Donavan traveled deep into the nearby woods until he came to a small clearing. The power from the full moon and it being close to midnight were all that he needed. Donavan set up four candles in each of the four directions and then drew a circle of salt. He left an opening in the circle to step through. A knife was in the waistband of his pants. Once Donavan closed the circle, the candle wicks burst to life.

There's nothing to be afraid of. The night only holds wonders and nothing more. The line went through his thoughts. His mother used to tell him that before she died. *If only that were true.*

The power in the circle was building. Donavan smiled sadly. *Please take me. End my torment and protect them. Anything to keep them safe from harm.* He reached into his waistband, and pulled out the knife. In a quick motion, he brought the blade against his arms and sliced his flesh. The blood gushed onto the ground as he raised his arms to the night and stared at the moon, which now had a crimson caul over the silvery surface. The rays pressed down upon him.

"Oh, Great Darkness, I call to the ancient ones. Accept this sacrifice to protect my wife and child from the ones bound to me. Cover them in shadows. Bind them inside my heart and soul so no evil touches them. Grant me the serenity to know they will be safe from harm's way. Keep them from my brother, Alexander. Keep them from the dark one who haunts reflections and my soul.

"Take my blood to seal my pact. Take my soul and my life if need be. Keep Rachel and our child out of harm's way." A great gust of wind swept up inside the circle and knocked him to his knees. Invisible mouths latched onto the wounds he had sliced into his flesh. They lapped at the blood, sucking it from his body. Unseen forms cleaned up the spilt blood on the ground. The invisible spirits, the ancient gods who would keep Rachel safe, drained the life from him. Darkness played on the edge of his vision the more they took from him. *Yes, take my soul. Rid me of this existence to keep them safe. Anything to be free.*

Dawn's light caressed his face, warming him. He opened his eyes slowly to see the candles were stubs. The salt scattered by the wind. There was now a black ring in the grass where he had cast the circle. Birds chirped overhead. Squirrels chattered in the branches fighting over nuts. Donavan got up slowly. The wounds on his arms were an angry red. He looked at the debris, whispered an incantation, and everything from his ritual burst into flame.

Donavan made his way slowly back to the sideshow. When he passed the mirror maze, he shuddered. A pang of sorrow hit his heart when he heard the screams of the trapped souls inside. Alexander sat on the steps of the trailer waiting for him.

"Where did you run off to last night? We were summoned."

Donavan blanched. *If I didn't hear the demon's call, then that must mean it hadn't sensed Rachel.* That gave him hope, but he had to play it off that he was not concerned. "I wasn't aware. I needed to be by myself last night."

Alexander gave him a half-smile. "Really? The stir of magick was in the air last night. I sensed it was connected to you. When I reached out, there was emptiness. I was worried that something had happened to you." Alexander leaped off the steps and tackled him. "Don't you ever do anything without me again. Do you understand?" he growled.

Donavan laughed. "Why? So you can be in its favor for the rest of eternity? Remember what we used to be, brother. We used to have morals. Don't you ever feel guilt for killing our father?"

For the first time, Donavan saw a flash of true emotion go across his brother's face. Alexander was hiding behind a façade. "The past doesn't matter. Only the present, Donavan. You—" He looked around and lowered his voice. "You must be careful. He knows about you and Rachel. He knows you're married. He's only letting you have your fun because when he calls for her soul he expects that you will do the right thing and give her to him."

Fear chilled Donavan's heart. *The demon knows! How is that possible? How could I have been so careless? Did I let my guard down?* He kept his mind blank. "So what if he knows. She's mine. He'll never lay a hand on her."

Alexander's grin widened, contorting into a twisted smile that was beyond the scope of a human face. His eyes burned. Donavan saw the outline of his skull. This wasn't his brother. It was the demon. A long forked tongue licked the side of Donavan's face. A sudden quake of ecstasy seized him. His brother's features melted away only to reveal the demon standing before him. Wherever Alexander was, he was not present. The demon had someone gotten free of the mirrors and taken on human form. "But you forget, Donavan. Everything that you are, I am, too. You are not free of me. Did you really think I was going to let you have your pretty little wife and play human without asking for my dues? You pledged your eternal servitude to me. You gave me everything that you were. That includes everything you own or covet. Rachel is sweet. I've been there in the corner of your mind when you fuck her. I've enjoyed every minute of it." He drew Donavan close. Once the demon touched Donavan, he was under his power.

The demon kissed his cheek. A shiver of delight moved through Donavan. The demon could punish him for keeping Rachel from it and Donavan feared that, but at this moment, that terror was driven away by the demon's overwhelming lust. Donavan's cock stirred under its power. The jester smiled, showing him pointed teeth and green burning eyes. It ran its hand over Donavan's shaft. A shiver of pleasure marched up his spine. His eyes fluttered shut from the caress. He cared about nothing else, but that was the demon's power.

It rubbed his cock through his pants. Donavan grew harder and harder while the demon enticed him. The smile didn't leave its face. It worked him faster and faster until he was on the brink of release. Then it stopped. The demon trapped him in a loop of sensation. It backed away, crossing its arms over its chest and watched Donavan suspended with need and wanting. Phantom hands caressed his length. A wet mouth took him in, teasing him, playing with him. The demon held his body immobile as it mind-fucked him, plunging his whole body into an orgasmic circle, but right when he was about to come, it started all over again.

The demon walked around Donavan. Donavan grated his teeth against the moans building in his throat. The demon wanted him to break down. *You can't have me anymore. Rachel is all I want.* The jester kissed Donavan, parting his lips, snaking his tongue into his mouth. Donavan hated that he responded to the demonic power, but he had no choice. Finally, the joker pulled away.

"You really love this little filly of yours?"

"Yes," Donavan forced out.

The demon tapped a finger on its cheek. "It seems we have a little bit of a dilemma on our hands. Alexander thinks that you should let the both of us fuck the bitch, but I can have whatever pussy that I want. Screwing your wife isn't going to satisfy me. I know you don't want me to have any part of her because she's so sweet and innocent. Do you know how many bitches put on the naive act and then fuck you over in the end? Donavan, Donavan. What we have is so much better than what Rachel can give you. Yeah, she can give you free pussy, but what I offer is so much better. I offer you power. Alexander knows the meaning of that. He's been ever so cooperative in giving me whatever I desire. Why can't you do the same? Are you unhappy with our arrangement?"

"You can't have her. She knows nothing about you. I haven't told her anything."

The demon shrugged. "I wouldn't give a shit if you told her I was the Second Coming of Christ. What really pisses me off is that you're keeping me from her. I want to taste her, Donavan, and I want to be with you when I do it. I can easily appear to her and fuck her while you watch, but I assume that you still want her body intact when I'm done with her."

"Please, I'll do anything. Leave her be." A tear slipped from his eye. *Please, God. I don't know what else to do.* The orgasmic fugue he had been in was growing painful. His hips thrust forward against his will, but he couldn't release.

The demon sighed and threw up his hands. "Oh, Donavan. I have such a soft spot for you and your brother. What am I going to do with you? How about this? Tell me what the hell you did last night. What did you conjure? I won't kill your precious wife. I can easily take away everything I have bestowed upon you. Is that what you want?"

The power that had animated Donavan's body collapsed around him. He dropped to his knees feeling empty. A great agony crept over his entire body. He stared at his hands. They shriveled before his eyes. Clumps of hair fell onto the ground. The flesh on his face shrunk over his bones. All the power and immortality the demon had given him was pulled from his soul. He glanced up at Alexander who now stood beside their master. He appeared unchanged. Donavan stared at his hands. Age spots and wrinkles had appeared. He ran his hands over his face, feeling the drooping jowls. He had no hair left and his clothes barely fit him.

The demon knelt down beside him. "Do you enjoy this new existence, Donavan? This is what you would look like if I hadn't given you and your brother my favor. Granted, you're still alive in your human lifetime, but image what it would be in, say, another fifty years. You'd be dust and bone by now. I can give you back everything I took away from you, but you have to be good to me. You have to tell me what you did last night. Do you want your power back?"

Rachel will never accept me this way. She'll run screaming from this horrid old man. I've never been so weak and so alone. But I can't go back. With this I'm free of the demon's wrath. But then Rachel will be his. I can't leave her to his whim. I have to protect her no matter if it means condemning myself to eternal servitude. Forgive me, my love. "Yes."

"What did you say?"

"Please."

"Oh, no. I want more than that. Tell me, what were you doing last night? Why are you protecting your beloved from me?" The demon wrapped his bony fingers around his throat and squeezed.

The demon hoisted Donavan up with little effort dangling him a few inches off the ground. His hands grasped the joker's, but he wasn't able to pry the fingers off his throat. Donavan heard a snap. He had broken one of the demon's fingers. Green fire ignited inside the demon's eyes. The energy moved down his hand, swallowing Donavan inside of its cold light. Donavan felt the power start to pull on him from the inside. Pain erupted inside his chest. Donavan screamed.

"Alexander, help me please!"

"Now, now. Alexander can't help you right now. He's taking care of something for me on the other side of the circus. He agrees with me though that you've been a bad boy. You taste so good. You would make such an excellent addition to the carnival. How about we make you into one of the sideshow acts?"

"No. Anything. I'm sorry. I beg you."

"Begging is good. Now what did you do last night?"

Defeat washed over Donavan. Alexander had turned his back on him. He couldn't break the demon's hold. He had no other choice if he ever wanted to see his wife again.

The pain vanished, but the demon was in his mind. It would know if he was lying. "I performed a spell to protect Rachel from you. I didn't want you to have her. I just wanted a little slice of my life to be mine. Please!"

The demon smiled a toothy grin and dropped Donavan. He hit the dirt hard and heard his ankle snap. "You've been a good boy. It's so much easier when you obey me. I'll give you the little slut. But each time you fuck her, I get a taste of her. Every instance when you hold and caress her, I'll be there with you. You can't block me out. I made you into what you are. Remember that."

Donavan sobbed into his cupped hands. There was no use. Everything he had hoped to have would never come to fruition. He was alone in the world and now, because of his weakness, it would have Rachel, too. "Yes."

The demon patted him on the head. "Good boy. Now come here and kiss me to show there's no hard feelings. We can't have you going back to your wife looking the way you do."

Donavan got up slowly, trying to balance and think through the pain of his broken ankle. The jester leered at him. The demon's skull was bone white with a few wisps of hair clinging to it. Green embers burned in its eye sockets and the grin he was used to, painted his mouth. The scents of decay and mildew clung to his brother as Donavan met the demon's lips. Instantly, the demon clasped Donavan to him, pulling in all the air from his lungs. Its tongue snaked in between his lips. Green light erupted behind his eyes. The energy infused every part of his being. He felt the itching of his hair regrowing. His ankle knitted itself back together. The demon continued to kiss him and run its hand along the bulge in his pants. Donavan had the sudden urge to fuck anything that came at him. The demon smiled.

You know who I want, don't you? It whispered in his mind.
Yes.
And you'll give her to me of your own free will.
Yes. Please don't hurt her. He hung his head in defeat.
I wouldn't do that. She's precious to you, so she's precious to me. I only want a little taste of her.

When he opened his eyes, the demon had vanished. His brother stood on the other side of the clearing by the wagons near the circus tent. The look in Alexander's eyes was one of pity.

"Why, brother? Why would you tell him?" Donavan asked, crossing the space to his brother, wondering what he had been doing while their master was punishing him.

"Nothing is safe from the demon. You knew that when you made a pact with it. He would have found out. Besides, I knew you would do the right thing and let him have Rachel. For a minute, I thought I had lost you."

Donavan closed his fist and punched his brother. The impact against Alexander's cheekbone split his knuckles. Rage seethed through Donavan. His brother didn't even remember what it was like to be human. "You don't give a shit about me. All you care about is placating our demonic master. You're the one who likes to be fucked by it all the time. At least I have a wife who loves me, to make me remember how it feels to love."

Alexander smiled, catching the blood on his lip with the corner of his tongue. "Think whatever you want. It's better to give him anything he wants than to try and fight him."

"One day, brother, you'll know love. When that day comes, you will rue the day you ever made a pact with the jester. Mark my words."

Chapter Five

During the months of Rachel's pregnancy, the jester had come into his body sharing his lovemaking with his wife, bringing their intimate moments to something darker and more depraved, but his wife never complained. He regretted every moment of the demon tainting the sanctity of his marriage, but he was too afraid of what it would do to him and his wife if he did not obey. However, the demon kept his word and didn't lay a finger on her. Finally, she gave birth and he was overjoyed. Seeing the infant had made his heart soar above the clutches of the demon. Now he would do anything to protect them.

Donavan stared at the picture of himself and his family. It had been taken only a couple of days ago in front of the circus tent. He placed it on the mirror inside his wagon. Then he turned his gaze to the tiny form in his wife's arms. Both of them were sleeping. He had a child. A son. He still couldn't believe it. The spell had worked. The demon still didn't see the child. Donavan wasn't sure how long the spell would last, though.

Donavan ran a finger over the smooth, pink skin of the newborn. A crown of dark hair poked out from underneath a bonnet. The baby's flesh was so warm. So alive. They had named him Jonathon after his father. Pride surged through him. *I'm a father.* There was nothing that anyone could do to them. He prayed the ancient gods would protect his son long enough that he could find his own way in the world and never know anything about the creatures that lurked in the darkness.

Donavan leaned over, brushing his lips on the baby's forehead and then on his wife's lips. Rachel stirred from the soft gesture. Her eyes fluttered open. She gave him a warm, sleepy smile.

"I didn't mean to wake you," Donavan whispered.

"It's okay."

"How are you?"

Rachel's gaze darted to the baby. She placed a hand on his cheek. Donavan grew worried when he saw her concern. "There's something we must discuss."

"Do you wish me to quit the sideshow? Whatever it is—"

She put a hand over his mouth to silence him. "No, Donavan. I know it would kill you to part from your brother. I also know that it would be impossible for you to leave. Ever."

His eyes widened. *Rachel knows.* "Whatever do you mean?"

She hugged the baby closer. For the first time Donavan saw fear in his wife's eyes. "I know about the creature in the mirror."

The warmth was stolen from his body. The demon stirred in the darkness. However, they had restocked the Hall of Mirrors with more souls so the jester should remain occupied for a few more days. He hadn't wanted the creature to be tempted by the innocent soul of the infant.

"You can't know anything about it."

"But I do. I know what it is. It told me what you and Alexander do for it. I know about the Mirror Maze. I know everything."

He grabbed her shoulders. "When? How? I've done everything I could to keep it from you and away from the baby."

"The night after I told you that I was pregnant, you came back inside and you were not yourself. I could see something with you. All these months that we've been making love, it's been with you."

"Has the demon hurt you?"

"No, love. But it speaks to me. I see its green, fiery eyes burning behind mine when I go to sleep. He whispers to me in my dreams. I've felt it touching me."

Fury and grief clutched his soul. *It's my fault that the demon latched onto Rachel. I let it win. I was too weak of a man to give up its power.* "I'm so sorry, Rachel. I've tried to keep it from you. I performed magick to hide you and our child, but the spell only blankets our son. The demon withdrew his power from me and left me to rot. I couldn't stand it. I was so alone, so powerless. I had to give in to it. It's been a part of me so long. I—"

"I know. It showed me exactly what it's done to you. It knows about the baby. The spell you wove didn't work. It wants me to join you and Alexander."

He grabbed her shoulders and implored her to understand. "No. You must never give in to the demon. You must never sacrifice your soul to it. All it wants is power. It will consume you. Only evil can come of the union between you and the demon. I would die before I let that happen. You and our son are the only things that matter to me now. I do my master's bidding, but you are the most important thing in my life. You're the other half of my soul. God gave you to me so I could be redeemed."

"It will save our son." Donavan saw the pleading in Rachel's eyes.

"No, Rachel. It says that, but it only wants you to give into it. I will take care of this. Don't leave the wagon. Don't let it inside your mind."

Donavan ran out of the door, ignoring his wife's cries. Fury tinged his vision. Donavan could live with it having his soul and his brother's because they had foolishly bound themselves to the joker. They were the ones who should be paying the price. The evil should have been contained in the mirrors, to them, to the souls that the demon fed on, but not to his family. He was not going to curse his wife and his son to an eternity of hell.

Darkness loomed on the horizon like a hideous wraith coming to capture the whole sideshow. Everywhere Donavan looked he saw the green tinge of the demon's power. It was the first time he noticed that another realm hovered over the sideshow. Where there was an empty space, he saw the wavering form of a building outlined in green. When he focused, it solidified in his mind's eyes. One building was a small stage. He saw a skeletal creature with a top hat pointing over to another figure lying next to it. Donavan walked closer to the ghostly platform. The figure was a naked woman, but her bottom half was that of a reptile. The skeleton gave him a toothy grin and bowed. Donavan felt a shiver caress his spine. He nodded at the skeleton. It would do no good to anger the spirit when it was probably under the control of the demon. Donavan backed away. The fury in him had subsided a little. The demon was getting more powerful than he had thought originally. They had been feeding it souls now for decades and sharing its power. Donavan now suspected the creature had been holding back on them. It was changing and shaping the world around it into a realm that only the demon could enjoy.

The energy he felt coursing through him gathered between his palms. It crackled in the night. He gritted his teeth, squelching the power. Seeing this new world gave Donavan a different perspective. *Soon he won't need us at all.* Donavan looked behind him, glancing at his wagon. There was a glow there, too, but it wasn't as severe as the other attractions in the sideshow. His eyes drifted toward the Mirror Maze. It pulsated with green energy. *Why hadn't I noticed this before? Why hadn't I seen what the demon was doing?* He shook his head and walked over to Alexander's wagon.

He barged in knowing that it was time to have a serious conversation with Alexander. Inside, his brother was getting dressed for the night. His dark hair was tied back in a ponytail. Even now, their performers in the sideshow had trouble distinguishing them from one another.

"What do you want, Donavan?" Alexander scowled.

"We have to talk."

Donavan watched Alexander's reflection. He stretched his mind out and sensed his twin's thoughts. It was only him sitting in the chair and not the both of them. He sighed and sat down on the bed, pushing some clothes aside.

"What is it that *we* have to talk about?"

"The demon."

Alexander threw up his hands. "We've had this discussion before. You can't break your servitude to it. You saw what it did to you last time. Would you rather it to do something worse?"

Donavan waved his hand. "I'm not talking about breaking our oath. More likely I think the demon might be thinking about breaking its ties with us. Have you seen the carnival lately? There's another one underneath it of his own making."

"What are you talking about?"

"Just look outside. Look at the Hall of Mirrors. You can see the power pulsating off it. We've given the demon so many souls that it has its own sideshow going on without us. He's trying to break free. He's even trying to get to Rachel. He knows about my son." Donavan dropped his voice to a whisper. A lump of emotion choked him off.

"Your son? When did Rachel have a child?"

Donavan realized then that the magick that he had performed so many months ago had blocked the child from Alexander's view. What good was the magick that he had performed now? The demon already knew about the infant. Donavan hung his head in his hands and telegraphed the images of Rachel's pregnancy and the birth to his brother. Once he did that, Donavan felt something snap inside of him.

"Well that explains the blind spot I've been seeing every time I look at you and her. I knew something was missing. Congratulations. We should celebrate."

"What is there to commemorate if the demon desires Rachel and my son? What are we going to do?"

His brother sat down next to him. "We will do nothing. I'll see if he will let Rachel go. He's been showing me things he wants to do with her. He is quite infatuated with her. He is furious that you give her all of your attention. I understand you cherish her and the child. I have grown to love her as if she were my own sister. But she *is* human. She will die eventually. We will not."

"We are still human, too. Or have you forgotten that?"

Alexander stared at him with intense blue eyes. "We are no longer mortal. You might have gazed upon the carnival and seen the other world the demon has created, but have you gazed at your true reflection of late?"

Donavan looked at the mirror. "There's nothing different."

"Look again, brother." Alexander waved his hand over the glass. Donavan felt a pulsation of energy pass through the both of them. The candle light dimmed. When he stared at his twin, a gasp escaped his lips. What he saw in the mirror was not his brother any longer. It was something else. Instead of Alexander's face there was a blank skull staring back at him with hollow eyes. Inside the eye sockets burned bright blue flames. Donavan switched his gaze to himself. His eyes were sunken into his flesh. His skin was pale white and tearing away from the bone. His hair was almost gone, only hanging in splotches on his head. His eyes were empty with only green flames staring back at him. When he smiled, all his teeth were sharp. He touched his face seeing his fingers were only bony knobs with no more flesh on them. He was rotting away.

"What has it done to us?"

Alexander waved his hand. The mirror rippled and their normal reflections stared back at them. "It's making us into its image. We've given it our souls and it is fashioning us to be just like it. Haven't you noticed the increase in our power? Haven't you noticed that you can do things without the aid of the demon? Whatever magick it gave us in the first place, we have burned through it. Sure, we can draw on its power, but we have become something akin to it. We have taken in so much of its essence I don't think it even realizes how much we are a part of one another."

"Then we have to do something about it before it gets too strong. Before it breaks free of the carnival. Before it consumes Rachel."

"There's nothing that we can do."

"We can destroy the Mirror Maze. There has to be something in the book we summoned him from."

"We won't do anything."

"You'll just sit here and let that thing consume you! How is that?"

Donavan felt his brother's anger rage through his mind. His twin stood up. "I have accepted my fate. I thrive on the power the demon has given me. I revel in it, just as you should."

The fury burning within Donavan erupted. He focused it into a large ball and hit Alexander square in the chest. The energy bolt slammed him back into the mirror, cracking it and knocking him out. The only way to be rid of the demon was to destroy the Mirror Maze. Once it was depleted of souls, it would have no more power. Then he would use the book they had summoned it with and banish the jester back to hell where the thing belonged. He stormed out of the wagon and headed toward the Hall of Mirrors. The stench of rotting flesh around the Mirror Maze was overpowering. He had never noticed it before, not until now.

He took the steps two at a time and entered the realm of the demon. He and Alexander had painstakingly fashioned the mirrors to the demon's specifications. Each mirror was a gateway to the demon's domain, a one-way doorway. Once the person stepped through, they couldn't get back. There was only one mirror in the maze that was a two-way door for the demon to travel back and forth through. Donavan knew that he had great power at his touch. He could heal if he chose to. He had healed Rachel after the baby.

Inside he sensed the darkness of the demon. It was feasting. The first hallway of mirrors wouldn't look out of the ordinary to a human, but when he wound around to the second hallway, he saw all the souls that were trapped inside the mirrors. The people pressed against the mirrors staring out at him. Some pounded on the glass begging to be released. Others had given up hope and were crouched on the floor of their cell already dead or mad. The energy in Donavan's fists crackled.

He placed his hand over one of the helpless victims, the glass separating them. The soul stared at him. Its body had died years ago. It was in storage waiting for the demon to either consume it or use it in the ghostly sideshow. *Forgive me. I'm so sorry. If I had known this was the sum of my life, I never would have gone through with it. If I could give you back your life I would. The only thing I can do now is free you from this torment. I swear I will try.* Pulling the energy from deep inside of him, Donavan let it loose upon the mirrors. A green bolt shot from his palm. It hit the mirror. The soul's eyes widened and its lips formed into a scream. It covered its face waiting for the glass to explode. The magick of the mirror hit him. The barrier created to protect the mirrors was like hitting his hand against a brick wall. He redoubled his concentration, pouring his will into shattering the mirror. A minute crack appeared on the glass. Sweat beaded on Donavan's forehead. He channeled his power, reached out to link with his brother and pulled on Alexander's reserves also.

When the extra power hit him, Donavan opened his other hand and shot the extra energy toward another mirror. The cracked mirror splintered. The glass exploded into dust. The soul inside breathed a sigh of relief and then disappeared. Donavan felt its gratitude and peacefulness when it winked out, going wherever it was that free souls went after they died. Once that mirror cracked, the barrier of magick around the other mirrors collapsed. A second mirror shattered. He smiled, walking down the hall and releasing the souls bound in the glass one by one.

The power he had pulled from his brother left him. Alexander had woken up. The full force of his brother's power hit his mind. He staggered. Never before had his twin fought against him. Donavan wondered if the demon had been waiting for the brothers to annihilate one another, squabbling over power. That had never happened until now.

Alexander, you will not win this. This place must be destroyed. We must be freed of the evil that has taken over our lives.

Would you give up everything that you have, Donavan? Would you sacrifice your wife and son? Would you have the demon leave you a decrepit old man?

I'll do whatever it takes to free them. I'll go to her an old man and live out my days if she accepts me. I don't care. God, forgive me. I don't care anymore. My soul will go to hell, but I can't live with this bloodshed on my hands anymore. No more innocent people will die.

He smashed another mirror.

I would stop doing that if I were you.

A blur of green appeared in the mirror before Donavan. He stopped listening to the tinkling glass and watched the image before him grow clearer until the demon was standing before him, in its jester guise. What skin it had was gray and peeling off its bones. Strings of hair clung to its balding head. A leering, red grin curled the corners of its mouth up. It was dressed in a green and white harlequin suit. Tarnished brass bells lined the front of the suit where the buttons should have been. It even had on curly shoes to match its outfit.

"Why would I want to stop? You deserve to go back to where you came from. Alexander and I should never have bound ourselves to you. The power isn't worth it."

The joker scowled. He wagged his finger at Donavan, scolding him. *Tsk, tsk, Donavan. You, of all people, should know what your life will be without my power. You would be nothing.*

"I'd rather be nothing than bow to you any longer. You had no right to reveal yourself to Rachel. You will not take her!"

The demon pressed his hand against the glass. Very slowly the demon tested the barrier of the magick. His hand popped through into the real world. He backed up a step when the demon pressed his face against the glass.

"How are you doing this?" Donavan asked.

It was easy once I had enough souls. Enough power. All thanks to you. Alexander has been such a wonderful enjoyment. He'll continue to be my faithful servant, but you, Donavan, have been such a disappointment. I had such high hopes for you. Your lovely wife is a good fuck. She's called for me in the night when you weren't there. Did you know that she desires me over you?

"Shut up!" Donavan drew back his hand to release a bolt of energy.

The demon waved his hand and Donavan was paralyzed. Heavy footfalls sounded in the hall of mirrors. Alexander was behind him. The bond between the two brothers sparked to life. He felt Alexander's surprise seeing the jester before him. Stunned, Alexander sank to his knees before the demon. Donavan felt his brother's sense of awe and fear. Disgust from seeing his brother bowing at the things feet shook his soul. After this was over, he would never call Alexander brother again.

Get up, Alexander. You don't have to bow to me. You and I have always had a good understanding of each other. You *have been loyal. Your brother, on the other hand, is really starting to piss me off. I know you care for him since you're blood and all, but I'm afraid I'll have to sacrifice him.*

"Whatever you wish, but I ask that you give him one more chance to see the error of his ways."

Donavan couldn't move or even speak. The demon had cut him off completely. He sensed the demon contemplating what Alexander had said. The demon walked toward him, now completely free of its dimension. It placed a finger underneath Donavan's chin, jabbing the bony knob hard into his flesh. The demon's other hand rubbed his crotch. Donavan felt his cock stir under the touch of the demon. The jester smiled.

We've had such fun together. It really would be a shame to let you go. Alexander loves you so. Don't you love me anymore?

The demon released some of its hold over him, allowing him to speak. "Go to hell."

The jester cocked his head so that it fell onto his shoulder. Donavan heard the sickly crack of breaking bones. *Been there. Done that. Not going to happen again. You've given me so much here I have my own little reality going on. Did you really think that by destroying a few pitiful mirrors that you could dent my power? I've grown beyond the mirrors. I'll give you one more chance to get back into my good graces.* The thing zapped Donavan with a charge so hard that he screamed in pain and sank down to his knees.

Alexander, what do you think is punishment enough for your brother to make him see reason again? He's too used to pain. He enjoys it too much.

"I could not begin to—"

Donavan's gaze switched to his brother. Alexander now stared at him with a defeated look on his face. *I'm sorry.*

Donavan tried to figure out what the demon was going to do. Then he heard the screams. Horror washed over him when he heard the numerous cries. The shrill screams of animals and people blended with the sound of heavy footfalls. Something horrible was going on outside.

"What are you doing to all those people?"

The demon giggled. Its crooked smile grew even wider. It shrugged its whole body and its head went back to sitting on its neck again. He waved his hand over an untouched mirror. Slowly the scene outside came into view. The circus tent was burning. Terror filled Donavan as he watched the fire engulfing the tent. It had spread to half of it. People were running out from the entrance. Inside he saw the stands were going up with the flames, consuming anything in their path. Some of the horses had escaped along with some of the other exotic animals, but there were others in there that were trapped and burning to death.

"I think you should let him go now, Master." Donavan glanced over at Alexander who didn't meet the demon's eyes.

The demon waved his hand. The power holding him captive evaporated. *I would go check on your wife, Donavan.*

His whole body froze as he got to his feet. The demon wouldn't. Alexander knew how much his family meant to him. His twin looked up and met his gaze. He saw the truth there. Rachel was inside the tent. Donavan raced out of the Hall of Mirrors.

Outside, the sideshow crew was trying to put the fire out, but they didn't have enough water. Donavan rushed to his wagon across the lot and found it empty. The heat generated from the fire would eat up anything in its path. He reached out with his senses and felt for Rachel. She was still alive inside the burning tent. He rushed headlong into the tent even though part of it was starting to collapse. He followed the link that he had between him and his wife. Rachel was trapped underneath a large beam that had fallen. It had landed diagonally across her, crushing her. He knelt as tears welled up in his eyes. *Please, God, no.*

"Donavan," Rachel moaned.

He glanced at her. The heat from the fire was slowly creeping up on him. "Shh, love. I'll get you out of here."

"No. Too late. Don't let him take me. Please."

Donavan took her hand and kissed it. "No one is going to take you, precious."

"But I-I promis—" Rachel breathed her last breath and lay very still.

A wail sounded from his lips. He pushed the beam with all his might, freeing his wife's body. He scooped her up and rocked her back and forth. Dripping pieces of tent fabric fell down around him. He glanced over to the door of the circus tent and saw Alexander hovering on the edge with a look of sadness on his face.

How could you let this happen?

It was the only way to keep the jester from taking you. I won't lose you.

Laughter echoed above the roar of the fire. Donavan's head shot up. From an opening in the tent, he saw the joker's face peering down at him. *You should have been a good boy and listened to me. Now your precious wife's soul is mine. We struck a bargain before you started destroying my mirrors. You could have had her forever. Now she's my plaything.*

The jester disappeared. Before Donavan could draw another breath, a piece of burning fabric settled on the side of his face. He dropped Rachel to the ground screaming. The fire began to engulf all of him. At that moment everything inside of him died. Blackness took over where his hope had been. His angel was gone. His hope was gone. All that remained was darkness and guilt. It was his fault his wife had died. *You were my soul mate. I should never have gone after him. I should have quelled my anger. I'm so sorry, Rachel. Please forgive me.* It didn't matter what the demon did to him. His soul was already forfeited. He was beyond caring. Hands dragged him out of the burning tent. Cool water was thrown on his face, putting out the flames, but the pain remained. There was nothing left of him anymore. The world was surrounded in darkness and hazy shadows. The light inside of him was dead and the only thing that remained was the demon.

Will you submit now? The demon asked triumphantly.

What else was there to do?

"Yes," he whispered and fell into unconsciousness.

Chapter Six

For the last fifty years, Alexander and Donavan had taken their traveling sideshow across the world. The demon had so many souls in storage that he had an unending supply of power. The demon was powerful enough now to leave the mirror maze and walk among humanity. For the last ten years the demon had been loose upon the world. The only thing that remained was the world he had created with all his souls that traveled with the sideshow. The demon still shared Alexander's and Donavan's souls, merging with them when it felt like it, bringing them in on its sexual escapades, keeping them in agony for hours until it decided that it wanted to move on. Most of the time now it possessed Donavan, leaving Alexander alone.

Alexander found it hard to look upon his brother. Ever since Donavan had been burned in the fire, he had taken to wearing face paint all the time. However, even the white makeup couldn't hide the mass of twisted scars on the side of his face. Alexander could have healed the burn scars, but the demon wanted Donavan to have them. Whenever Alexander tried to bring up Rachel, Donavan flew into a rage. His guilt and wrath fed the demon allowing it to bond further with his brother's soul.

After the fire something happened to Alexander. His lust for power had dwindled. The eternal life and bending other's will faded away. He did what he had to do in the sideshow and retreated to his wagon getting lost in books. One day he wandered the back streets of London seeing the homeless and the orphaned children. He happened to walk by a mill where all the workers were children. His first response should've been luring the children to him to mark them for the demon to consume their souls. Instead, he stopped and stared at the taskmaster who was about to beat a child for arriving late. Alexander felt rage. It wasn't right. He used his magick and slipped inside the gated courtyard shoving the man from the little boy. From there he marked the taskmaster for the demon and gave the child enough money so he could at least buy food for a couple of months.

From that moment on, he kept his feelings hidden from his brother and from the demon. He had constructed an impenetrable wall between himself, his brother, and the demon. Lately, though, it didn't matter with the demon because it was hardly ever around. The power that it had imparted to them now burned inside of their souls. If the demon was ever vanquished it would not be able to take the power from them. He wasn't sure if the immortality would last, but he suspected that it would.

Now he stood in the Mirror Maze gazing at all the lost souls. They all cried out to be released. There was only one in particular that he truly desired to free. It was his brother's wife, Rachel. The demon had claimed her soul the night their tent had burned down. The soul inside was no longer the woman that his brother had loved. She was now an old hag with flaming red eyes. She leered at him, sensing that he was on the other side of the glass. The demon had kept Rachel around using her for a plaything and to keep Donavan in line.

I'm so sorry I ever let this happen to you. Alexander placed his hand on the glass. *I finally understand what we've done. We've seen one hundred years. New inventions have taken the world by storm.* Electricity was the newfangled gadget that the populace craved. Carriages had been replaced with automobiles. *The world we know is gone. We are trapped as the souls in these mirrors forever twenty-five. And all this was accomplished because I wanted power.*

Alexander shook his head, turning his back on Rachel in the mirror. She was trapped. So was he. He had been searching the book they inherited from their father, which had originally summoned the demon for a way to conquer it. There was no exact spell to destroy it.

He could send it back to hell if he chose, but he would need his brother's help. Donavan would not assist him in that endeavor. For now, Alexander endured living within the haunted circus that had come to be known as Circus Diabolique.

He left the Mirror Maze heading back toward his wagon. A horse's whinny caught his attention. There was nothing there, but the sound came again. It was Nightmare, his steed. With a small current of his power, he brought the horse into his reality. The horse was tied to him, sensing his emotions that he was disturbed. The creature had been fashioned out of shadows and darkness. An ebony masterpiece materialized before him with a black mane and glowing red eyes. A faint blue glow outlined the creature. Alexander ran his hand over the horse's flank feeling the powerful muscles underneath. Nightmare could outrun a normal horse and if needed, carry him anywhere he wished. When she was not attached to Alexander, she was part of the carousel the brothers had within the sideshow.

"We've known each other for decades, girl." Alexander patted her materializing a carrot out of thin air. The horse took the treat and munched on it. A green blur caught Alexander's peripheral vision. It was one of the souls bound to the demon's sideshow. Alexander was so used to seeing it that he barely noticed the twisted circus underneath the real one. He only caught glimpses of it here and there.

"She's a fine animal, brother."

Alexander looked up to see Donavan standing before him. He hadn't heard his sibling come up even with the bells on his harlequin jester suit. Fresh white makeup covered his face. Red accented his curled up lips widening his smile to impossible proportions. His eyes had a spark of green fire to them. The demon was in his brother's nature more than usual.

"Thank you. Where have you been these past few nights? I have not seen you."

His twin's smile stretched over pointed teeth. This was not his brother. Immediately, Alexander dropped to his knees before the demon. His gaze remained locked to the earth noticing the green mist that clung to the grass. "Master, forgive me." The demon's will pressed on his mind. Alexander did not fight the invasion. He knew better than to show any resistance around their demonic taskmaster.

"Alexander, get up. I only come here to congratulate you and your brother."

Alexander hesitated for a moment and then rose. The demon could be playing a trick. It always had other motives. "For what?"

"You and your brother have been serving me for over a hundred years. Most humans make it about twenty or thirty before I tire of them. Both of you have become outstanding students, allowing me to create my own carnival from the souls I have gathered. You have permitted me to leave my otherworldly dimension and travel among humans, picking and choosing who to eat and who to fuck. For that feat alone, you shall be rewarded."

Alexander was stunned to hear this from the demon's lips. Its evil chuckle spread through the night and stopped the workers in their tracks. The jester even did a couple of back flips and then disappeared. Hands came down on Alexander's shoulders a couple of seconds later. "Boo."

Alexander smiled. He saw his true brother emerging from his wagon. When Donavan saw the demon, he bowed. The demon strolled over, placed its fingers under his brother's chin, and drew him to his feet. The demon kissed him. His brother returned the kiss, sharing tongues with the demon. He bit his lip from disgust, watching the demon caressing and fondling his brother. Finally the tension eased and he was able to breathe again. The demon motioned for the brothers to walk with him.

"You boys have become something like children to me. You're good to fuck with and you've created such a wondrous world for me to play in. I wanted to reward the both of you."

"Master, we are unworthy of—" Donavan started.

The demon waved him off. "Shut up. I don't feel generous all the time. My reward to both of you is your souls. I give them back to you. You are still tied to me, of course. Our pact can never be severed. You are my minions for eternity, but I give you back the spark that you freely gave to me in the first place."

When the demon said that, a jolt of intense pain seized Alexander's body. Warmth spread through him again. He heard his heart beating. For more than a century, it had been cold in his chest. Donavan had experienced the same thing. The demon placed the palms of his hands over each brother's heart. Desire so intense swept through Alexander it was ten times what he had ever felt from the demon. Blackness dotted his eyes while he struggled to hold onto consciousness.

"Now, my beauties, you will do whatever I ask, won't you?" the demon purred.

"Yes," the brothers answered in unison.

"Good. I want more than a Mirror Maze this time. I want a place to settle down. Being around these humans has given me a sense of wanting roots. We will travel until I deem a place is worthy of me. When I finally find a place, we will build the greatest circus the world has ever seen. And the souls that come will all be mine. Will you build this for me?"

Alexander tried to think clearly. He tried to mentally connect with his brother, but found it impossible. If the demon took more souls he would be indestructible. Its will pressed down on his, searing his newly won soul. He clutched the ground burying his fingers into the earth, trying to stay conscious.

"Yes," Donavan answered.

"Alexander?" the demon asked.

He shut his eyes feeling his hips rise. "Yes, Master."

The demon rubbed the length of Alexander's cock through his pants. The light touch made him instantly come. "Good boy."

The demon withdrew leaving the brothers exhausted and nearly unconscious. Alexander struggled to stay awake, but the intensity of the experience still gripped him and he let darkness take him away.

Chapter Seven

The sideshow made its normal trek across the country. The demon hadn't yet found a worthy place for them to build their sideshow. Alexander was relieved. Every time they left a town, the people had been spared from becoming slaves of the demon.

On their journey, they had picked up a few stragglers. One of them was a young woman who claimed to be psychic. Donavan hadn't liked her the instant he saw her, but Alexander was taken with her. Her name was Endora. To Alexander, she was an angel. Her hair was blonde, almost white. Her skin pale and her eyes so clear blue he wondered why God had created such a being. She had stolen his heart the first time he laid eyes on her. The first time he had touched her, there was an instant connection between the two of them. Alexander knew this was his soul mate.

Ever since the demon had returned their souls, the complexity of human emotions washed over him more and more. His body was warm to the touch now and not cold. He could feel easier. His judgment wasn't clouded any longer. If he hadn't had his soul, Alexander knew he never would have felt the spark between them. Alexander tried his best to stay away from Endora. Once the demon or his brother found out about the feelings he had for the psychic, then she would be at risk. Alexander was not going to risk that on Endora so he kept his distance and remained aloof, always the ringmaster of their little carnival and treating her coldly even though in his heart it killed him to do so. The longer she stayed at the sideshow, the more she was in danger.

Alexander sighed, pulling his long hair back into a ponytail. They had set up a stage to hold their acts. The audience was always thrilled and awed by the feats that he, his brother, and the other carnival members performed. And among each of them was a family or two that would return home only to be found dead a few days later when the demon collected their souls. His heart went out to each of these innocents more and more.

A slight headache formed in his temples. He squinted against the glare of the candle flame in his mirror. Someone knocked on his door.

"What?"

The door opened. "I-I'm sorry to bother you, Mr. Rosin, but I was wondering if I could speak with you."

Alexander glanced up to the intruder. It was Endora. She had never come to his wagon before. "What do you want?" He kept his tone cold.

Her hands shook. Her pulse fluttered on the side of her throat. Alexander caught himself staring at the swells of her breasts from her corset pushing them up. Her dress was tattered, but it was all part of her costume. Her blonde hair was woven with different colored cloths and was bound, hanging down her back. A pink flush accentuated her cheeks. It was cold outside for a normal human, but he wasn't bothered by the weather anymore. She closed the door behind her. "I-ah-this might sound a little strange."

"Endora, I don't have time for games. I have a business to run. Get to the point."

She clasped her hands together absently twiddling her thumbs. "Okay. These past couple of weeks, something has been trying to get into my wagon."

"Someone has been bothering you?" Alexander asked, wondering which one of the sideshow hands he should throw to the demon.

Endora stepped forward. "No, not someone. Some*thing*. It's been trying to come through my mirror, but I've stopped it. It still tries, though."

"Endora, whatever monster you *think* has been trying to come through your mirror is only a nightmare." Alexander turned in his chair knowing full well the demon had taken an interest in the psychic.

She scowled and stepped even closer. "I don't *think* anything. I know what I see. This creature presses its face against my mirror. It resembles your brother, Mr. Rosin, when he dresses as the jester, only more evil. Its eyes are green flames and it reeks of decay. It longs for my soul. It wants my body, too. It tries to touch my mind, but my amulets keep it at bay."

Alexander was intrigued to hear that there was something that could keep the demon out. "Endora, it's only a dream. There is nothing to fear here. But if you wish to leave—"

"I'm not incompetent. What I've seen is real. You know it. I know it. I don't want to leave the sideshow."

"Why?"

"I can't."

"That didn't answer my question." Alexander watched her in the mirror. Endora closed her eyes drawing in a deep breath. She reached out slowly, her hand trembling, and touched his shoulder. The spark between them was still there. A momentary feeling of calmness descended over him.

"I can't leave because I'm in love with you."

The shock to hear those words uttered from her lips stunned him. *What can I do? If the demon finds out he'll want Endora all to himself. Just like he did Rachel. I can't let that happen. I won't let that happen. But I want to tell you how I feel. I need to tell you I love you, too.* Alexander mourned for the loss of his brother's family, but he was not about to let the same thing happen to him. He turned slowly keeping his face hard. "Your crush on me is flattering, but I do not get involved with any of the employees. My brother and I have been running this carnival for a long time. I don't believe in monsters or evil jesters. Please go back to your wagon."

Her fingers moved from his shoulder to his cheek. Her soft touch stopped his heart. The connection between them was growing. He swallowed back the emotions swirling around inside of him.

"Stop lying to me. I'm not some fake psychic who tricks people for money. If I was, you wouldn't have hired me. I know what you are. I know what your brother is. I've seen what you've become. I've had dreams about you for years. When I touch anything in this place, I see another world underneath it. You and your brother bound yourselves to something so dark that it wants to consume the world because you've been feeding it souls. At first your brother tried to fight it, but his wife was killed and you felt nothing. Now your roles are reversed. While his soul is twisted from guilt and rage, yours has seen regret and love. You wish you'd never made the pact with the demon. Tell me I'm not right."

How does she know? Alexander was shocked when he heard the truth. *None of the other psychics have ever been able to see into our future or our past. Maybe things have changed now that I have a soul. Or maybe they changed because I have hope.* He shook his head. *No matter what it is, I can't show her any kind of favoritism. The demon will only twist it until she's gone. At least from afar, I know that my hope is still alive.* "Endora." He moved her hand away from his cheek. "I appreciate your candor. However, there is nothing between us. Yes, we hired you because my brother and I sensed you were the real thing. Now go back to your wagon. There's nothing that I can do about your dreams. Nothing can be done to change the past or whatever destiny you think you see for me. Do you understand?"

Endora crossed her arms over her chest. She was stubborn. He liked that about her. He wanted to smile, take her into his arms, and claim her, but he knew better. *This is for the best. Trust me.* He would never be able to hold her. Never be able to tell her that she made his heart stop when she walked across the courtyard. Or how when the sun hit her hair it shined like golden wheat.

"I understand that you're trying to protect me, but there's something about me you don't understand. I'm not afraid of it. I know the magick to bar it from my wagon, my mind, and from my dreams." Endora placed a hand over his heart. A zing passed over his skin.

He found himself drowning in her eyes. The words froze in his throat. His whole body went rigid. She leaned in place resting her lips on his. Her mouth was soft and velvety smooth. It took him a moment before he responded. Alexander tried to hold back the well of emotion surging through him. He tried to dam his feelings up, patching any holes there was in his mental armor, so his brother and the demon wouldn't be able to detect what was sliding through his mind. But once the warmth of her flesh pressed against him, the wall broke. He crushed her against him, praying her delicate body wouldn't break under his hold. He parted her lips hungrily with his tongue. Her hair smelled of mint and apples. Heat flushed his body so that he was trembling. Alexander released her lips, hearing her gasping for air. When he searched her eyes for the disgust he thought he would see reflected, there was none. Endora had told him she could see what he truly was. If that were the case then she would know that she was kissing nothing more than a skeleton.

Endora moved a piece of hair away from his face. "I thought you said you don't get involved with employees. That it's bad for business."

"I know what I said. And it has to be that way. We can't have this between us. We'll be found out. I don't want you to suffer the consequences of what will happen if we are discovered." Alexander unwound himself from Endora. Already the emptiness filled his heart with sorrow.

She stepped forward pushing him even farther into the cramped space of his wagon. He held up his hand. She still advanced. "I'm not afraid. You give the evil that has haunted you all these years too much credit. There's still good in the world that can defeat it. That will eventually destroy it."

What had she said? Did she know a way to completely vanquish the demon? "How do you know that?"

"Because I've dreamed about it. Just as I dreamed about this moment in time and so many other things I've wanted to share with you."

"Then why don't you?"

Endora's voice dropped to a whisper. "It's not safe here. My wagon is protected from the creature. Come to me tomorrow night, and we will discuss what I've seen."

Alexander smiled. Hope started to bloom inside of his heart. Could he even dare to think he might one day be free of the evil that haunted him? "All right."

Endora nodded. He noticed that she glanced over his shoulder into the mirror. He turned to peer at the glass. There was nothing in it. The man staring back at him was not the normal skull with blue flames for eyes, but his true reflection. One he hadn't seen in years.

"How did you do that?"

Endora smiled. "I told you. There is magick out there that can defeat the demon. I can't take away the pact you made, but I can give you back a little bit of yourself. We're meant to be together. Hope has given you something to believe in. Love has given you more power still."

He crushed Endora to him. Wetness formed in his eyes. He didn't know the last time that he had cried. He had forgotten he could cry. With Endora in his arms, he finally knew there was a ray of light in his very dark tunnel.

* * * *

Alexander tried to keep his mind focused throughout the next day. The sideshow was moving again. The demon hadn't made itself known to him and Donavan, had not popped up to ask him anything, either. He hoped neither of them had sensed his connection to Endora.

His thoughts strayed to their brief encounter. Her scent was intoxicating. The feel of her body pressed against him stirred his lust. He wanted to bed her no matter what. Images of depravity flashed through his mind. She was tied up. The demon was impaling her from behind while she sucked his cock. Red welts showed where they had beaten her with a riding crop, but she loved every minute of it. She begged them for more. The jester and he were sharing her over and over again while Endora cried out for them to keep fucking her. His dick hardened while he rode Nightmare letting his mind play over whatever other things he wanted to torture her with. She didn't look like the type who would be delicate. Her flesh appeared to be supple and could take whatever tortures the brothers thought up. The demon would be with him, of course, sharing his mind while he rode Endora and she was bucking against him while she was tied spread-eagle to the bed.

"Oh, Alexander, I love the train of your thoughts."

Alexander snapped out of his fantasy, realizing the demon and his brother must have caught the scent of his lust and wove their minds with his. He didn't want to see her tortured at all. In fact, he vowed no harsh instrument would touch her skin. Only his lips, fingers, and hands would caress every intimate and hidden part of her. A forced smile touched his lips when he glanced over at his twin. When he did, Alexander nearly gasped, but bit back the reaction. What stared back at him was not the man he had grown up with. True, Donavan's outward appearance looked human along with the burned side of his face, but what Alexander saw now was the demon. The evil had reformed his brother in the demon's own image. Alexander knew he could not balk. He had to keep up appearances.

"I don't know what you mean, brother." Nightmare snorted. The horse sensed Alexander's thoughts and was laughing at the lie he had told.

Donavan threw back his head and chuckled. Alexander heard a loud crack when he did. "I've seen you looking at the new psychic.

She is a sweet piece of ass. I don't blame you for wanting to sample it. I could keep him out of the way. He understands we enjoy a good fuck by ourselves once in awhile."

"Donavan, I appreciate the offer, but I want the bitch. I can have a little fun, can't I? Or is our Master unhappy with me that he would begrudge me a little pussy without him?"

Donavan slapped him on the back. "Unhappy? No, he's ecstatic. He's found the place where we will build his great circus. Imagine it, Alexander. He will feed on souls and we will have more power than we can ever imagine. He does warn you to be careful of the human bitch you have your eye on. Our Master says she is a powerful witch. He's happy that you want to fuck her because then he'll have a way in to steal her soul. He already has a special place lined up in his carnival for her."

Cold fear ran down Alexander's back when he heard that. There was no way the demon was going to get his hands on Endora. But the worst news was that it had found a place to settle down. "A special place. Like Rachel has a special place?"

His brother's eyes narrowed. Alexander thought he saw a flash of green fire inside of them. "What did you say?"

Alexander smiled. Now was not the best time to rehash old wounds. Donavan might have given himself over to the demon, but the one thing that stirred his humanity was the mention of his wife. "Nothing. Forgive me. My mind is not where it should be. Please tell our Master I will be careful. I wouldn't desire anything to come between me and him. All I want is pussy. It's been a long time since I've had anything good." He reached over and touched his brother's arm. "When we settle down, we must find time to share someone. I miss the days of old. What do you say?"

Donavan grinned. The demon curled around both of their minds looking forward to whatever debaucheries the twins would hatch. "It's wonderful to hear you say that. I've been worried about you, brother. These past few years, you seem to be withdrawing from me and our Master."

"I am weary from traveling. I, too, desire to find a place to settle down. I have dreams of the circus we can build. Humans will come from all over the world to see the feats our troupe will perform. All the while, they will never know what awaits them once our Master chooses them for his Circus Diabolique."

The demon wormed around in his thoughts trying to see if he was telling the truth. On some level, his speech was true. He had thought about what would happen with the circus. The backlash he waited for from the demon did not occur. Instead, his demonic master withdrew from his mind, satisfied with what he had found there.

"Good. I too have many dreams for the circus. Soon we will begin to plot what we can do to keep our Master satisfied. He has chosen a small sleepy town called Crow's Creek. From there we will build the most diabolical carnival. We will celebrate soon with the new filly from our troupe being the main course. Break her in first for me, Alexander. When I'm ready, I'll fuck the life out of her."

Donavan kicked his horse and rode to the head of the wagon train. Alexander watched his brother depart. Endora had said she had seen a way to destroy the jester. If they were going to be constructing his carnival, whatever that was would have to be soon.

Chapter Eight

The sideshow wagon train had pulled off the road for the night, setting up in a field not far from the main road. Alexander wasn't afraid of anything happening to the carnival since it was protected. Sitting before the fire, he watched green fog flow out of the Hall of Mirrors wagon, blanketing the ground, overlapping the other wagons, and spreading out even farther than he had seen it before. The crack of whips against ghostly horses sounded. A low din of voices perked Nightmare's ears while she munched on some grass nearby. Once the fog touched the horse's hooves she snorted and then faded away into the green mist. The steed was only loyal to him and not the souls of the demon who tried to boss him around. Green, blurred shapes drifted past Alexander, erecting tents, stages, and games for any customer who was dead enough to want to play. He spied Rachel floating along unaware of him, but hovering outside of Donavan's wagon. He wondered if the soul had any shred of humanity left. Did she even remember she loved Donavan?

The phantasmal circus spread out around him unaware of the living workers. The only place the green mist did not touch was Endora's wagon. Whatever magick the psychic had, was obviously working because the demon's minions were unable to penetrate her wagon. He had put off going to her wagon as long as he could. He hoped Donavan would find some distraction before he ventured to see Endora. The heat from the fire did not warm him. It only made him colder now that the demon's souls were around him. When they would leave tomorrow, the field would be dead. Alexander couldn't help but think of all the devastation they had left behind in the places they had traveled over all the years. *How many souls has the demon consumed? How many lives have I helped to steal away? How will I ever find redemption for the things I've done?*

"Alexander."

Someone touched his shoulder. An energy ball gathered in his palm. He turned and saw Endora. He squelched the ball. "What are you doing here?"

"Are you going to come and join me?" The psychic smiled, but her gaze was fixed on something beyond him.

Alexander followed Endora's look. Donavan leaned against his wagon staring at the two of them with an evil grin on his lips. His brother was expecting him to claim Endora tonight. He nodded over at his twin and then rose, yanking her into him. A small gasp escaped her lips. She went rigid in his arms. The power inside of him wrapped around them both scorching the ever expanding link he and Endora shared. She began to fight his grasp, but he held her close, kissing her deeply, grasping for her breasts. His cock stirred the more she tried to fight him.

"Go with me on this. You know I won't hurt you. We have to give them a show," he whispered to Endora.

He swung her around so Donavan had a better look. His brother's thoughts and lust merged with him. *Fuck her good and hard. She's a fighter. Those are always the best. Mmm, she smells good, too.* Alexander grabbed Endora's ass, hiking up her skirt. Donavan's velvet laughter slid through his mind. His twin went back into the wagon and shut the door. When he did that, Alexander released Endora. She slapped him across the cheek. There were tears in her eyes. He felt her shame, but part of her mind was blocked to him. He'd never had that happen before. Where she hit him, he tingled.

"Never do that again! I don't care who you have to fool. I am *no* man's plaything, even yours. Is that understood?"

Alexander nodded, dumbfounded.

"Good. Now please come into my wagon so we can talk freely. The screams of all the lost souls hurt my heart."

Endora walked to her wagon. Alexander followed. When he got to the steps, he noticed the runes carved above the door and the stained glass window in the door with the same symbols. *Are these the same symbols Father used to keep the demon at bay so many years ago? Is it that simple? Why hadn't we thought of this? Because we never wanted to bar the demon.*

Alexander stepped inside and closed the door. There wasn't much to Endora's wagon. Her mirror was covered with a black cloth with the same symbols painted on it that were on every opening in the wagon. Once he was inside, he felt the pulsation of magick. It was light against his skin. She had said there were other forces greater than evil. Love and hope. *Where does her magick come from?*

Endora sat on the bed. Alexander didn't trust himself being so close to her. His entire body throbbed with need. It had been a long time since he had thought about being gentle with a woman.

"Forgive my behavior outside. Donavan wishes to bed you when I am over my attraction to you. The demon wants all three of us to claim you."

Fury built in her eyes. "Is that how you truly feel, Mr. Rosin? That I am some wench who spreads her legs for a demon. Am I to be turned into your whore?"

Alexander's anger awoke to its full force. He gripped the back of the chair and closed his eyes against it. The demon loomed within the anger ready to join Alexander if he let it, but he took in a breath, controlling the emotion. "No, Endora. It's not how I feel. I wanted you the first time I saw you. But I stayed away. You were the one who came to me last night professing your love. You told me you understood what I was. But I truly don't think that you do. I'm sorry for forcing myself on you, but it was the only way to have them be satisfied." He stared at her.

She was shaking. "I rehearsed my conversation with you over and over again until I had it right. I told myself I wasn't afraid. But I'm terrified of what I've seen, of what I've dreamed. The things you've done with that creature. What it's done to you." Tears slipped from her eyes.

Alexander's anger vanished. He dropped to his knees before her. Seeing her cry cut his heart to the quick. She was afraid of him. His palm caressed her cheek and he wiped the wetness away. "Please don't fear me. I can't—I won't let anything happen to you. Please know that."

He leaned up and kissed her gently. The link they shared flared to life. The current hummed between them. His magick washed over her skin, electrifying her in a blue glow. Endora broke their kiss. Her back arched and a gasp escaped her lips.

"What are you doing to me?"

"I can't control it. My power, the demon's power, it stirs lust. It's a part of me now. Don't be afraid."

Alexander trailed his hands over her face feeling the satin-smooth cheeks. His fingers were outlined with the power leaving blue lines over her flesh. Her breathing quickened. She struggled against the power moving through her, fighting it, but his power was winning. He could feel the battle from the link they shared. Endora desperately wanted to give into the passion, but she was frightened. Her whole body was tight and that was when he realized that she had never been with a man before. She was a virgin, an innocent. *No wonder the demon has its sights set on her. He wants to corrupt her purity.*

"Alexander, I can't. I—"

He claimed her lips, cutting her off. The tension between the two of them stimulated by his power had grown. He couldn't push her, but everything in him screamed to take her right there on the bed not caring anything about her purity. Her lips fought against his, but not to stop the kiss, only to expand it. Her arms slipped around his neck when she pressed her body against his. Their tongues met. Hers was inexperienced, but Alexander didn't care. He let her explore his mouth while her fingers stretched over his shirt fumbling to feel the skin underneath. His cock was already hard. The heat deep inside of her scorched his flesh. Through the link he sensed how ready she was for him. Finally, he was the one who broke the kiss. He had to remember that Endora was going to tell him how he could vanquish the demon.

Endora gave him a look of longing, but then smiled. Her hand found its way underneath his shirt. She bit her lip. Alexander chuckled. He wondered if he was seeing the making of a monster. "Are you sure you want to stop?"

He removed her hand and kissed the back of it. "For now, yes. Originally you invited me in here to talk and not for me to ravage you."

"You don't want me?"

"I've desired you from the first moment I saw you, but I'm not going to give into my nature, into the demon, and take you without you being completely ready. Right now, I would hurt you. I don't want that. Will you tell me how to vanquish the demon? I've been trying to think of a way to do that for ages."

Endora straightened her dress and then stood up. She reached over the bed to a shelf and drew out a box. On the box were carved the same runes that were above her door. Her hands ran over it, caressing the cracked wood. The box looked old and the lock on it black with tarnish. "This belonged to my mother and her mother before that. It goes back at least fifteen generations. There are rumors that it came from the isle of Avalon, that one of my ancestors was a priestess there. That was where our power came from. She was near the end of the isle being in this reality. The runes fused together were a symbol of our family and used for protection." Endora pulled out a medallion from around her neck. "This was my grandmother's. She gave it to me the day she died. She told me it would keep out all the evils of the world and an even greater one still that would come and try to conquer me, but that the evil wouldn't be able to penetrate it. So far the demon hasn't."

Alexander listened to her tale with interest. It would make sense that her power came down her family through the female line. He had heard of this before. This was one of the reasons that during the Inquisition women had been burned. He wondered if any of her family had been taken to the stake. The amulet, her belief in it, and the magick inside of her had kept the demon at bay. *How much power does she truly have?* Alexander reached out and tried to touch the box, but Endora pulled it away from him.

"Why did you do that? I won't hurt it. I just wanted to see it."

Her cheeks flushed. "Of course. I'm sorry. It's really the only thing I have left of my family."

Alexander understood. The only thing he had left of his family was his brother and the book which had summoned the demon. The only belongings he had now were in his trailer. His hands ran over the wood of Endora's box. The carving in it was crude, but there was power even in the small box. He opened it carefully not sure what he would find and the only thing inside the satin lining was another amulet.

"The other was supposed to belong to my sister, but my mother died giving birth to her. My grandmother raised me. My mother didn't believe in the old legends. My grandmother taught me to embrace my power. I can't really do much magick. My gifts are more in my mind, seeing ghosts, talking to them, predicting the future, feeling the emotions of others. I have prophetic dreams. I've been dreaming about you since I was a child." Endora took the box from Alexander. She placed it on the bed taking his hand in hers. "I knew you and I were meant to be together. My grandmother knew it, too. When she died, she gave me her blessing and her protection to come here and follow my destiny."

"Endora, you being here is not a good idea, even if your amulet keeps the demon out. One day, the evil will find a way in if you're with me. The demon will lay claim to you as the way it did to my brother's wife. It grated on her mind, enticing her, possessing her until she made a pact with it. She almost became like us, but Donavan wouldn't have it. The jester punished him by killing Rachel. Now her soul is part of the ghostly sideshow. I don't want this to happen to you. I love you too much to even think about it. I don't want the evil to corrupt you."

"Alexander, I know my own mind. You can't persuade me to leave when my place is by your side. The demon won't take me. I'm here to be with you and to let you know that you can be free."

"How? If I try anything, Donavan will know. We can't destroy it. It's become too powerful over the years that we've been feeding it souls. No spell will send it back to hell."

"You have to burn down the sideshow. Destroy it and your brother with it. You have your soul, Alexander. You can be free of the demon. I can help you purge it from your system."

Alexander drew back from Endora. He would happily set fire to the carnival if it would drive the demon away. But there was no way he could kill his brother. He was bound to his older brother. It didn't matter how twisted his twin had become. Somewhere, buried beneath the demon's influence, was the brother he had known and loved. They were still connected. He would never abandon him.

"Endora, I'd be happy to light a match to this God forsaken place tonight if it would mean the end of the demon. But I can't desert my brother. He's all I have. We have shared everything together. If it wasn't for me, Donavan would never have gotten involved with the demon in the first place. I was the one who insisted he join in the ritual. I begged our father to let us worship the evil. I was the one who the demon cultivated first. I killed my father and sealed our fate. Deep down Donavan hates me for what's happened to him over the years, but I can't kill him. Underneath the man you see is the brother I love. But if I could take it all back I would. This was never what I wanted."

"What if he's not your brother anymore? What if he's nothing more than a slave to the demon? What would you do then? Would you sacrifice him to save yourself?"

Alexander was silent. Her conviction to rid the world of the demonic jester for good was evident. She truly meant to take Donavan with the jester. If his brother wasn't even there anymore, could he? Alexander had never contemplated the thought. "I don't know. There's no way to find out if my brother is still there. What you see is the way that he has been for ages. It's him, and it's the demon. They are one in the same now since Rachel died. Donavan gave up hope."

Endora opened the box again. She withdrew the amulet and placed it in his hands. "If you can get him to wear this, even for a few minutes, then you'll know if some part of your brother is still alive." She closed his fingers over the metal. It was warm against his palm, vibrating with the power that it held.

He took their combined hands and brought them to his lips. He kissed Endora's fingers. Maybe there was still hope for Donavan. "I'll try. Thank you for this. I still fear for you if Donavan approaches you. He might corner you while I'm not around."

"Kiss me then. Brand me with your power."

Alexander's eyes widened. More surprises were coming out of her lips than he had ever imaged. She was willing to open herself up even to a little of the demon's influence. He nodded. The power gathered inside of him. He wrapped his hand around the back of Endora's head and pulled her to him. Without warning, he let loose the wall around his magick and placed his lips on hers. A searing heat burned through him and into her. Her lips worked frantically to keep up to his, but when the blast of magick hit her, Endora's fingers clawed at his arms. He knew it hurt her, but he did not release his hold. He kept kissing her. Endora squirmed against him. He felt the wetness of her tears against his cheeks. His magick was attaching to her soul, burning his brand into it. The more it scorched her, the more their link expanded. He could really see now that they were destined to be with one another. Alexander saw her mind and knew her words had been true. They were soul mates. Finally he pulled away. Endora collapsed on the bed. She wiped away her tears. When she opened her eyes, they burned blue from his lingering magick. She was his. His brother wouldn't dare touch her now.

"Are you all right?"

"I'll be fine. You're so much stronger than I thought. So much power. But you have hope. You should go for the night."

Alexander nodded. A lot had been said between them. He needed time to figure out how he was going to approach his brother. He clutched the amulet in his hand. Its power raced up his arm. Having it and Endora gave him more hope than he'd had for a long time. In her, he finally saw a path for his future.

Chapter Nine

The sideshow would not reach its final destination for another couple of weeks. Donavan had decided to make an unscheduled stop at one of the nearby cities. Alexander was left to watch over the sideshow. While he did, he stayed away from Endora. It took all of his will. Now that he had branded her, he could feel her ever so close to him. If he concentrated on their link, he could feel her heart beating. Each night he dreamed of her. Tonight, with his brother and the demon distracted, would be the perfect time to claim her. But he would not tempt her. He would leave that decision up to her. Now he stared at himself in the mirror and he saw his true face. The amulet she had given him hung on the corner of the mirror. He had contemplated slipping the necklace around his brother's neck while he slept, but the demon would feel that. He had to keep the plan secret. The solution of burning down the sideshow was something that he was in favor of. If he could destroy the mirror maze then maybe they would drive it back to its own dimension.

"I don't know if it will work. But it has to."

"You don't know if what will work, brother?"

Alexander looked up. He hadn't heard his brother come into the wagon. He hadn't even felt him come back. He extended his mind and found only his brother was standing before him. "I was thinking of a new act, actually. I don't know if it would work. Something about living puppets and no strings. Our master would have to have some influence of course, to pull the trick off. Maybe have them walk through a freestanding mirror. Once the audience member passes

Carnival of Souls 69

through the mirror, their soul will be caught. I haven't worked out all of the details yet."

Donavan smiled. "I'm sure that our master will love it." He straddled a small chair that he pulled out from the corner. "Have you bedded Endora yet? I see that you marked her soul as your own."

Alexander shifted uncomfortably in his chair. He stared at the reflection of his brother and then reached up, taking the amulet. He had to know if his twin was still inside of the man in front of him. He used a small amount of power and masked the symbols on the bronze amulet. He didn't want to get his brother suspicious. "No, I haven't fucked the bitch yet. We got into it, but she got feisty. I didn't want to pressure her. I didn't want you trying to sneak in and take advantage of her. I know how you work, brother." Alexander turned giving his brother a know-it-all grin. He remembered when he used to banter with Donavan in the old days, when they could laugh about whatever evil deeds they did together and nothing else seemed to matter.

"You're holding out on me."

"I don't know what you mean, Donavan." Alexander got up and sat on the bed so he could be next to his brother. "I have something for you." He held out his hand with the amulet on it. Instead it was an elaborate C and D fused together for Circus Diabolique.

Donavan gave him an eye and did not take it. Never before had his brother been wary of what he was giving him. Alexander held his mind blank with a smile on his face. After a moment, his brother tentatively picked up the fine, silver chain and held it up to the light. "What is this for?"

"Nothing. When can't I give my brother a gift? It is something I was fooling with. A trinket to show our new partnership when our Master settles down. If you don't want it—" Alexander reached for the necklace. Donavan smiled and pulled it back.

"Forgive me, brother. I've been on edge of late. Our master has been making more and more demands on me. He did not want to make this stop, but I wanted to be sure that Crow's Creek would be a good place for us to build the carnival the way that he wants it. I wanted to get a lay of the land." Donavan took the amulet and placed it around his neck.

Once he did, he slumped over in the chair. Alexander didn't know if he should touch him. But after a moment, Donavan began moaning. "Donavan."

His brother looked up at him. "Alexander? Where am I?"

Alexander dropped to the floor. "Donavan, is that really you? Or are you the demon?" He stretched out his mind and sensed along the link he shared with his twin. He didn't sense the taint of evil. It was true. The man before him was truly his brother. Endora had been wrong. The demon hadn't fully taken him yet.

"Yes, brother, it's me. Where's Rachel?" His green eyes pleaded with Alexander. Donavan didn't remember anything about the fire. Alexander realized then that was the last time his brother had been truly sane.

"She's dead. I'm sorry. But you have to listen to me. Time is short. Do you remember anything that the demon has done over these past decades?"

"No. Only he's planning something big."

"Yes. He wants to make the carnival a permanent fixture in some sleepy little town. I have a plan that can finally send him back to the realm he came from. But I needed to know you were still there. I had to know you were worth saving, too." Alexander felt wetness in his eyes.

Donavan's hands curled around the wood. Alexander sensed the power of the amulet was waning. The evil which had twisted his heart was returning. He had to be quick. "Destroy him. Send it back to Hell. And kill me while you're at it."

Alexander's face fell. He was not going to leave his brother behind. "I can't do that."

His twin gritted his teeth and screamed. His hands groped around his neck. He snatched the necklace and threw it away from him.

Alexander knew then that the power was gone. His brother had been taken over by the demon once again. He reached out to touch Donavan again. But he snapped back up. What had returned was not his brother. "Tsk. Tsk. Tsk. Alexander. Trying to pull Donavan away from me. Now that is bad, bad form."

"Master, please. I only wished to speak to my brother. I meant no disrespect." Alexander played on being humble.

"No disrespect! First you keep that bitch from me, and then you try and take your brother away from me as well. What are you planning?"

Pain sliced through Alexander that made him writhe on the floor of the cabin. His entire being felt like he was being pierced with mini-swords. They burned when they stabbed into his flesh. His mind was being frozen. "Nothing!" he screamed.

"Nothing." Donavan kicked him in the stomach. Alexander's fingers scraped along the wooden floor. Slivers embedded themselves in his flesh. He began to feel the demon withdrawing his power from him. Only he was doing it slowly. His body was starting to die. He could feel the life leaving him cell by cell. His internal organs, skin, and everything else was dehydrating. This must have been what his brother had experienced when he had confessed his love for Rachel to the demon when he had been punished, only Donavan had been within his mortal lifetime. Alexander was beyond the years of a normal human. If the demon kept this up, he would be dust and bone.

"Tell me before you don't have a mouth left to."

Alexander stared at his hands. They had curled up and were old. His fingernails were yellow and had grown several inches. "Nothing, I swear." His voice came out in a rasp.

"Swear you are my loyal servant as always. Swear you will give me that pretty bitch in the trailer I can't get into. Find out her secret. I want her. Is that understood?"

"I...swear." There was nothing else that he could do. He was losing consciousness fast. His whole body felt like it was dust.

"Good boy. Fuck her good. Do it tonight and then remove your brand. I don't enjoy things being kept from me. Use her. I'll grant you tonight to have your way with her. When we build the carnival, I'll use your idea. Keep thinking of things like that."

Cool air rushed into Alexander's lungs. He breathed and felt his body returning to normal. Power flowed back into him. The demon had let him off lightly. He could have punished him worse now that the pain had fallen away. In his soul, he knew what he would do. Endora was correct. The sideshow had to burn. They had a few more days to reach Crow's Creek. He had to do what the demon said. He had to play along. Only for a little while longer. And then, once he knew it was safe, he would burn the place down and there would be no one that would stop him.

Chapter Ten

Alexander stood outside of Endora's wagon. The power that emanated from it brushed against him. It was so good and pure but his was dark and evil. Together they were complete opposites, but when he thought of her, his soul sang. Tonight he had to claim her body or the jester would punish him again. He raised his hand to knock, but she opened the door.

"Come in, Alexander." Her voice was a whisper.

He brushed past her into the small wagon. He turned to face her. What he saw made him stop. Heat washed over him. She wore hardly anything. A sheer, emerald robe covered her body and was tied at her throat with a green ribbon. The material swept over her form, accentuating the curve of her hips, the swells of her breasts, and the line of her entire body. His cock tightened. She had known that he was coming to her.

He stepped toward her, but she held up a hand between the two of them. There was fear in her eyes. *What did she have to be afraid of? If she knew that I was coming, she should know that I would never dream of hurting her.* The closer he got to her, the stronger the connection grew. Already it tugged on his heart. He tried to read her thoughts, but she was keeping him out of her mind. The more he pressed he would be able to break into her mind, but he didn't want to scare her anymore. She didn't need to feel any threat from him whatsoever.

"I won't hurt you."

"I know that, but I've never done this before. I've never felt this way before about any man. Since I was a child, I've been fantasizing about you, about this moment, but I never thought that I would be this scared. Part of me never really believed that you were real until I came here. Then I saw you. Then I saw your brother and the evil that was inside of him. I couldn't run away. I had to face my fears. Even last night when I dreamed and my guides spoke to me about what was going to happen this night and what the jester was going to do when he found out you were going to burn down the sideshow. It all frightens me, but this one moment, before you touch me, before I feel your caress, I'm more terrified than anything. Already my body aches for you."

Alexander took her hand in his. He turned it over and brought her open palm to his lips. He kissed the center of it lightly. When he did, a tickle of energy passed over his mouth. Her flesh was soft. He could only imagine how the rest of her body felt. How it would move against him. He craved to hear her groan his name.

"I can cure your woes. I can make your body sing. I can make you do a lot of things, but I want to be sure that you want this. The jester has deemed I must ravish you tonight. But I won't do anything that you do not wish. If you want me to go, if you push me away anytime, I'll understand. I want to be gentle with you. I pray that I can be, but I've been under the jester's power for so long, I don't know if I still have the sincerity to be the human that I once was, the man that I lost so long ago."

Silence spanned between them. Her heart beat in time with his. Her skin was flushed underneath the robes. Her hard nipples pressed against the cloth. They wanted to be released from their sheer prison. She slipped her hand from Alexander's and pulled on the ribbon that held her robe closed. She didn't take it off. He sensed she wasn't ready for that.

"I want you. I won't tell you no." Her jaw was set. She kept his gaze.

Alexander smiled. He reached out to her slowly, gently running his finger along the line of her stomach. She quivered underneath his touch. He stopped above her heart, sliding his palm over her left breast. The firm globe fit as if it were made for his hand. Her nipple hardened instantly when he brushed his thumb over it. He moved her robe away from her right breast taking the pert pebble into his mouth, running circles over her areola while he pinched and massaged the other. Endora groaned. Her body leaned into his. This only encouraged Alexander more. He bit down, gently tugging on her nipple. With his free hand, he rubbed the inside of her thigh slowly, parting her legs. His nimble fingers slid between her pussy lips discovering her hidden treasure. He began to rub her clit slowly. She was already wet from the anticipation of their coupling. The more he aroused her, the more her walls were crumbling. Her fear was ripe and sweet. She wasn't afraid of being with him, but he was more afraid of being without her. No one had ever made his body smolder the way that she had.

He flicked his tongue over her breast again before releasing it and claiming her lips. Endora pushed herself against him. Her tongue spilt his lips, probing. He was pleased that she didn't fear the desire sparking between them. He met her tongue with his, tasting her. Their tongues caressed and fondled one another while he rubbed her harder. Endora's fingers clawed at his clothes trying to find a way under his jacket and shirt. When she couldn't, she settled on cupping his cock through his pants. She gripped it and squeezed it, feeling him. Each of her caresses was clumsy, but he didn't mind. He was holding back. He wasn't about to scare her.

Alexander sensed her body trembling more and more with his quickening strokes of her hard node. Already, her pussy was slick with her own juices. She rocked against him when he kissed her. He broke the kiss and held her gaze. The power inside of him was building just as an orgasm trembled inside of her. He settled his palm against her belly button right over her womb. He slowed his pace and sent zaps of energy running through her. With each small burst of his power, and his manipulations on her clit, she was going to come hard and fast. Her eyes widened. Her breath quickened. She tried to hold back moans, biting her tongue. His power overwhelmed her body.

"Do you want me to stop?"

"N-no."

He leaned in close to her ear. "Are you sure? Because I can make this go on for hours. Tell me what you really want. What do you crave?"

He stopped the flow of his magick running through her and rubbed her more slowly, now trying to ease her down from the edge of her orgasmic precipice. Alexander kissed the spot under her ear. His tongue licked her lobe and his teeth nibbled the end of her ear. Alexander felt the gush of wetness from between her legs, dying to dip his dick into her pussy.

"Alexander."

"Yes, sweet one."

"I need you. I need you inside of me."

She blushed when she admitted her longing. The perfect roses on her cheeks only made him want her more. He backed away and slipped the robe from her body, letting it pool around her feet. He undid his jacket and threw it on the chair. Endora watched with fascination glistening in her eyes while he undid the small buttons of his shirt. He tried to stay focused on what he was doing, but it was getting more difficult with each passing second seeing her flushed and so ready for him. The shape of her body was sublime. Equal to any artist's rendition of Aphrodite. As pure as the Virgin Mother herself carved from stone, but underneath the innocence there was a vixen waiting to emerge. He tossed his shirt onto his jacket leaving him topless before Endora. He paused. She worried her lips. The small creases on her forehead made her more adorable to Alexander. *She is so human. So delicate.* Seeing her before him, Alexander realized that he loved her. He understood what it was that his brother had felt for Rachel. He had been in love.

After a moment, Endora crossed the distance between them. She laid her hand flat on his chest, running her hand over his muscles, feeling the hardness of his body. The body that the jester had granted him. But the demon wasn't here. Endora was his. She trailed her hands over his pecs. Her feather-light touch drove him crazy. He dropped his head, inhaling the scent of her hair. The strands smelled like lemons. Her fingers moved lower, tickling him until they came to rest on the waist of his pants. She hesitated, not sure what to do. Alexander cupped her chin, drew her lips up to his for a brief kiss, and then stepped away. He pulled off his boots and socks and then undid the buttons on his pants. Once he stepped out of them, Endora's eyes grew wide staring at his saluting cock.

She tried to back away, but he caught her wrist, gently guiding it down to caress his length. "It's so soft. And so warm it's almost burning."

Alexander chuckled. "It is burning. For you. I want to feel your legs wrapped around me. I want to hear you screaming my name." He lowered his lips to the hollow in her throat, sucking on the little indentation while her inexperienced hands slid over his shaft. With each of her butterfly strokes, he desired her more. The tightening in his groin was getting hard to control. His balls hurt from the longing of wanting to fuck her.

Endora's arms wrapped around his back. Her nails dug into his flesh, running furrows, marking him. She pressed her body against him. Alexander couldn't take the wanting anymore. He scooped her up and laid her on the bed. She stared at him with trusting eyes. Alexander looked deep into her gaze and saw himself reflected there. He saw and felt his soul through her. She had given him back a part of himself by being able to love him.

"Thank you," he whispered.

Her brow furrowed. "For what?"

He brushed a strand of hair away from her face. "For believing in me. For seeing me as I should have been if I had remained truly human. The jester might have given me back my soul, but you have given me back my heart."

Her smile made the darkest and bleakest time in his whole existence worth it. This was why he had existed for so long. He had moved through time to find Endora. "I love you, Endora. I mean that. I don't want anything to happen to you."

She touched his face. "Oh, Alexander. I love you, too. I always will, no matter what happens to me."

He reached down and claimed her lips one more time. His hand stretched down her body, caressing her calf and then her thigh. He wrapped her leg around his waist. Endora leaned up and kissed him again. Her arms wrapped around his neck. When he pulled away from her, he saw her fear.

"Do you still want me, love?"

"Yes."

He nodded, knowing he could hurt her if he was too swift. Already she was so slick that he wanted to have his way with her, but slowly he guided his cock into her pussy. His gaze searched her face. Her eyes widened when he entered her. Alexander pushed a little more into her well, forging in inch by inch, letting her expand around his cock. Endora was so tight. She felt so good. He gritted his teeth, struggling for control. His magick threatened to overtake him again.

The demon sat on the edge of his consciousness pleased that he was ravaging a virgin. The evil jester wanted Endora screaming in pain. It assumed that once she got a taste of sex, she would want to be fucked and toyed with until her soul was dried up, maybe even bonding with her so it could have another outlet. Alexander wasn't going to let that happen.

"Ahh-Alexander," Endora groaned his name.

His balls contracted when he slipped inside of her further. He had come to her barrier, to her innocence, and he was about to break it. He called upon his magick and laid his palm once again on her stomach.

Immediately Endora arched off the bed. The pleasure that rode her body reverberated through him. He sensed her longing.

He sent another pulse to consume her and mask the pain. Right when the wave of passion gripped her, Alexander plunged his cock deep into her pussy. He felt the flesh of her barrier break with only a slight hesitation. He removed his hand and began a slow rhythm between them. He watched Endora's expression. It took her a moment of rising against him and pushing him away that their bodies synched together. At each plunge of his dick, he lost himself to her. The link between them flared to life. He was inside her mind, and she was inside of his. Her pants and moans joined his when she took control of their mating. Her fingers dug trails into his back, through his hair, along his ass. She wanted to consume all of him. Alexander wanted her, too.

"You feel so good," he whispered.

"I'm-ahh, I don't know—"

"I do."

The coupling was frantic. He was surprised they hadn't broken the bed, let alone the wagon. Everywhere he touched her sent sensations racing through Endora's body and then back onto him. Alexander had never felt anything like it. Not even being connected with the demon. Her touch, her emotion was so light that it made his heart soar.

They were almost there. Sweat had covered the both of them. Their bodies fit together so perfectly. He would do anything to hold onto her forever. Nothing was going to drive her away from him. He pushed into her again. All his nerves clenched and tingled from being with her.

"I want you with me always."

"Always."

At that finally moment, he came, releasing inside of her. Endora clenched her legs around his waist and finally relaxed under him. He pulled out of her and lay beside her on the small bed.

"Did I hurt you?" Alexander asked, concerned that he had damaged her in some way other than stealing away her innocence.

She gave him one of her beautiful smiles. "No. I'm just basking in you. That's all. I feel what you feel. You're so free. So light. There's no weight on your soul and it's wonderful. I want to remember this moment forever."

Alexander smiled, kissing the side of her cheek. "We can, love. We have until the end of time. I'll make sure of that. No matter what happens. You and I will always be together."

Chapter Eleven

Alexander stared at the field where his brother was building the permanent Circus Diabolique. They had arrived in Crow's Creek only a few days before, and construction was already underway. The attraction was located at the end of a dead-end road with woods all around it. Donavan wanted to set up in the field for now while the workers felled trees to start construction. Every night that had gone by, he'd put off his twin as to why he hadn't claimed Endora for the demon. However, his brother hadn't asked him because he was so busy setting up the sideshow. Once it was completed, the demon would have a foothold in this world, and he couldn't let that happen.

"Brother, we must celebrate."

Alexander turned and saw his brother emerge from his wagon. He looked happier than he had in a long time. Almost like he did when Rachel was still alive. "What are we celebrating?"

"Our master is pleased with the location and the construction. Once the sideshow is complete, he will be able to travel between this world and his own. He won't have to rely just on souls. Others will travel with him. Imagine all of the power we will have. Can't you feel the stirrings of magick?"

"I feel them. It's good that our master is happy." He sighed. "Forgive me, but I have much on my mind."

Donavan clapped him on the back. "You have feelings for this woman, don't you?"

"Am I that transparent?"

"Of course not. I understand you want to keep her all to yourself. But don't let the witch fool you. She wants nothing more than to turn you against our master. To turn you against me. That will never happen, will it?"

"Of course not. Our master will have a taste of her soon. I promise."

"Good man." Donavan smiled and walked into the night.

When he was gone, Alexander saw Endora beckon him from the outskirts of the woods. He slipped into the shadows and met her there. He pulled her into his arms and kissed her before hugging her tightly. The scent of fresh earth hung around her. He backed away and saw that her fingers were caked with dirt.

"What did you do?"

She smiled. "I've made sure that things will be okay."

"What does that mean?"

Endora leaned up on tiptoe and pressed her lips to his. The love he had for her captured his heart. "Nothing you have to worry about. Do you know how much I love you?"

"How much?"

"Enough that if anything ever happens to me, I'll make sure you'll be happy."

"You're starting to sound cryptic."

"Only because it's time. We have to take out the demon now before it gets any stronger. You have to kill your brother."

Alexander stepped back. Donavan was still good deep down. He was bogged down by the regret and guilt of losing his wife. "I can't. The demon doesn't have total control of him. I saw that with your charm."

"Then we burn down the Hall of Mirrors and close the doorways. The demon isn't here. It's out traveling the world dining on souls."

"Fine. Tonight it is then. How are we going to do this?"

"I'll distract your brother, and you set the wagon on fire from the inside. Once the mirrors are destroyed it won't have anywhere to run." She gave him one more kiss and hurried toward her wagon. Alexander's gaze followed her. Already the neon green of the demonic world was settling over the real carnival originating from the Hall of Mirrors. He saw his love go into her wagon and saw one of her protective windows was gone. He walked toward the wagon, but she came back out dressed in the same green robe she had worn for him. He understood her intentions then. Grabbing her arm, he hugged her to him.

"You can't sacrifice yourself to him."

"It's the only way for you to have a shot. Trust me. You have my heart, and neither your brother nor the demon will have my soul. Now go." She pushed him away. There was no way of stopping her. He knew that. She was stubborn. He sighed and prayed that she would be okay. Alexander backed away and watched as she climbed the steps to his brother's wagon.

* * * *

The door opened, and Donavan glanced at Endora. She then caught his eye.

His twin smiled and he felt his pleasure in his thoughts. *You sly devil. You sent her to me didn't you? That's why you've kept her from me. You wanted to train her.*

Yes, that's right. Have fun with the bitch. When you're done, we'll both enjoy her like the old days and then feed her to our master. Alexander choked on his words. He hoped that Endora could distract Donavan long enough for him to destroy the mirror maze. The door closed. Alexander ran to the supply wagon and grabbed a bucket full of oil along with a paintbrush.

Green fog swirled along his legs when he went up the steps of the maze. He dribbled a little of the oil on each one before he entered. Inside, the wails of the dead pressed down on him from all sides. He didn't look into the mirrors. If he did, his guilt would overwhelm him at the wretches and abominations that stared back at him. Quickly he emptied the oil along the floor of the wagon. He dipped the brush into the remaining oil and began spreading it onto the mirrors. He worked quickly.

At first the trapped souls did nothing, but soon their cries turned to ones of warning. He was almost done. There was only one more section to go. He wiped the sweat from his brow and threw the bucket aside. It had to be enough.

"What do you think you're doing?"

Alexander saw Donavan standing in the hallway. Endora wasn't with him. "Something that I should've done ages ago. He needs to be stopped. He can't get any stronger."

Donavan laughed. "You really think that you can kill our master."

"I'm sure as hell going to try. At best, I'll send him back to hell." Alexander focused his magick into a bright blue flame into the palm of his hand. Donavan's gaze narrowed.

"It won't work."

Alexander formed the flame into a ball, turned, and threw it at the mirror at the far end of the hall. Once it hit the glass, the mirror erupted in flames. Donavan landed on top of him knocking him to the floor. The face that stared down at him was not his brother, but the demon inside his twin.

"You can't destroy me. I'll live on even if this place is reduced to ash." His hands went around his throat and choked Alexander. He sent another blast of magick into his brother's chest. Donavan screamed and pulled away. There was a scorch mark in the cloth where the blast hit him.

Around them the fire began to spread and the glass to crack. With each new crack, souls escaped the mirror maze. Hope filled Alexander watching this. He was sure they would find their rest. His brother whirled around and shot a bolt of energy at him. The blast only knocked the wind out of him. The demon was losing its power. He kicked Donavan back against a mirror. When he did, he saw Endora standing in the doorway fully clothed.

His eyes widened, but she smiled and shook her head. He stepped toward her, but his brother opened his eyes and grabbed his leg.

"Your little bitch is clever. Don't worry, I never tasted her. Shame really because you won't be around to see what I do to her once you're gone." He twisted Alexander's ankle hard enough that the bone snapped.

Alexander fell to the ground. The heat of the fire was upon them. The flames were only inches away. He landed with his back against an unbroken mirror. Hands caught him around the back and began to pull him in.

"You're mine, Alexander. I'll make you my bitch for what you've done to me," the demon hissed.

"No!" Endora placed her palms on the glass. The demon wailed and Alexander felt solid glass behind him. Before he could thank her, the demon was behind Donavan in the mirror. He reached out, but the jester pulled his brother into the glass.

The flames licked the top of the wagon now. He looked at Endora and then at the darkness yawning before him. She bent down and took him in her arms. Their lips met in a kiss.

"You knew this would happen, didn't you?"

She nodded. "I knew."

"Then you know I can't leave him to the whims of the jester."

"I know that, too."

He held her close. "What happens from here?"

"The carnival is destroyed as you've wanted, the demon imprisoned in the other realm. And I'm there to make sure that you'll be happy."

Alexander swallowed back the emotion choking him. His ankle was almost healed. He forced himself up and stared at the darkness. *God forgive me. Watch over Endora.* "I have to go in there."

She pressed her lips to his. "Then I'm going with you."

He clutched her hand and they both stepped into the darkness of the other realm. Alexander prayed that no matter what happened

Donavan would be safe, and the jester would finally meet his end, but if not, then no matter how long it took, he would see the evil fiend destroyed.

THE END

SIREN PUBLISHING *Allure*

Crymsyn Hart

Circus Diabolique

THROUGH THE MIRROR

THROUGH THE MIRROR

CRYMSYN HART
Copyright © 2010

Chapter One

The haunting music of the calliope stuck with Rhianna as she woke from her nightmare. Her eyes snapped open. Her breath came in pants. Her heart thumped inside her chest. A shiver snaked up her spine, chilling her sweat-covered body. Something snapped outside, like a tree limb breaking, causing her to jump as the threat of her nightmare hung in the air. Rhianna reached over her nightstand, turning on the light, wincing at the sudden brightness. It helped calm her speeding heart but out of the corner of her eye, one of the shadows moved. Instinctively, she clutched the sheet to her chest. Her throat was dry. She drew in a breath quickly as her body poised on the edge of fear. It seemed her nightmare had pursued her out of the dream world. Now, like a silent predator, it stalked her bedroom, waiting for her to slip into sleep once again.

This is silly. I'm scared a dream will come and get me, like I'm six all over again. A smile appeared on her lips as she thought how foolish she had been. Her body began to relax as she stared at the bedside clock. Neon green numbers told her it was only three in the morning. She sighed and flopped back down into the bed and pulled the covers up over her head. When she did, something suddenly jumped on her stomach.

Rhianna sat, throwing the covers off. She closed her eyes and tried to catch her breath. Her heart was back in her throat once more. Opening her eyes, a midnight black head peered at her with blue eyes.

"Snowball! Stupid cat! Scare me to death!"

The cat gazed at her. "Meow."

It settled onto the empty space next to Rhianna and began kneading the covers, walked around in a circle a couple of times, curled up, and started purring loudly, thinking nothing of scaring its owner to the point of turning her hair white.

Rhianna said nothing but reached over and shut off the light. The music of the calliope from her dream played in the darkened room. It was faint and sounded like an out-of-tune music box. The melody was the same one she had heard in her nightmare. *Why would I be hearing it now? It's not like anyone lives close by.*

Curiosity drove her to get out of bed and peer out the window into the deserted street. She was in a quiet neighborhood at the end of a cul-de-sac, where no one bothered her. Her parents had lived in the house when they were first married and then left when she was only six never telling her why. All her mom said was the house was unlivable, so they had rented it out. Her parents had died in a fire five years before in a freak accident. Lighting struck the antenna on their house, sparking a fire, when they were sleeping. It devastated her, but she had coped with the loss. Rhianna had always known about the house and finally decided to consolidate and sell the one she had lived in for years. Besides, there were too many sad memories she had to live with in the old one and she wanted to put the past behind her and move on.

Only a few houses dotted the same road, but the nearest one was a mile away. What was great about the old house was behind it and to the side, the land spread out into acres of fields and woods that had also escaped being sold to the highest developer. Still, as she stared out into night, there was nothing there. In the sleepy town of Crow's Creek, even on the outskirts where she lived, no one ventured out late.

Finally, she shook her head and decided the tune was all in her imagination. *I'm overtired, overstressed and now I'm hearing things. It's what I get for moving out of the city.*

Rhianna settled back down into bed, trying to ignore the faint music. Even as her head hit the pillow, it would not leave her. Tossing and turning in frustration, sleep eluded her. The tune would not leave her alone. After listening to Snowball purring like a mini-engine for a while, her eyes grew heavy from watching the daunting shadows, and the calliope song was fading with the coming dawn. Her body was heavy, and the music almost muffled.

"Rhianna." A whisper came from near her bed.

She thought it was only her imagination getting to her. A cold shiver passed over her from the open window. She searched the shadows for an intruder, but there was no one there. Oddly enough, the darkness seemed more tangible, like something was going to jump out and get her. Maybe it was hiding behind that chair. *I'm losing my mind.*

"Rhianna."

This time she didn't look into the darkness, but gazed at the full-length mirror nestled in the corner of the room. She clutched the sheet to her body, wondering why she was not seeing herself in the reflection like she expected to. Instead, a new image greeted her. A man dressed in turn-of-the-century clothes stared back at her. An eerie blue glow emanated around him like a twisted halo. He had dark brown hair and dark eyes. From inside the mirror, he reached out to her.

I'm dreaming.

"Please help me, Rhianna. Help me before he comes back."

Mind-numbing fear kept her frozen in place like a frightened animal. Her gaze slid toward her napping cat, which purred and was probably dreaming about catnip mice. Snowball was not sensing anything out of the ordinary. *Stupid cat. I thought you were supposed to sense spooky stuff like this.* Staring at the specter in the glass, the desperation in his eyes tugged on her heart strings. Something inside her knew she had to help him, and there was something else. An aura of familiarity surrounded him, yet she had never seen him before. A piece of her soul recognized this man. A deep sense of loss and love washed over her that brought tears to her eyes. Before she knew it, she was kneeling on the edge of the bed, not realizing she had moved, and reaching out to him as well.

"Who are you?" she asked.

"Who is not important now. You have to free me." The fear in his tone moved her heart, and tears of frustration formed in her eyes.

"I don't know how. Tell me."

The apparition looked behind him. Rhianna heard something like a branch breaking or a whip cracking. Outside, the calliope music seemed closer.

"Help me. Please!" he pleaded again.

"How? Who are you?"

"Beware of the jester. Please. Free me!" The figure gazed behind him again and then disappeared.

"Wait!" Rhianna leaped off the bed and touched the glass, expecting the image to show the stranger again. However, its cool surface reflected only her. She listened for the music again and didn't hear it. She shook her head and checked outside. No one around on her street. It was what she got for living on the outskirts of town with only fields, wildlife, and the night to keep her company. Groaning, she climbed back into bed. The strange encounter had made her forget her nightmare. However, fear still made her tremble from the recent encounter. It wasn't every day a ghost, or whatever, appeared in her mirror. She wasn't sure the whole thing wasn't part of a waking dream, but in the back of her mind, Rhianna knew she had experienced something few people did.

What does he want with me? Why me? What the hell is going on here? Is he the reason why all the renters moved out within a couple of months? Why we left when I was just a kid? Rhianna shook her head and tried to settle back onto the pillow and get some sleep.

The next morning, Rhianna opened her eyes to the birds singing and the sun warming her face. It took her a moment for her eyes to adjust. Her gaze swept the room, looking for her crazy cat, which must have gone off in the middle of the night again. Finding nothing, she got up and stared out of the window, wondering if he was in a nearby tree. She didn't see her cat, but what she did see was a very odd sight. Sitting in her gravel driveway was a horse and wagon. The horse she could understand, as there were several horse farms along the road, and as a child, she had seen riders going through the field across from the house. The wagon looked like it belonged in another century, with a circus promoting its sideshow. The horse was happily munching on grass, and underneath the wagon, Rhianna saw a pair of legs and heard the echo of metal hitting wood. The banging ricocheted through the field next door and off the windows, making it seem louder than it really was.

Things just keep getting stranger and stranger lately.

"Hey!" she called out the window to the pair of legs. The pounding stopped. The horse swung its head up from its meal meeting her gaze with ebony eyes. Its ears flicked. The steed ignored her, deciding the grass was tastier than her voice. The hammering started up again after a minute.

Rhianna glanced at her clock. It was only seven. Whoever was banging was on private property, and she was going to make him aware of the fact.

"Hey, hammer boy!" she screamed again.

This time the pounding stopped, and the pair of legs came out from behind the wagon. Instead of the dreamy, gypsy thief she envisioned, with dark hair and enthralling eyes, what she saw made her scream. The man attached to the pair of legs stared at her with rotting flesh and one eye hanging from its socket. The sun gleamed off the top of a bone-white skull. Tattered and torn clothing hung on a decaying frame. The thing opened its mouth to say something, but only a groan came out. Rhianna noticed a deep slice around the zombie's vocal chords. Her gaze darted to the horse. Instead of the ebony beauty, there was now nothing but a putrid corpse with only patches of skin left on it, revealing muscle and bone. The one thing lively about the animal was its eyes, and those burned absinthe green. The wagon cover flapped in the breeze. The cloth in tatters like it had been torn by a thousand raven claws. Rhianna backed away from the window.

This isn't happening! This is not real!

She continued backing up until her foot hit the side of the bed. The pain brought her back to a little bit of reality, and her eyes met her reflection in the mirror. Instead of seeing herself, she saw a jester. He was dressed in a harlequin suit and a hat with bells. One-half of his suit was emerald green, and the other was white. He even had the curly shoes with bells on the end. In his hand, he held a scepter with a miniature head on top of it. Her head with an expression locked in terror. She wore a hat with three strands dangling from it, all with bells. Her gaze met the jester's face. It was painted white, like the color of death. His grin held pointed, brown teeth and thin lips. His eyes burned the same green as the horse outside.

The door downstairs slammed shut. It had been locked. The jester's grin grew wider. The jingle of bells echoed in her bedroom as well as the jester's menacing laugh. Her throat grew dry. Her heart raced. Whatever was outside was coming to get her. The stairs were creaking from the weight of the thing, the zombie creature mounting them one by one, getting closer to her room. Her gaze whipped back to the joker.

"What do you want?" she asked.

The jester put his finger to his lips to shush her. He jumped. The horse whinnied outside. Her heart was doing the tango from the beat of fear coursing through her. She tried to back away but was paralyzed. It was almost to the top of the stairs. Rhianna's eyes couldn't leave the jester's face. She reached out to the mirror, knowing she would have to act in a second. The jester's hand didn't mimic hers.

Her fingers were centimeters from the glass. The zombie gypsy was coming into her room. The overwhelming stench of death and decay filled the bedroom. She had to cough to keep from choking. Her palm hovered near the mirror's surface as she watched the dead thing coming toward her with an outstretched hand. The flesh had worn away on his fingertips, and there were only bones poking out at the knuckles. In his other hand, he held a hammer.

Rhianna was about to dodge out of the way, when something grabbed her. She spun around, and the jester grasped her hand closest to the mirror outside of the glass. She struggled against him. There was no where to go, because the zombie was in front of her. Then the gypsy seized her as well, and she screamed.

Chapter Two

"Are you okay?"

She blinked. The gypsy was no longer a zombie but a normal-looking guy in jeans and a black T-shirt. His skin was beginning to go from a lobster sunburn into a nice bronze color. He had dark wavy hair, curling around his ears. He had a gold nose-ring and tattoos of dragons and fairies covering both arms. A braided goatee adorned his chin and his ears had plugs in the lobes to stretch them out.

"Yes, God." Rhianna grabbed her chest and waited for her heart to settle down. Something weird was definitely going on with her. "I'm sorry."

The guy shrugged. "Whatever. You screamed. I wanted to be sure you were okay. Look, I didn't mean to trespass. I didn't know anyone was living here."

"No. It's fine. I guess you surprised me. I heard you nailing something to the tree outside. What was it?"

The guy handed her a rolled up flyer he pulled out of the back of his jeans. The flyer was neon green with black writing. It read:

CIRCUS DIABOLIQUE
Enter a realm of nightmarish wonders to indulge in your darkest dreams. The marvels will mystify, haunt, and entrance you.
Come if you dare…

"Is this for a sideshow?" Rhianna asked.

"Yup. I'm putting them up all over town. You should come. They'll be here this weekend. It's a regular gig for them. They've

Through the Mirror 97

been coming this route for decades. At least that's what my pops tells me. Look, you okay, cause I still got like a million of these to post."

She shook her head as she read over the flyer again. On the bottom was a picture of a court jester. His toothy grin reminded her of the apparition she had seen in her mirror. "Yes, I'm fine, I think. Thanks for coming up to check on me. I didn't mean to scare you. I wasn't expecting you."

The guy smiled, making him look more like a schoolboy. She lifted her hand and waved bye as he turned and walked down the stairs. The front door slammed shut, and from the window, she heard his shoes crunch along the gravel road. Rhianna waited a few more minutes and ran down the steps to lock the door. She didn't want any more strangers coming into her house. Laying her head against the front door, relief flooded through her. She was still jumpy from seeing the hideous jester in her mirror. Rhianna didn't hear a car engine rev to life or a car door slam so she glanced out of the window. When she did, she saw him riding down the road on a bike. Rhianna breathed a sigh of relief

The guy was not really a zombie. He was a regular guy putting up flyers for some two-bit circus.

Something was going on she couldn't put her finger on. It wasn't like she woke up in another world. What was happening to her was not normal. She didn't have anything to drink the night before, and she hadn't even had her morning coffee. Maybe there was something in the air. Maybe she was still dreaming, and this was all a nightmare like the other one she had before. It was a logical explanation. *There is no way creepy-looking jokers and zombies came to life and out of mirrors in the daytime. Monsters lurk in the shadows, in the darkness, where fear is what they thrive on.* Normally, Rhianna wasn't afraid of the dark, but as she looked down at the flyer and then back at the mirror, she knew something was wrong with this house. There had to be.

Now her parents were dead, and she couldn't ask them. She had been so young, her memories of the house were blurry, although she remembered she used to love to walk in the field at night. Her parents would get so worried about her. Her mother had told her stories of how she had slept walked. However, that had stopped when they had moved. Rhianna shook her head and decided maybe she was overtired and would dismiss everything, as she had a lot on her mind and didn't need to be scared.

Later on in the morning, she had made a dent in the dust in the living room, and figured it was time to head into town to get some supplies. As she did, she saw paw prints on the roof of her car in the gravel dust.

Hope you're having fun, silly cat. Snowball was still missing from earlier, but she wasn't worried about him. He always had a mind of his own and hunted for birds and whatever he could find. He always brought her a souvenir and left it for her to step on. Rhianna shivered at the thought of all the cold, dead mice that had squished between her toes. She figured he was off exploring his new hunting ground and would return when he wanted his fix of catnip. As she got into her car, her gaze caught the poster the guy had been putting up earlier. She got out of the car and walked over to the tree. As she got closer, a chill ran through her.

The flyer was printed on paper from a bygone era. It was yellowed, worn, and torn on the edges. The ink was faded green. It showed the same tagline, but there were two jesters mirroring one another, juggling over the headlines. Her hands touched the paper and a piece broke off in her palm. The nails were rusted and could have been mini railroad spikes. Rhianna felt her throat go dry, like old sandpaper. Her hands came away shaking. Not thinking, she ran back into the house, flying up the stairs to look at the flyer she had gotten earlier. She had absently laid it on her bed after she had gotten dressed and dismissed the events of earlier in the morning.

The leaflet was the same as the one on the tree. It was worn and faded, from olden days. Fear shivered her heart as she sat on the bed and stared at the mirror. The events all had to be tied in.

Why would a ghost, a handsome, eye-popping spirit, appear in my mirror begging for help? Why and how would the phantasm know my name? Then there was the crazy, leering jester. How was it he had appeared in her mirror as well? Was he attached to the sideshow advertised on the handouts? There were jokers on the leaflet, and oddly, they looked like the creepy joker in her mirror. How could they affect her in the daytime? Next time, she wasn't sure what would happen.

Rhianna rubbed her wrist lightly as she stared at it. The jester had grabbed her through the mirror. It was not possible for a ghost to clutch anything. Unless the jester was more than a ghost. Maybe it was why the man had called her name. Her instincts told her that coming back to the house might have been a mistake. Rhianna closed her eyes and tried to remember what had happened to her in the past when she lived in the house, but try as she might, she came up with a blank. Maybe the guy who had come in here earlier was a ghost, too. Maybe he had appeared normal only so as not to scare her, and before, she had seen his true identity. She quivered thinking about it. Rotting-flesh zombies and horses were not her cup of tea. Pushing the image from her mind, she focused on her past. The only memory that came up was the faint sound of music, which she had heard before. Rhianna couldn't place it, either. Groaning, she crumpled up the paper, stuffed it in her jeans pocket, and decided it was time to find out some more information on the house she inherited and maybe even on the town, itself.

* * * *

In the afternoon, Rhianna found herself among the dusty shelves in the stacks of Crow's Creek library. She had searched through hundreds of documents and old newspapers but had come up with nothing. Her fingertips were dry and paper-cut. Her eyes were aching from the lack of bright light and strain of reading fine, faded print. Even as she skimmed the pages, she found nothing on traveling circuses or sideshows. She even looked for references of jesters and jokers; heck, she even looked at weird news around Halloween, but nothing. Finally, after hours of checking, it was time to go back home. Part of her dreaded it though. She was in no mood to see what the long shadows of dusk would bring, but her stomach was growling. Her next avenue was to scour the town records and see if anyone in the past had owned the land the house was on. Or see when it was built. She knew very little about the structure, just that her parents had bought it.

Her mother had never told her specifically not to go back to Crow's Creek to live in the house; but she had steered Rhianna away from living there, telling her it was better she stayed in the city. Now she wondered. She swallowed as her body yearned for water. Her mouth was dry no matter what. Looking at the pages of all the old newspapers, seeing the happy faces of brides and grooms and the sad memories of the obituaries had gotten to her. Her mind reeled as tears rimmed her eyes. The pages on the table became blurry. The world started to fall away. Her mind brought her back to the night when the police came to her door, and the happiness in her heart abandoned her.

Chapter Three

Jingle Bell Rock was the tune floating through Rhianna's head as she finished putting the last gingerbread-cookie tray into the oven. The Christmas song was on the radio, but her mind was reworking the song into a dark rock ballad suitable for a heavy metal band. She could see it now, the lead singer of *Korn* head-banging to the happy melody as the bass guitarist's fingers flew off a rift. The thought made her smile. She had such a perverse imagination.

I am such a twisted sister. It was seven, and her guests would be arriving any minute. She had been planning the event for a couple of months, and it was unusual to get all her friends together in the same place at the same time. They were either off doing their own thing, working, or not getting along. She couldn't help it if there was fighting in the gay community, and someone was mad at someone else because they said something about so and so. It was exhausting sometimes to keep up with all the gossip running around. And it had been three months since she had seen Jason, her finance. He had been away at school, finishing up his Master's Degree in British Literature and had gone to London to dig up some ancient manuscript for his dissertation. Whatever. Better him than her. She was happy at home with her laptop, designing websites for a living.

Rhianna figured she had gotten the artistic side from her mom, since her mother had painted in her spare time. They were gallery-good, but her mom never displayed them. Rhianna liked technology more and was getting her own business up and running, thanks to some of her friends, who had gotten her odd jobs. Soon, she would be a full-fledged designer. The thought of her mom stabbed her heart. It had been several years since her death, but it still hurt around Christmas. She was glad her parents had met Jason because she knew they would be happy with her choice to marry him. She only hoped they were keeping an eye on her, and she imagined they were.

The scent of gingerbread filled her small, one-bedroom house. Her house looked like Christmas had exploded inside. Candy canes adorned her windows, and paper snowflakes hung from the ceiling. She had even bought fake snow and sprinkled it around her floor. It would be a bitch to clean up later, but she didn't mind. She had always loved the holiday season, probably got it from her mother, who was more over-the-top than she was when it came to decorating. At least she wasn't like her dad, who stapled lights all along the gutters and trim of the outside and had tacky light-up ornaments on the front lawn. Rhianna didn't know how many times she wanted to kick their plastic rendition of Frosty when she was a kid. Of course, the one time she did try, her mother caught her, and Rhianna was grounded until Christmas.

Rhianna smiled to herself. Her gaze took in the layout of her living room. Snowball, her black cat, was curled up underneath the tree next to the metallic wrapped presents. Todd, her ex-pain-in-the-ass boyfriend, had given Snowball to her for a Christmas present the year before. She hadn't known what to name the feline until she had watched the kitten pawing at some snow and making it into small balls. Rhianna checked her watch. It was quarter past seven, and the cookies would be done soon. The candles still had to be lit, and the caramel popcorn balls put out. She began to head back into the kitchen when there was a knock on her door.

Her heart thumped in time with the knock. "Coming!"

The buzzer went off for the cookies. They could wait a minute while she got the door. Instead of Meredith, who was supposed to be bringing the cheesecake, a pair of officers stood on her stoop. Her heart sank at the sight. Everything in her froze like the ice on her windshield. The draft coming from the door snuck under her skirt, chilling her even more. It wasn't snowing, but the breeze lifted the loose snow, flinging it around like a flower girl with rose petals at a wedding. Some of the white dust settled on the female officer's hat and shoulders. The look on the officers' faces was grim, like they had it in with Death himself. Tonight, they were the dark angel's messengers.

"Can I help you?" she whispered, forcing herself not to shake. However, sugarplums danced in her stomach.

The two officers remained forlorn and stepped inside. She closed the door hoping it would also bar the cold from entering her heart. The taller of the two, the male cop with a pock-marked face, thin lips, and strong jaw, took off his hat. Rhianna noticed he started to go bald from his thinning hairline. His green eyes were sad as his gaze darted over her living-room decorations and back to her. No one liked to invite Scrooge into their house around Christmas. He always heralded bad news.

"Ma'am, I'm sorry to have to tell you this, but tonight..." he trailed off as he looked at his partner to finish his sentence, but she wasn't going to give him any help.

From the kitchen, Rhianna smelled the burning gingerbread men, but her mind was not on the cries for help from the cookies. The officer moved his lips. However, she did not understand what he said. It sounded like he told her Jason had been in an accident. His car had hit a black-ice patch, skidding off the road, and gone into a telephone pole.

"What? What did you say?" she whispered. The smoke alarm rang in her ears, and the heavy smoke of burnt cookies was filling her kitchen since she could smell it in the hall. Her gaze darted to the cops and then to Snowball. He was still purring under the picturesque tree among the presents, waiting for Santa to bring him plastic balls with bells in the middle of them.

"Miss, I'm sorry, but your fiancé. There was an accident. We need you to come with us to identify the body."

The candles flickered. She had to get to the gingerbread men before they were completely burned to a crisp. "Why? I can't. I have a party. People are coming over. I have to get to the oven."

There was a knock on the door, and then it opened. It was Meredith and her fiancé, Terrance. The look of utter surprise was wiped off their faces when they saw the cops. Meredith's eyes met Rhianna's and then immediately went to the smoke filling the kitchen. She brushed past and went to turn off the stove.

"Come with us. Please. We have to make an ID. You are the closest next-of-kin we could find for him."

"Rhianna, go with them. I can take care of the party." Meredith had put her coat around her friend's shoulders. The wool of the coat scratched against Rhianna's neck. She barely felt herself nod, but she knew she was following the cops. The door slammed shut behind her. She followed the cops and sat in their car, absently watching as the street blurred by all in a white storm of her emotions, until she got to the morgue. The coroner pulled a sheet away to reveal her fiancé's face. Rhianna turned her head quick enough to see his face was almost flawless, except for the hairline cracks marring the perfection along Jason's cheeks. His blond hair needed to be re-bleached, as she saw the brown poking through, and his lips were tinged blue with death. Rhianna nodded, acknowledging it was him. She tried not to let the smell of death get to her, but she couldn't, and it was making her sick.

What am I going to do without him? He had been on his way to see her. He had gotten back only a couple of days ago, and she hadn't seen him yet since he wanted to get things squared away with school. She had only talked to him a couple of hours ago. He said he loved her. Now because of her, he was dead.

The next few days went by in a blur as her house was transformed from an over-decorated, picturesque Christmas card to a black, dark Halloween replica. People filtered in and out of the house. She hardly paid it any mind and tried to hold it together. Jason was the only one she had left in the world. No brothers and sisters were there to help warm her heart or ease the burden of the grief she felt. Her friends were being great and helped her organize the funeral, but no matter how many casseroles they stuffed in her fridge or words of kindness they uttered, her mind was focused on one thing—the scent of burning gingerbread and their cries of helplessness as she let them burn. If she tried to tell Meredith about it, her friend would think she was crazy. Perhaps she was, because in the past few nights since Jason had died, besides the cries of the screaming gingerbread men, she had been hearing the melodic, slightly out of tune song of a calliope, and it reminded her of being on a carousel. But the carrousel had nightmares on it instead of horses, and there were strange characters from a dark, twisted dimension riding it she had never seen before. When she woke up, the melody faded.

Chapter Four

When Rhianna got back to the house, she pulled up in front and stared at the structure. It was an older house. Three stories, old wood, well-built. Why had her parents bought it in the first place? At first glance, you would never know there was something wrong with it. Crow's Creek was a quiet town where nothing ever really happened. Hours of digging through back issues of the Crow's Creek Chronicle, the local rag, told her that. She had gone back one hundred years, and still there were more issues to go. The town had been around for almost three hundred years, and she was not up for digging in musty, old, spider-webbed documents when she had her own dusty, spider-webbed house to deal with. Now, as dusk settled on the horizon, you would never know the house was haunted. As she had been thinking about Jason's death, she was surprised she remembered her old dreams about the crazy carousal and the melody attached to the merry-go-round. The song sounded as familiar as the one she had heard the other night. Maybe her nightmare and the music were connected. Rhianna didn't know, but staring at her bedroom window, she saw a figure leering down at her. She blinked, but was not sure if what she saw was from the sun glinting off the windows.

Rhianna heard the whinny of horses, and when she looked into the field, expecting to see a rider following a trail, she didn't see anything. She was not going to be scared away from her own house. This was the only place she had left to go. It had taken her a year to get here, and she wanted to start a new life in a quiet town and get her business up and running. She was okay for a little while with the sale of her former house and paying off the debts. She still had a little bit left to live off of for a while. The only good thing about her job was she had discovered she had an eye for graphic design.

Besides, Crow's Creek held a fondness in her heart, because she had fallen in love with it as a child. Maybe it was the nostalgia that had brought her back. Rhianna wasn't sure. A shiver moved over her flesh, and she rubbed her hands over her arms, feeling the goose bumps. The house was deserted and so was the field. The thought of seeing another zombie horse was not something she desired at the moment. Finally getting up her courage, she walked up to the door. Once her hand was about to touch the knob, the door swung open. She stared at the keys in her hand and then at the door.

I know I locked this when I left. I know I did. I am not going crazy.

She swallowed back her fear and drew on the courage she had in her soul. Nothing was going to scare her away from the house. Tentatively, she pushed the door in. It creaked on its old hinges. The smell of popcorn and cotton candy faintly clung to the air. Neither thing was in the pantry or the kitchen cabinets, because she had not gotten a chance to properly stock them.

"Hello." Her announcement echoed through the house. Rhianna listened, and heard something upstairs. It sounded like bells. Bells from a jester hat. She stepped in, and the door slammed shut. The aroma of popcorn and cotton candy faded, replaced by decay and must. Sweat broke out on her forehead. She backed up against the door. Her hands were behind her, fumbling for the door knob. When she tried it, the knob turned in her hand, but it was locked. Her gaze stayed glued to the stairs as she heard the bells coming closer.

Before her eyes was the same jester from the other night. He was dressed the same, except he had no hat this time. The jester took the steps one by one. As he did, the bells on the curls of his shoes jingled. The smile on his face was devilish. The corners of his mouth were turned up so far into his cheeks it looked like his face was frozen, showing all of his pointed teeth. His lips were painted dark red, like dried blood, and his skin was so pale it could have been his skull, if not for the wrinkles she saw underneath the white paint.

He was dressed as before in a dirty green and white harlequin suit with bells for buttons. Each jingle echoed through the house. His hair was dark brown and stringy. He was on the second step when he stopped, staring at Rhianna. Her heart banged against her chest like a bucking pony. *This is not happening.* She was seeing something that should not be real.

Laughter echoed in her mind. The chuckle was low, menacing, like the jester knew a secret, and he was not going to share it with her, just taunt her with it. She desperately tried her hand on the knob once again, but it would turn and then do nothing. He lifted his finger and wagged it at her like a mother scolding a naughty child. The grin never left his face. The green fire in his eyes glowed brighter as he gestured at her.

Rhianna felt herself nod and let her hands drop limply at her sides. Whoever, whatever this phantasm was, she was not about to piss him off. Her breathing increased as he leapt into the air and flipped, landing inches from her. When he came out of the flip, it took him a few moments before he came up and met her gaze. His movements were slow, deliberate, as if he had to get used to being able to control a body, or if he figured out what it was like to be alive again. Either way, the creaking and cracking of his bones and joints made her shiver more. She was going to lose it.

The being and Rhianna stared eye-to-eye. He really had no eyes, only the green orbs. Where his nose should have been was an empty socket. His suit was covered in dirt and cobwebs, like he had dug himself out of the grave. He smelled like it too.

"What do you want?" she asked. Rhianna tried to pull her gaze away from him, but it was locked there, like he had stolen her will, since all her muscles were rigid.

The jester cocked his head to the side. His lips didn't move, but she heard the low gravel of his voice in her mind and echoing through the house. It was a whisper and yet a shout, all directed at her.

"A warning."

"What warning? I don't know who you are or what you want."

The jester brought up his hand. She noticed there were holes in his gloves. He touched the side of her face. Part of his hand was soft from the satin of the glove, and the other was rough from his chafed and peeling skin.

"Do not follow. Stay away. Have this house if you wish, but he is mine."

Rhianna blinked and tried to pull away from the caress of the jester. However, she was locked to her spot. "I don't know who you're talking about. I—"

He cocked his head to the other side with a loud crack. The fire in his eyes burned neon green. His hand trailed along the line of her jaw and settled on her chin. This time his hand crunched on her chin. Rhianna swore she heard the bones breaking, but the jester didn't seem to be in any pain. His grip was firm, and she was not getting away from him. A shrill hiss and growl sounded behind them. Snowball was on the stairs, staring at the two of them. The cat's hackles were raised, and it looked like he was a pantomime of a Halloween cut-out she had seen on windows. The jester turned his head all the way around in a pantomime of human life. Rhianna knew then this thing in front of her was no longer alive. Not that there had been any doubt in her mind in the first place, but this cemented the fact that the joker was not of this earth, and she was in way over her head.

Snowball meowed at the suddenly display. The joker's head turned back around, and he cracked his neck to get it back into place. His smile seemed to have faltered a little bit. The light in his eyes now glowed around his teeth, giving them a light glow, and his skin was now tinted green. Rhianna was trying to keep it together. She took in a deep breath, noticing the aroma of decay had lifted slightly from the house. Snowball's appearance seemed to have jarred the ghost's concentration, because his grip was not as tight on her chin. A surge of adrenaline pumped her forward, and without thinking, she shoved the joker out of the way. It was easier than she thought, because he weighed no more than a balloon. She didn't think of anywhere to go but ran up the stairs, following Snowball's lead. She made it to the second floor only to hear the jester's bells right on her tail. The door to her room was open, and she saw a green glow around her mirror. There was no way she was going back into her bedroom. Then she heard a slight creaking sound. The attic door swung open a little.

"Rhianna." It was her name whispered on the breeze blowing through the house; however, it wasn't the gravelly voice of the jester. She glanced behind her, and he was walking up the stairs slowly, knowing there was nowhere to go. The smile was no longer on his face. He was pissed.

She didn't have to think twice and ran towards the opening in the door and up the attic stairs. She took the steps two at a time, and when she looked behind her, she saw the creature, jester, whatever he was, at the bottom step. Tripping, she tried to get up, but her legs were getting wobbly, and she was almost out of breath. Looking around, she ducked behind an old dresser she never knew was up there. The bells were coming closer as his shoes stepped on the carpeted stairs.

"Rhianna." Again, the voice was not the joker's. There was another door at the end of the attic, only a few feet from her. The joker was searching for her. The bones in his neck creaked and cracked. The voice had come from the door. The door was open. Something was leading her to salvation. What other choice did she have except to get attacked or eaten by the zombie joker or go through the door and see what was on the other side. She only hoped it was nothing like what was in front of her now. Without another thought, she dived from her hiding place.

The joker saw her and reached out. His fingers grabbed her shirt, but her momentum kept her going, and she sailed through the air and slid across the threshold of the attic room. As soon as she made it, the jester stopped on the edge of the door. His fists came up, and he pounded on air. He couldn't get through. A wave of serenity washed over her. She was going to be safe, at least until she discovered what the hell was going on.

Finally the creature stopped and stared at her. Whatever power he had reached through the doorway and caressed her spine. Suddenly, she was dipped in ice water. "I warned you. Now even your soul will be mine."

Rhianna watched as the jester did a continuous cartwheel to the stairs, and disappeared. The attic door slammed shut, and the whole house quaked from the impact. Not knowing what to do next, she lay on the blue braided rug, curled up, and let herself fall into a fitful sleep.

Chapter Five

The first thing Rhianna heard when she closed her eyes was the music of the calliope that had been haunting her. Her dream was taking on a dark tone as she found herself in a landscape of blackness. The darkness was thick and soft, like a velvet curtain had been draped over everything. The melody was louder and closer than it had ever been. She took a deep breath and found it was like breathing in dust and cobwebs. It made her cough. The music suddenly stopped, and she heard hooves and the shrill whinny of a horse. There was no where to hide, and the sounds were near, so she followed them. Crazy as her dream might have been, she might at least find some answers in the darkness. What did this have to do with the guy she had seen in her mirror the other night? What the hell did the crazy clown want with her? She didn't remember him, hadn't come across anything like him, except on the flyers she had seen. Then it dawned on her that she was wearing the same jeans she had on yesterday, and when her hand went into her pants pocket, she pulled out the folded-up flyer. This time the flyer did not look like it was a worn-out piece of paper but like it had recently been printed. The ink was vibrant and smelled fresh.

Her eyes focused on the joker on the corner of the leaflet and saw him grin. The ink began to glow. It got brighter, and the paper in her hands suddenly burst into flames. When it happened, she dropped it and covered her eyes. When she opened them again, she stood among a sideshow with wagons like she had seen the other morning except they all had the same logo painted on the side in green writing:

Circus Diabolique

Rhianna stood and took everything in. She had never seen anything like it. If this was a dream, it was some dream. It seemed like she had been thrown into the past. The only familiar thing was the tree next to her where some of the horses were tied. It was the same tree that was in her front yard. The circus was setting up in the field next to her house. Next to the horses was a pipe organ attached to a wagon, something she would have seen on a carousel. She walked over to it and pressed on one of the keys. Her hand passed right through the piano. It was the calliope she kept hearing, moving through her house and in her dreams.

This is interesting. Rhianna followed the line of carts and wagons until she saw one outlined in green and painted with a jester on the side of it. Creeping up the stairs, she peeked in the wagon's window. Inside, she saw a man sitting in front of a mirror. Only one side of his face was visible. He had dark brown hair, tan skin, and dark green eyes. He was handsome. Without thinking, she wanted a closer look at him and entered the wagon. She passed right through the door as if she were a spirit. It was packed full of costumes, trunks, and flyers advertising the circus and the sideshow that went along with it. She stepped closer and saw one of the pictures on the mirror was an old tintype. In it a man was dressed as a jester with a female jester next to him, holding a small baby.

As she got closer, the man turned, and she saw the other side of his face. It was horribly scarred and melted, like someone had thrown acid on it. He had been badly burned at one time. She recognized the wound from the scars on her parents' bodies. His right eye was missing, and the corner of his mouth was frozen in an upturned smile. Her heart stopped. This was the same jester who had cornered her in the attic.

"Whoever you are, go away! I'm busy." His voice was gravely.

Rhianna turned and saw the door open, and another man come into the wagon. Her heart paused again. It was the man in her mirror, the one who had asked her for help. He could have been the jester's twin.

"Donavan, we need to talk."

The jester looked at the newcomer. It was such an amazing contrast, with one side of his face being angelic perfection and the other being so horrifically scarred. The jester who had threatened her didn't seem to have any scarring, but who knew what was under his face paint.

"Alexander, brother, you're not leaving the sideshow. I forbid it."

Alexander's fingers flexed into a fist. His forehead knotted, and the vein in his temple throbbed. "You cannot forbid me from leaving. I *will* marry Endora, and she *is* leaving with me. Nothing you can say or do will make me stay."

His brother turned back around and started to paint his face while staring at the reflection in the mirror. "You forget, brother, we made a deal."

"Screw your deal. That was ages ago. You will hold me to it now? After all we have been through, and I have finally found love?"

Donavan slammed his paint tin down on the dressing table. The entire wagon shook. His one-eyed gaze moved over his brother, and for a moment, locked onto Rhianna's eyes. It was almost like he knew she was there. "You know the price we will pay if we find love. Look at me! Is this what you want?" He gestured to the scar on his face. "We are in this together. An eternity, remember? You wanted forever, and the pact we made granted you that. I love you more than this life and the next. Nothing can come between us."

"What about Rachel? Did you ever tell her about the pact? Did you ever tell her the price of loving us? Did you? I've told Endora. She knows the risks. I will not end up like you." Alexander did not wait to see what his brother would do. He walked through Rhianna, and slammed the door. Rhianna wanted to turn and go after him, but something held her in the wagon with the jester.

She observed Donavan pick up the tintype and stare longingly at it. "If only you knew the price, my love. Then maybe my soul would not be damned like it is."

He might have been the jester, but once upon a time he had a soul and had lost the ones most dear to him. She understood that loss from her parents' death.

The air in the wagon grew thick and suddenly smelled like sulfur. The reflection in the mirror darkened and then changed. The melody of the calliope whispered in the background. The reflection took on a sinister face, mirroring the jester who had come to attack her, except this time, its eyes were blood red, and it had more of a skull outline to it than a jester's face. Donavan stopped and stared at the apparition in the mirror.

"You will stop him or I will," said the entity in the mirror.

"No. Please. I swear he will not go anywhere. We are your loyal servants."

A hand came out of the mirror and grabbed Donavan by the throat. "You have served me well except for the slip-up, but I made sure to remind you of that. No one comes between us. Your brother and you have eternity for our bargain. You give me souls, and I give you everlasting life. If either of you leave, you know the price!" The skeletal hand threw the jester back against a trunk. Rhianna watched as the demon's reflection faded and the mirror went back to normal. She swallowed and wondered what had turned the jester into the monster who now haunted her house. *Obviously something had happened with Alexander, because he showed up in my mirror. I wondered what happened.* She wanted to find out more, but the melody of the calliope was getting louder, sucking her away from the wagon and dragging her back into the darkness.

Chapter Six

Something warm rubbed against her face. It tickled her nose enough it brought her back to consciousness. "Snowball, get away," she mumbled to the cat.

"I don't think Snowball is here at the moment," a velvet voice whispered next to her ear.

Rhianna opened her eyes to dark ones and a man she had seen in her dreams. Was she still dreaming? Her eyes opened all the way as the sun streamed in the attic windows. The stained glass was blue with some kind of a symbol embedded in it. As the sun hit it, the rays shot straight at the door. She put her hand up to the light and felt the warmth and a charge go through her from the illuminated symbol. That must have protected her from the jester, from Donavan.

As her gaze swept the room, she saw an old-fashioned carousel horse. It had a gold, faded pole running through the center of it. It was completely black with red eyes. It was frozen in a rearing position, like it had been captured that way in the wood. Its eyes seemed to be alive. The saddle and bridle were also black and outlined in gold. Red jewels were embedded into the saddle and bridle. Rhianna got up, feeling like she had seen the horse before. The closer she got to it, the more real it seemed. It was almost if the braided mane would be silky under her fingers, or the coat would be like pressed silk. As she stared at it, she swore she saw an energy current running over it. Ebony black and a tinge of blue clung to the surface. It was a sheen no paint could have given it. Tentatively, her fingers touched the horse's flank. However, they came away full of dust, and there was nothing there. Only a piece of carved wood that had so much potential. Her gaze moved over the other objects in the room, as well as the man. She tried to ignore his presence, but it was hard. Her gaze kept trailing back to him as she took in his dark pants and the white tunic he wore. It was open to a v at the neck hinting at a defined chest. His dark hair was loose around his shoulders.

The other objects in the room were a doll house and a chest with a padlock on it. It was an old-fashioned lock, which appeared to be fastened tightly. She took a step towards it. Each item in the room gave her a feeling of déjà vu. She had seen them years ago. Her fingers closed on the padlock as she tugged on it. It was not coming off anytime soon. A wave of disappointment moved through her.

"I wouldn't open that if I were you. I don't think you're ready for what's in it," he whispered to her.

Rhianna jumped at the hot breath against her ear. "And why not?" she asked.

He laughed. "Because there are more important things to discuss than what is in the trunk when you have seen it before."

Rhianna turned toward him. "Really? And when have I seen this?"

He crossed the slight distance between them. His gaze graced her features as if she were a goddess. Rhianna felt as if his gaze burned right through her, like he saw her soul. The way he walked in those few strides were full of confidence. He was like a wolf, honing in on his prey, but she didn't feel threatened with him, just aroused. The sheer thrill of being around him culled up buried memories, making her lick her lips. She placed a hand between them. Instead of passing through him, like it should with a ghost, her hand landed on warm flesh. A zing moved up her palm as she touched the space above his heart. She even felt it beating underneath her palm.

"What are you? Why do I feel like I know you? Why—"

He didn't answer her except to trace his thumb along the line of her jaw and curl the rest of his fingers under her chin, drawing her lips up to his. As soon as they met, her head lightened. All her fear of what had happened to her in the past few days melted away. She was safe in his arms. They were strong, and he would protect her. His lips were as soft as flower petals. His kiss was chaste at first, tasting her mouth, allowing her to make the decision if she wanted to go any further. It was up to her if she wanted to explore his body.

God what am I doing? He feels so real and so warm. Her hands entwined around his neck as if they had a mind of their own. Her body worked against her wishes. She pushed herself against him, feeling his hard length against her pelvis, waiting to be freed. Her breasts crushed against his chest, and she had to stand on tip-toe to meet his lips properly. Once they did, his tongue snaked between them, exploring. And she let him. Everything about him wanted her. His hands cupped the mounds of her ass and pulled her into him even more as he gave it a little pinch, and he laughed while he kissed her.

Alexander's lips left her mouth, trailing down the line of her neck. He nipped at her skin, above her jugular, and for a moment fear, eclipsed her lust. Maybe he was a vampire come to claim her. When he planted a kiss there and circled it with his tongue, she relaxed and let him rake his fingers under her shirt, over her spine, so she was shivering and moaning against him.

"What are you doing to me?" she asked.

He licked up from her collarbone in one long, slow stroke and then nibbled on her ear. "What we both want. Don't you want me? I can feel your desire sparking over your skin. It makes you taste so damn good, like champagne and strawberries. God, I want you, Rhianna. I've been watching you all these years, hidden in the shadows of your reflection. Every time you stood before the mirror, naked and admiring yourself, I was there, on the other side, looking back at you. I've loved you for years. Let me love you now."

Rhianna's head reeled from the spell he wove over her. Something was transpiring, and she needed more information on what was unfolding with the house and with him before she could commit her body to a ghost. But damn she wanted him. She sighed.

"Alexander, I'm flattered, and not that I don't want you too, but I need to figure out what's happening. It's not every day I have a gorgeous hunk of a ghost come on to me or his crazy, jester, twin brother try and kill me. What is all this? My dream? This room? The mirror? How is it all connected? How is it all real?"

The ghost, the man, whatever, peered long into her eyes. She could tell he was fighting his own desire for her, as well. He lifted her chin and pressed his lips to hers in a chaste kiss and pulled away, leaving an empty space between them that promised more.

"You are right. You do have every right to know about the events playing out in your house."

"Where did it all start? What role do I play in all of this? Am I caught between some war started by your brother and now I'm a pawn? Have I gone to another dimension? Cause dead, psycho jokers, zombie horses, and weird music following me in my dreams are not something I am used to."

Alexander laughed. "Even when you are serious, you are so beautiful. So savage, like a wild beast wanting to break out from its cage. Much like Nightmare here."

He patted the wooden horse's side, and Rhianna saw the horse's eyes blink. Once Alexander put his hand on the horse, a current of blue energy ran over the ebony paint and made it come to life. Her life was getting stranger and stranger.

"What are you? Are you dead? Why me?" she whispered, trying to fit the pieces of the puzzle together.

"Rhianna, please, I don't mean to scare you. There is not a lot of time. I wish there was more, but once the sun sets, I will be back in the mirror, and the night is his time."

"You mean your brother? The jester?"

Alexander shook his head. "He used to be my brother. Now he is my keeper. When he died, the evil we promised ourselves to took him and turned him into a twisted parody of what he used to be and what he loved to do. It blackened his heart and stole his soul. The only way to be free is during the day, when the sun is high, and in this room, I can be flesh once again. Like I was with you when you were a child. That was how I knew my time of imprisonment was almost over."

A child? She had known him as a child? She didn't remember, even though everything about this place felt familiar. "How come?"

"You can't remember. The fear of my brother wiped it from your young mind. Your parents first brought you up here to play, and your mother would paint. She had one side of the attic set up as her studio because the light was good. They bought the house and moved in. When they did, they discovered this room with the trunk, Nightmare, and the mirror you now have in your bedroom. Your mother loved the mirror and had it moved downstairs. That was when the trouble started."

"I figured the jester was the cause of my parents' moving out of this place. I always loved the house. I never knew why they moved."

Alexander left the horse and crossed the distance between them. "Can't we skip the rendition of the past for a little bit and enjoy the time we have together?"

He twined her hair in his fingers and brought it to his nose to inhale the scent of the strands. "There is so much I've dreamed about doing to you," he breathed into her ear.

Rhianna felt the warmth of the sun bathing her in its light. It held her like a lover, and Alexander was there to give her what the sun could not, what she had not had in so long. Someone to hold onto. Did it matter if he was a ghost? Her eyes half-closed as he pulled her into him, and his hands began to pull up her T-shirt from her jeans. His hands were not calloused, but smooth like an angel's, and she was falling under his spell.

"How can you be flesh? You're dead. How can you be whole and not like—?"

"Shh. I'm not like my brother or his dark minions. I wasn't twisted, and I never truly died. I fell into the mirror whole. The symbol in the glass connects this room and my wagon in the other dimension I was sealed in. It's a rune of protection combined with a rune for gateways. My beloved created it to keep out the evil, to keep out my brother. She wove it into the gateway rune to bar anything from coming through. When the sun hits the sigil here, it opens a doorway between my dimension and yours. I did this with your mother and when you were a child. Just like I'm doing with you now. I can sense desire, and it draws me here, so I don't need the mirrors since they are guarded by my bother's minions."

"My mother? You knew her?"

Alexander laughed. "Yes. I knew her very well. She had a great mind and a wonderful eye for art."

The mood was broken then. "So you and she did this same dance, and you seduced her too? Did your brother get jealous and drive her out of the house, along with my father? Is that what this is all about? You want the house for something?"

Rhianna moved away, backing into the corner. As she did, her foot hit the trunk. Alexander looked out the window. The blue glass reflected off his face, and for a moment, it seemed he became transparent. He lifted his face to the sun and placed his fingers on the glass, trying to draw warmth from it. "No, Rhianna. Your mother and I were not intimate. She was already in love with your father. They were soul mates. I lost my soul mate to the demon I made a pact with. Like the dream, if anything came between my brother and our duty, we would be punished. My brother's scar was a reminder, and he lost the two things most precious to him. With each passing day, his heart became more twisted, like the scar on his face. And I, after two hundred years of traveling and feeding souls to the blasted demon, had finally found my soul mate. Endora knew the secret of how to free me. Before it could happen, the demon discovered my treachery and forced my brother to act."

"I'm sorry," Rhianna whispered. "I know what it's like to lose someone you love."

"It's okay. I know you lost your fiancé only a year ago. Part of me died when Endora did. When I met you as a child, I knew you were my soul mate. You were my key to freedom."

"I thought you said Endora was your soul mate. Am I her reincarnation or something? Should I remember you or the past?"

Alexander turned, and there was a half-smile on his face. The sun hit the rune and cast a shadow as the orb sank below the horizon. "When Endora died, her soul moved on to a higher realm. Fate would have dictated it was her time, but at least I know the demon did not get hold of her soul. No, Rhianna, you are my second chance at life and at love. You are my soul mate. It's rare, but it does happen. God has heard my prayers in the darkness and has granted me you. Please free me from the hell I exist in!"

His plea was so heartfelt it drew her to him like a month to a candle. If she got close to him, he would singe her wings. Rhianna believed Alexander. Part of her knew every word he said was true. She didn't know how to free him, and being next to him was like feeling the pull of a roller coaster going downhill. She was falling, going with a force that defined gravity, and without another word, she was in his arms.

Chapter Seven

Rhianna could not wait for Alexander to have his hands on her. Rhianna did not protest this time when he pulled her shirt over her head and flung it across the room. Her hands dove under his tunic and felt the rock hardness of his defined chest. God, she wanted to lick every inch of his cock. Rhianna imaged herself for a second a madam in a trashy novel where Alexander was her hero and he had to rip her bodice to get to the flesh beneath it. He did not rip her away her bra. Instead he teased her nipples through the lacy fabric. They were already hard pebbles, and the flick of his tongue made them tighter, harder, as he pressed against the fabric. Her need for him made them hurt. His teeth nipped at her left nipple while his thumb and forefingers twirled the other, until she moaned for him to stop.

Rhianna's hands tickled his chest as she let him take her where not even Jason had taken her. Everything with Alexander felt so right, like they were made for one another. Maybe they were soul mates like Alexander had said. If that were the case then their coupling wasn't for nothing. Maybe this was what would free him. He looked up at her with a devilish smile and then kissed the tip of her nose.

"I want you, Rhianna. I want to feel your wet pussy and hear you call my name. Do you want that?" The desire in his voice matched her wanting and covered her like a velvet fog. His hands went behind her back as he undid the hook of her bra. She was falling under the spell he wove with his voice and his hands. His fingers gently guided the straps down over her shoulders. She didn't feel embarrassed standing topless in front of him. Experiencing his touch made her so hot, like the atmosphere in the room had thickened. Gently, he guided her to the floor, to the rug she had slept on the night before.

There he leaned over her and brushed a few stray hairs out of her eyes. His touch was light and made her shiver from the desire of wanting to feel him inside of her. The anticipation was killing her. She hadn't been with anyone since Jason. Her finance was good in bed, but there was always something missing, some piece she could not describe, and with Alexander, it was there. His eyes were dark as the horse's coat

"Do you want me, Rhianna? All of me?"

She didn't answer him but leaned up and kissed his lips. Her tongue met his, and they did a mating dance as her hands searched for the button on his pants.

"I need to hear you say it. I can only come so far over, but with your permission, I can be all the way here. Only if you want me body and soul. Do you accept me?"

His fingers undid the button on her jeans, and he pulled them down, along with her panties. Alexander slid two fingers deep inside her hot well, making her back arch, and a guttural, primal moan escaped her lips. Rhianna bit her lip as he moved inside of her. Her mind was blown at him entering her and finger-fucking her. Did she want him? God, yes! Would she free him from his prison and risk her life against the jester? Yes. She desired him in her arms forever. She wanted him to fuck her every way he could think of. With their lovemaking, Rhianna felt a bond forming between them. Deep in her soul, she knew it had been her destiny to return to the house and free Alexander. They were meant to be together. He had known it even when she was a child.

His thumb pressed against her clit, rubbing it slowly in a circle, heightening her passions. Her muscles clenched, and his movements were slow torture. With his other hand, he ran along the sensitive flesh of her inner thigh. She was so wet, it was easy for him to insert another finger into her pussy, moving them together in slow, steady thrusts as her muscles conformed around his flesh. Her back arched, and she was loosing herself to him.

"Tell me, Rhianna. Do you want me to fuck you? I need you to say it."

"Yes, Alexander, I accept you. Fuck me. Now. Please. I need you!"

His fingers slid out of her for a final time, and he ran one along her lips so she could taste her own juices. His mouth met her lips in soft kiss.

"Thank you."

Without another word, he slipped off her jeans and panties the rest of the way and then allowed his pants to fall off as well. Rhianna licked her lips as she saw his cock saluting her. She leaned back on the rug and took in all of him. He was definitely a fine specimen of a man, and she wanted him. He smiled smugly as he lowered himself down, using one hand to spread her legs even wider. There he knelt and touched his tongue to her open slit and licked her lovingly. With each stroke, Rhianna pushed herself into his face even more. His free hand rested lightly on her stomach, pressing her down each time she lifted off the rug, and her hips bucked wildly. His other hand cupped her ass and squeezed it as his tongue found her clit.

Rhianna was so wet, and the sensations of Alexander's tongue darting over her were throwing her into a frenzy she had never known before. Each time she closed her eyes, she saw blue energy sparking between Alexander and her. His free hand replaced his tongue as his fingers rubbed her hard node faster than his tongue had. She was on the verge and needed him, but he kept up the torture, and with each burn of his fingers, she clutched the rug, letting the ecstasy build inside of her. Her muscles were tight. She needed him to fill her. She needed it hard and fast.

"Alexander!" she whimpered. Her body was alive from his touches. His fingers moved over her clit lightning quick, and right as she was about to crash, he pulled his fingers away, grabbed her hips roughly, and buried himself deep inside her pussy.

"You're so wet. You feel so good, Rhianna."

"Take me. Fuck me. Hard!"

He smiled. He almost resembled the joker. A bolt of fear rode the ecstasy as he pulled himself out of her inch by slow inch. His hands held onto her hips as he pulled her into him. His balls hit the outside of her pussy as he sunk himself into her, slowly increasing his pace, until Rhianna wasn't sure where he began and she ended. With each thrust, even through half-closed eyes, she saw the same blue energy around him and spreading to her. Once the charge enclosed around her, something changed. The air seemed more alive, and she felt every caress of air on her skin. She sensed the space between him and her, and as he drove into her harder, she needed it more.

"Harder," Rhianna moaned.

Alexander quickened his pace until the slapping sound of skin meeting skin was the only sound filling the room. The energy between them was making Rhianna a little light-headed. Her hips were moving at a frantic pace to keep up with her lover. He pounded into her a little bit more, gripping her tightly so she would probably have bruises on her hips in the morning, but she didn't care. It felt so damn good, and she yearned for more of him. Her muscles were scrunched so hard they hurt, and she was on the verge again, and so was he. A sheen appeared on his skin, and he was getting a little breathless as she was panting and going out of her head. The energy between them was building. She could see it sparking.

"Rhianna. You…are…my…mate…" With the last word, he came in a long thrust. And so did she. It was like the sea had washed over her, and she let it carry her away. The energy between them hummed over her skin and his. He lay on top of her, catching his breath, and then looked down at her.

Alexander laughed and kissed her deeply and moved out of her to lie beside her. His body heat helped keep her warm. His fingers played over her belly. Blue energy ignited between them and left trails. It felt electric. Each time his fingers wandered lower, she arched her back as the energy reached the secret place in her, and brought her to the edge. Alexander seemed to have fun toying with her, like she was a yo-yo, and pulled the energy string away from her, watching as her hips lifted and then went back down as he came closer to her skin again.

"You're doing that on pur...pose." Rhianna swallowed a groan of ecstasy as she came from his movements. She couldn't take it anymore, and let the energy wash over her in a blaze of blue light as it infused her. Finally, Alexander ceased his torture.

She traced her fingers over his chest, watching the energy spark. "What is this?"

"A little bit of magick."

"And can you pull a rabbit out of your hat too?"

Alexander laughed. She noticed his eyes look out the window at the setting sun. "No rabbits. When my brother and I made the deal with the demon, it included immortality and a little bit of magick. Sometimes I wonder if it was worth the price." His expression grew grim as he and Rhianna dressed in silence.

"What was the price?"

Alexander looked at her sadly. "Besides swearing our allegiance to it? Anyone, if they would not be missed, who was not part of the carnival and visited the Mirror Maze was selected by the demon. He would wait and pick out those he wanted. He had the power to reach into the world and grab those he chose. If we continued to feed him and never left his service, we would have eternal life with a little bit of power to go with it. If not, then there would be consequences."

"And Endora found away to break the pact?" Rhianna asked.

Alexander nodded. "She was a soothsayer, a psychic, from a long line of witches in her family. She would tell me stories about how some of her ancestors were from Avalon. She had a little bit of magick of her own, which was why she made the window. She dreamed about the demon and how it could be stopped. She said an angel came to her and told her love was the only way to break the spell. If I could give my heart to my soul mate, and she could accept me for everything, good and bad, then she could free me from my curse."

"So how do I free you?" Rhianna whispered wrapping her arms around his waist and buried her face in his back, inhaling his scent.

"It's getting late, and I have to go back. There are still things about me you do not know, my love. Dark things. Please, as much as I want to be free of this curse, leave this place before my brother returns. Once you are away from this house, you should be safe. My brother cannot travel off the land where the carnival was set up. He cannot use the mirrors like I can to watch over you. His heart has forgotten how to love. Leave here, so the demon doesn't find you. Please!" He turned in her grasp and stared deep into her eyes, imploring her to go. "I can always watch you from the shadows and know you are safe. Wherever there is a reflection, I will be on the other side. Please."

Rhianna shook her head. All of this was happening very fast, and she was not sure she could deal with it. She didn't want to leave the house. She had no where else to go. Alexander needed her. She believed him when he told her they were soul mates. She felt it with the energy flickering between them. She was not going to lose him like she lost her parents and Jason. She had finally found something in her life that was good, and now her heart was opening for him. If it was crushed one more time, she didn't know if she would recover from it.

"I'm not going anywhere. I guess I have to figure all this out then. Facing demons was never in my resume, but neither was dealing with crazy jesters. So where do I start?"

Alexander opened his mouth to say something, but his gaze caught the setting sun. "I have to go. I'm sorry. Tonight, go to a motel. Please. Donavan will be here soon. Promise me that. I can find you in the mirrors." He placed his hand on her shoulders, and Rhianna saw the desperation in his eyes. "Promise me."

"I promise."

He looked behind him, as if he saw something in the distance. "Donavan is here in my wagon. I have to go. I'll buy you some time." He leaned in and kissed her quickly on the lips. Alexander turned, and then he was gone. Rhianna was left staring out the window at the setting sun and an empty room. A chill went through her.

What have I gotten myself into? She looked at Nightmare and saw the slightest movement of the horse's head. Rhianna had better go. She was in no mood to deal with the jester. Her gaze fell on the trunk. There was something in there that would help her free Alexander. It was a sense she got, but there was no time for her to explore it. She swallowed and would be back in the morning. First, she was going to do some more digging in the town hall to see why a whole carnival could suddenly disappear off the face of the earth and be sucked into another dimension. There had to be some record of it. There just had to be.

Chapter Eight

Rhianna threw some clothes into her bag and looked for her keys, keeping an eye on the setting sun. It dipped lower and lower by the moment. She felt like she was fleeing from a vampire about to wake up. *Shit!* Her keys were no where to be found. She didn't remember where she had put them. Hoping they weren't upstairs or somewhere lost in the house, she ran down the steps and opened the front door. As soon she did, she heard the jingle of bells coming from her bedroom. She resisted the urge to turn back around and investigate and see if it was Donavan. If it was, she was in trouble. So she slammed the door shut and ran to her car. As luck would have it, her keys must have fallen out of her pocket when she got out of the car, because they were by her driver's side door.

Thank you. Thank you.

She got in the car and put the keys in the ignition. When she looked up, there was the jester, half-kneeling, half-standing on her hood with his face pressed to the windshield. Rhianna screamed as her heart jumped from her chest. She shifted the car into reverse. Her tires spun gravel and stone all around her. Rhianna made a backward beeline down the road to get away from the house. However, the joker didn't move from her hood. It was like he was a fixed, oversized ornament and stayed there as she accelerated to over fifty, barreling the car backward. Glancing in the mirror, she made sure she was still on the road and not in some ditch. Then she looked back at the jester.

The expression on his hollow, white face was one of pure glee.

"Do you really think you can get away from me?"

"Leave me alone!" she screamed.

"How can I leave you alone when you want to take my brother away from me? You bitches are all alike. Your pussy and your tits do all the talking."

Fear and a little bit of rationality came back to her, and she slowed her car down as she saw the beginning of the field to her left. Alexander had said the joker could not go beyond the boundaries of the carnival. Rhianna figured the boundary was the field. She came to a complete gear-and-brake-screeching stop. Half of her car was over the line, and the other was not. She left the car in gear and her foot on the accelerator. She was not going to take any chances, but she was also not going to run for her life, either. She was not a wuss. She would stand and face her fears even if they were dressed in a dirty, dark green and white jester suit. Underneath it, there must have been a soul left of the man whom she had seen pick up the tintype. Somewhere in there, the demon, or whatever, had not completely gotten hold of Donavan yet.

"Finding a little backbone now, are we?"

"Donavan, I know you're still in there."

The jester pressed his face against the windshield so it pushed through the glass, stretching and ripping his skin, until the jester got his neck through and then turned to look at her. The green fire in its eye sockets dimmed. Rhianna swallowed and held her breath. Her foot was itching to slam down on the gas pedal.

"Sorry. Donavan isn't here anymore."

"Oh, really? Then if he was completely gone he wouldn't care about the memory of his wife and child. Do you remember them?"

The fire died in his eyes and the perpetual grin turned down some. A tear slid down the white cheek. He was still in there somewhere.

"They died because I was too weak to save them." The voice coming from the jester was not the same one she heard in her mind. This one was filled with pain and sorrow. The echo of it burned her heart, since she wanted to help the man who was trapped underneath.

"Let me help you. Let me help Alexander," Rhianna whispered.

Whatever compassion Donavan had from the mention of his wife vanished and the jester, the demon returned. "You bitch!" it yelled. "You think you can sweet-talk away my brother! I know you fucked him, whore! For that, I'll feast on your soul!"

The jester made a grab at her. She floored the car and watched in a silent scream as the jester disappeared once she crossed the boundary of where the field ended. Once she did, she stopped the car altogether and sat and cried as the shock wore off from everything going on around her.

Rhianna was coming off having the best sex of her life, finding out she had a soul mate who was trapped in another dimension because of his crazy twin brother who was possessed by a demon who not only lived off souls but that Alexander and Donavan had been granted immortality with. It was all very crazy and very supernatural, and she had no idea anything like it existed. She was going to do some research and hit the library and the town hall in the morning. There had to be some information she could dig up. For now, she was going to get some sleep and not even think about ghosts, zombies, or Alexander.

* * * *

No matter how much she tried, she could not get Alexander from her mind. She had checked into a small motel on the outskirts of town off the interstate. Now she sat staring at the television, watching the shows flickering in and out from the white snowy background. The reception was horrible, and there was no cable. No matter how much she moved through the shows, her mind wandered back to Alexander. Her eyes closed as she thought about how his hands had been on her body and his cock buried between her legs. It had felt so damn good; she wanted him again. She licked her lips and felt her breath coming in short pants as her mind replayed every sensation from a few hours ago. For a dead guy, he sure knew how to light up her world. A groan of frustration escaped her lips because Alexander was not there to touch her. She shut off the television and the lights allowing the darkness envelop her. He said he could watch her in the mirrors. Maybe he was watching her now.

She stared at her reflection as the only light was from the red glow of the digital clock by the bed. The little illumination made her able to see her outline and nothing more. A faint blue sheen surrounded her body. It moved with her when she moved.

"Alexander?" Rhianna asked, feeling slightly foolish talking to an empty room. Everything around her was quiet except for the banging of the bed next door. The heavy thudding and groaning of the occupants made her bite her lips and chuckle as the darkness surrounded her and made her feel all alone, even if her beloved was looking out for her in another dimension. She heard something rustling in the room. She swallowed as she prayed it was not the joker staring out of the mirror. A small yelp escaped her lips. Automatically, Rhianna backed away until the edge of the headboard was digging into her back.

In the mirror was the ghost of a woman. She had blond hair and blue eyes. Her skin was translucent, and the dress she wore was the same blue as her eyes, the same blue as the stained glass window in the attic. Rhianna didn't get a sense of malice from her, only warm friendship. The apparition did not move and only smiled at her and waited for her to be comfortable. After a moment, the fear melted from her body. Tentatively, she crawled to the edge of the bed as curiosity overtook her. Her life was getting stranger and stranger by the minute.

Rhianna looked at the peaceful expression on the ghost's face, and the longer she stared, she realized who the specter was. "Endora?"

The woman nodded. "Yes, Rhianna."

"Did Alexander send you?"

Endora shook her head no, and a sad look marred her features. "No. I only wish he had. I would so love to see him. We are as separated as you are. Worlds apart that can only see each other on different sides of a mirror. His world is dark and filled with pain. My world is joyous and filled with wondrous things, but—"

"But you still love him, so it makes your heart sad, weighed down."

"Yes. The others tell me it will pass if I let go. It's the only thing truly holding me back from moving on with my afterlife. I had to be sure he was okay. You can understand that, can't you?"

Rhianna nodded. It was hard for her to believe she was talking to Alexander's long-dead lover, but then again, she herself had talked to a demonic joker who wanted her soul. So in retrospect, it was not such a strange event for her to be talking to a ghost. "I understand. I know what it's like to lose someone you love. I'm sorry, Endora, but why are you here? This is getting a little too weird for me. My nerves are about as frazzled as they get, and I need to be sure you're not Donavan here to trick me."

Endora laughed and floated out of the mirror. "No, silly. I'm not a trick of the demon, because that is what has inhabited Donavan. I'm here because I felt something change in Alexander. We are still connected, since we were soul mates. And his joy drew me from the void. Joy and hope let me follow the link between us, and I felt the cord between you two. When I saw you through the mirror and felt your pain just now from being separated from him, I knew my days of mourning for him were over. I can move on now. But I wanted to give you a few words of warning."

Rhianna moved over a little bit as the ghost sat on the bed next to her. The light Endora gave off warmed Rhianna's skin. Rhianna didn't have to squint to look into the brightness of the aura surrounding Endora. As Rhianna looked at the spirit, she was able to see more details of her dress. The blue was actually a peasant shirt and skirt with small teardrop jewels sewn into the fabric, so when she moved, they winked. Her hair was blonde but not as white as it seemed due to the glow. Her nose was delicate, and her fingers were long, like she could have played the piano.

"What's the warning?"

"The demon is very cunning. He will use your love for Alexander against you if you are not careful. You must not let him escape the other dimension. If he does, he will wreak havoc in this world."

"Great, now I have to save the world too?"

Endora laughed. "No, not really. You can't let him out. Right now he is confined to where the carnival was. As you saw, he can't get past the boundary of the field, which was where the sideshow used to be. I used to think it was a glorious place when I first joined up with it. Alexander and I fell in love, and he begged me not to tell his brother, who ran the sideshow. It wasn't until Donavan lost Rachel and the baby that he became more twisted, and the demon took hold. You saw in the dream what he had become. When he found out about us, Alexander wanted to run away. He was tired of the sideshow, tired of feeding souls to the demon. He told me the truth. He wasn't like his twin and didn't want to end up like him or have me end up dead, as well. And I saw how we could escape. In my cards and in my dreams, angels came to me and showed me how to bar the demon from entering through my mirror, to keep evil away."

"The runes in the attic window. Alexander said you made them. How did they survive? How did the carnival disappear? I can't find any records of it in the town. Something that big would draw attention and a crowd. What happened?"

"You won't find anything in the town records. There is nothing. When the carnival disappeared, it was completely wiped away from the history of man. A fire destroyed the whole thing. A fire I started to rid the world of the demon. I did not know how far his evil had spread. He had claimed all the souls of the carnival as his. He was barred from my wagon because of the runes I had on my door and I had drawn on my mirror. The only things that remain from the past are the trunk in your attic and Nightmare."

Rhianna nodded absently. It made sense a fire could destroy the whole carnival. When the carnival was destroyed, the demon was trapped until someone built a house on the land. Until her mother moved the mirror from the attic room, like Alexander had said. "How did the window get into the house?"

Endora smiled. "I made the glass and buried it away from the sideshow in the woods. I had a dream one day a house would be there and thought it might need some protection, since I was not going to need it anymore. When they were building the house, I assume they found it. Rhianna, you have to go back to the house and up into the attic. There are more answers in the trunk than I can ever give you. Here, take this."

The ghost pulled a key from the folds of her skirt and handed it to Rhianna. It fell heavily into her hand. The metal was cool against her palm. This would open the trunk she had tried to open earlier in the attic. "What's in the trunk?"

"You'll have to find out. As the sideshow's motto says: Some things will mystify you. Some will haunt you, and others will entrance you. You have to enter a world of nightmarish wonders to see your darkest dreams come true. It will help you to understand what the carnival and sideshow were, how they started, and give you a weapon to use against the demon. Maybe you can free Donavan with it."

"Why are you telling me all this? I mean, you failed. Alexander said you were psychic, and you knew a way to free him. How do I free him? Will the answer be in the trunk?"

Endora shook her head. "Your love is the only thing that can free him. You have to see what he is." The ghost started to fade.

"Wait!" Rhianna cried. "What do you mean I have to see what he is? I love him. He said it would be enough. I'm his soul mate like you were."

"Soul mates or not, Rhianna, some things cannot be told. They must be shown before the heart and mind can truly accept all of one person. We all have demons to face. I faced mine ages ago and didn't live to tell the tale, but I didn't fail my love. I only gave him hope for you. There is magick inside of you. There was when you were a child. You have to find it again. Go back to when you first felt the power inside of you. It came from your ancestors, passed down through your mother."

"What are you talking about? I don't remember…"

The ghost had almost disappeared becoming transparent. The warmth of her presence was dissipating fast. "Remember before the demon touched you and stole your memory. Find the power inside…open…mirror…" Endora was gone and had left behind more questions than she had answered.

Rhianna screamed in frustration as her hand wrapped around the key. The last thing she wanted to do was go back to the house, but it was the only place where she could find some answers. *Before the demon touched me? Had I seen the jester before? Alexander said he used to talk to my mother and he had known me as a child. Mom, I wish you were here to tell me what happened before you left that house. Why didn't you ever tell me? Probably because Mom was scared something would happen to me and was protecting me. God, Mom, I need you here right now. I hope you're watching out for me, 'cause I'm going to need all the help I can get. What did Endora mean about accepting the darkness in Alexander? Is there something I'm not seeing? Is he really the jester and Donavan is some image he created? Is he really the demon?* Rhianna shook her head. This train of thought was getting her nowhere. She looked at the clock again. Its numbers stared at her like demonic eyes. It was still early, but if she wanted to go back to the house, she had to get there early without running into the jester. Thankfully the room was safe from him.

I guess I have to be a hero tomorrow. Right now, I want to be the damsel in distress. Rhianna settled back on the bed. Her head hit the pillow away from the glare of the clock. As her eyes closed, she tried to calm her mind into something peaceful. Once she did, she didn't see the blue outlined form in the mirror, watching over her as he had promised.

Chapter Nine

Rhianna found herself staring at the light streaming in the attic window. It was bright enough she had to put up her hand to keep the glare away. *Great, another crazy dream.* As she looked around the room, there were three other figures in it. One of them was her mother, and she was standing over an easel, painting. Her mother was young, the same age as Rhianna was now looking like an angel with the halo of sunlight surrounding her. Tears welled in Rhianna's eyes as she saw her mother. She tried to touch her, but her hands passed right through her mother as they had when she dreamed about Alexander and Donavan.

Rhianna heard her mother laugh, and it brought back all the warm feelings she had and the loss of her parents. Rhianna was closer to her mother, since her father had worked all the time while Rhianna was growing up. It was only in the years before his death did she really start feeling comfortable with him. Now she looked at the scene and took it all in.

The trunk sat in the corner. Alexander was holding her up on the horse. The portrait her mother painted was the view she was looking at of her on the horse and Alexander making sure she didn't fall off. Her heart broke since she did not remember it. Alexander had said she had seen him before and played with her as a child and spoken to her mother. Here was proof of that.

"Claire, you are such a wonderful painter. You should really think about showing the pieces."

Her mother laughed. "Alexander, you are such a flirt and such a liar. You know I'll never show these. They are doodles that keep me busy with Jim not being around."

"Mommy, look. The horse wants to go outside. Can't we take him out?" young Rhianna asked.

"No, honey. He has to stay in this room. You know that." A look of concern flashed across her mother's face as Rhianna looked on. Her mother put down her brush and stared at Alexander. "Will she be safe? I've starting hearing things at night. He wants her. I don't know how to protect her."

"Bring the mirror back upstairs or smash it, Claire. It's the only way to keep her safe."

Her mother shook her head. "I've tried both. I can't. I picked up a chair, and it only bounced off the glass. It won't budge from the floor. I've even brushed the glass with paint, tracing the runes over it, but nothing. The paint disappears the next morning. What am I going to do?"

Alexander took her mother in his arms and gave her a hug and kissed the top of her head. He took her shoulders and stared at her. "I will protect her. I promise. When she grows up, she will be my soul mate. If not, I would not be able to be here."

Claire nodded. "I never would have believed any of this was true until I moved in here and saw this room. I always thought my grandmother's stories were just stories. My mother assumed my grandmother was crazy, but my grandmother had this symbol carved above all her doorways and would always tell me it kept the evil out. I would sit by her knee next to the fire, and she would tell me stories about the magick passed down through her family. She said we were elemental witches. And I watched her light candles without matches. She tried teaching me some things. Told me I was a water witch, but before we got too far, she died. Everything was lost with her. My mother never believed in any of it, and I don't know about Rhianna."

"She is a witch. It runs in her blood. You named her after your grandmother, didn't you?" Alexander asked.

So that's where my name came from. Mom, why didn't you ever tell me any of this? Not that I would have believed you, but it might have come in handy now! I need a little bit of magick to be able to deal with my situation.

"She will find her magick when the time is right. I only hope she can see past the darkness to find it." Rhianna heard Alexander whisper as he kissed the younger version of her on the head lightly. Even as she watched in the memory, he loved her.

"Take care of her, Claire."

Alexander turned and vanished. As he did, the scene grew dark, and suddenly she heard screaming. Rhianna looked around her and realized she was in her parents' bedroom. The mirror in which she had first seen Alexander was pulsating with an eerie green glow. Rhianna reached out and touched the glow. She was zapped by the energy. She pulled her hand away quickly and looked around the room, wondering what had happened. A sense of urgency filled her. She ran out of the room and into her old bedroom.

Her younger self was crumpled up in the corner of the bed, staring at the very same jester who had come after her earlier in the day. He was perched on the footboard of her bed like a bird, balancing on the balls of his feet. As Rhianna stepped into the doorway, the joker turned his head all the way around and stared at her. The grin on his face was even wider than when she first saw him. She was not afraid of him anymore. She stepped in and lunged at him as he leaned over, slowly reaching out his bony fingers to the younger version of her.

"You can't save her. She's mine!" the jester voice echoed in the room, followed by a high-pitched laugh.

"Mommy!"

Rhianna spun around to see her mother standing in the doorway. Her mother rushed in and threw herself between her and the jester. "You will not have her."

"She is mine, bitch! What would you do? Give me your soul instead?"

"Yes," her mother whispered, "anything to save her from you."

"A mother's love. How quaint!"

The jester reached out and touched little Rhianna's hand. He stopped and stared at Claire. Her mother noticed the change in him. Donavan was fighting the demon who had wanted her. Something about the scene or her mother's love had triggered an emotion in him. "Run. Go from here and keep her away. If she comes back, I can't promise what he will do. From my touch, she won't remember anything. Go. Now!"

Donavan ran the back of his gloved hand over Rhianna's tiny cheek. She heard herself whimper and touched her own cheek where he had touched her. The poignant moment was broken when he screamed and clutched his face. The bells on his outfit shook and jingled. A green light appeared around him as he seemed to be struggling with the demon inside. Claire and little Rhianna stayed where they were and watched what happened.

"I said go!"

Claire scooped up the child and ran out the door. The front door slammed. The car started and burned gravel as she had done earlier in the day. Suddenly, the sound of the calliope was blasting in the room. Rhianna watched as Donavan let go of his head and then turned and sniffed the air. He clapped his hands together like a happy child. "We have company."

Rhianna looked around the room, and there was no one else there. He stared directly at her. As he waved, a green balloon appeared in the middle of her room and floated there. Outside, she heard the sound of horses and people walking in the gravel, a lot of people, like there was a carnival in her driveway.

"I'm dreaming," she whispered.

"It's only a dream. It's only a dream." He waved his hands in front of his face like he was freaking out. Then his demeanor grew menacing. "He's mine!" He jumped, and Rhianna tripped and fell backwards onto the floor, banging her head on the hardwood.

"Oh, shit!" she said as the jester stood over her.

"HAHAHAHAHA. You can't escape me that easily, girlie. I might have been a memory before, but now this is my world, and you can't do anything to get away from me." He straddled her, and in an instant, produced a rope. He bound her feet first and then crawled over her until his face was even with her own. He kissed her on the lips. His tongue squirreled into her mouth. All Rhianna tasted was death. Getting her mind back, she shoved him away, but he only did a back flip and landed on the bed.

"Alexander," she shouted.

"My brother won't hear you. He won't come for you. You're mine, now. All mine! And I'm going to have so much fun with you."

He reached down and grabbed her arm. Panic and fear flooded her thoughts. She was not going to give up that easily. Rhianna closed her eyes and tried to gather her wits. Her mother and Alexander said she was a witch. Then somewhere deep inside her she had to have some magick. This was her dream, her memory. He was not going to twist it. She looked into the recesses of her soul and felt the tie between her and Alexander. She felt the energy coursing through her, and as it did, it felt like something that had been blocked with cobwebs or ivy, waiting to be opened. With a creak of hinges, the power inside her fluttered to life, and she felt it move down her arm. Her eyes flew open enough for her to see a purple glow move over her and into the jester. His head snapped back around, and his upturned smile formed into a perfect o. A howl of pain filled her head, and he let her go. He hissed at her, and without another word, did a couple of back flips and crashed through the bedroom window. Rhianna slumped to the floor as exhaustion washed over her, and as it did, she heard the tinkling of glass as it hit the dirt, which turned into a loud, overbearing beep.

Chapter Ten

Rhianna opened her eyes and stared at the clock. It was seven in the morning. She turned off the alarm, and decided she'd had one messed up dream. She flung the covers off not remembering crawling under them, and when she did try to stand, she nearly fell. When she looked down, her feet were bound with cord, which was old and frayed. Her butt fell back on the bed, and she undid the rope.

Okay, not a dream. This is getting even stranger. If it was true, then I did magick. I'm a witch. She looked at the night stand and saw the key Endora gave her. She had to go back to the house and see what was in the trunk. First, she drew in a deep breath and took everything in she had learned. All the information, dreams, memories, from all the ghosts was true. *If I'm a witch, then how does that work?* Rhianna closed her eyes and raked her fingers through her hair. As she did, she felt energy sparking between her fingers, and when she looked at her hand again, she saw a faint purple energy around it, like in her dream. *This is cool.*

Even though she didn't know how her power worked, she didn't want to be burning anymore daylight. She grabbed her stuff, threw it in the passenger seat, and headed off back to the house. Her fingers were itching to rifle through the trunk and see what was there. She hoped Endora was right, and it did bring her some answers.

Back at the house, she turned the handle on the door and listened. Nothing. She poked her head in the doorway, and there was still nothing. She went in carefully and let the door close with a soft click. Fear thundered in her mind louder than her heartbeat. Her gaze swept the living room and dining room for Snowball. She hoped the cat was okay and smart enough to hide from the crazy jester. She made her way upstairs and into her old room. None of her furniture remained. As the long shadows retreated, she noticed the window was broken.. Rhianna gripped the key tighter. She checked her bedroom, and the mirror showed nothing more than her reflection.

Tired and baggy eyes stared back at her. Lanky black hair was thrown up in a ponytail. *I look like hell warmed over.*

Rhianna went up to the attic. The house was still silent. Once she entered the other room, it was like walking into another world. Where the rest of the house was dark and eerie, like it should have been in a gothic novel, this room felt like it was light and airy.

"Hello, Rhianna."

She spun around, and there was Alexander. Without a second thought, she pushed herself into his arms, forgetting about the key and the trunk. Her lips met his in a heated kiss. Her tongue snaked into his mouth as his hands wove through her hair. He was already hard and ready for her. For a long moment, they kissed, feeling and holding one another. Rhianna didn't want to let him go, as if he were her lifeline back to reality. However, it was a strange reality; she was not sure where it fit into her world. As they kissed, she saw and felt the energy sparking between them. His blue and hers purple.

When they parted, they were both breathing heavy.

"I was afraid for you. I felt your distress last night. I couldn't come to you. I'm sorry. Forgive me." He kissed her again, gently this time, and lifted her shirt off her head.

"It's okay. I handled it."

"God, Rhianna, I need you right now! I need you so bad."

His lips went to her breasts, as she had forgotten to put her bra back on. He brought his lips to one breast and cupped the other. Alexander bit down hard on the nipple enough to make her moan.

"Alexander." She drew out his name in a breathy groan, accentuating the syllables. Her hands dove under his waistband and gripped his rock-hard cock. She needed him to fuck her so bad. She needed him to remind her that nothing else mattered in the world except her and him. Rhianna fell to her knees and pushed his pants down before he could protest. Her lips found his dick and then encompassed it as her hands gripped his bare ass. He was so warm as she nestled into working her tongue around his shaft, pulling her mouth up along him, creating a vacuum effect. He quaked against her as his hand gripped her shoulder hard, and his legs wobbled a little bit as she brought her free hand around and cupped his balls.

She dared a look up and saw his eyes were closed, and he was breathing heavy, trying to hold onto control. She liked that he wasn't. It meant anything went, and she could do whatever she wanted with him. Her tongue rode his cock in one long stroke until it balanced on his spongy head where she tasted the salty essence of his pre-cum. She licked around it, like savoring whipped cream, and let the edge of him rest on her bottom lip as she tickled his scrotum until he opened his eyes. The lust in them made her see how much he was about to lose control. Through the strange connection developing between them, Rhianna got a sense of him. Alexander could be an animal if he wanted. He wasn't ready to unleash what he kept hidden inside, since he didn't want to frighten her. Not yet.

"Please," he whispered. Rhianna smiled, liking that he was begging her for something.

"Only if you're a good boy," she answered.

He grabbed her hair and yanked her head back. "Suck it," he ordered.

She batted her eyelashes at him and smiled innocently. "Only if you say the magic word." She licked her lips.

Alexander growled in frustration. Rhianna answered by running her hand slowly up the length of his cock, enjoying the soft and smooth skin of it. She always loved that about men's anatomy. It was so soft and yet so hard. Her palm wrapped around his penis and held it tight as she moved up and down in slow tantalizing motions, making him want release. Each quick inhale from him made her wet and hot.

"Come on, baby. What's the magic word?"

"Rhianna, please!"

"All you had to do is ask, baby."

Alexander let go of her hair, and she nested between his legs once again, letting her mouth take him all in. She was so happy she didn't have a gag reflex, because she wanted to taste all of him. He grabbed her shoulders and pushed her away from him. A little dazed, she looked up at him as the sun surrounded him like an off-kilter halo.

"Jeans. Off!"

In a second, her jeans were on the floor, along with her underwear. Alexander had her leaning against the carousel horse with his hand around her waist so he could fuck her from behind. Rhianna gasped as he plunged deep into her pussy. She was so wet he slid in easily. As before, they fit together like two pieces of a puzzle. His left hand gripped a breast, and he pounded into her.

"Fuck me."

"Rhianna, my dick loves your pussy." Alexander pumped inside of her.

Every time he pounded into her, her muscles wrapped around his cock, and it brought her closer to the brink. Her eyes were closed as her hands gripped the wooden mane of the horse. The energy between them was building. As it did, she realized the hair underneath her fingertips was not completely wooden anymore. It was coming to life, but she didn't care. She was getting exactly what she wanted.

"More, baby. Please, I need it!" she screamed.

Her juices were flowing between her legs as he was near to coming. She could feel it as he tried to stay in control, but he was losing the battle. "Rhianna, I'm coming. All for you, baby. All for you." With one more hard buck, he met the skin of her ass and spilled himself deep inside of her.

"Alexander!" Rhianna cried as he released. It was wonderful to be filled and know she was wanted. They were soul mates. She could have him any way she wanted. It almost seemed like he could read her mind and know what she wanted from him. She hoped he also knew what she wanted in the future.

He withdrew from her and backed away. Rhianna unclenched her fingers from the horse's mane and felt it was now wooden again. *Strange. I guess it was magick.* After a moment, she caught her breath, turned, and gathered her discarded clothing.

"Hi." He ran a thumb over her cheek and kissed her.

"Hi, back. I didn't expect to see you here. I mean—I wasn't sure."

Alexander smiled. "I know, but I was able to sneak away. I figured you would be here. I hope you don't mind."

Rhianna shook her head as she adjusted her shirt. She sneaked a look at him again and wanted to have another marathon session. However she was taking up daylight and had to see what was in the trunk. For now, her body was humming with the aftermath of their loving-making. She fished the key out of her jeans pocket and knelt down next to the trunk.

Once the lock opened, a sense of anticipation washed over her. Whatever was in here would help her unlock the puzzle and hopefully free her soul mate from the dimension he was imprisoned in. She swallowed and opened up the trunk. Her first reaction was to scream. On the top of the trunk was a white and green harlequin suit. Her breath quickened, and she waited for the suit to spring to life. Alexander put a hand on her shoulder and pulled out the suit.

"It's okay, Rhianna. This was Rachel's costume. See the colors are on different sides than Donavan's. It's not him."

His fingers moved over the soft fabric for a moment, as if they were remembering his sister-in-law. Underneath the suit was the tintype she had see in her dream with Donavan, Rachel, and his baby, all staring back at them happily as if nothing had happened. She gazed at the happy family and wondered if Rachel's soul was at peace or if the demon had gotten it. Underneath the photo were tons of old flyers promoting the carnival and sideshow. All of them had the jester on the logo but displayed different cities. The same one that was tacked up on the tree outside. And underneath that were paints and makeup she had seen on Donavan's dressing table. As she lifted out the tray of makeup, she discovered a large leather-bound book. The book was old and as big as the old-time Bibles. The cover of it seemed to pulsate and call to her. Rhianna went to take it, but Alexander seized her wrist tightly before she could touch it.

"Don't. That is what got this whole mess started."

"What do you mean?"

"The book belonged to our father. He had gotten it in his travels in Europe. He began to dabble and called up the demon. The demon devoured my father, promising him more and more magick for a part of his soul. Until it was too late, and nothing could save him. Donavan couldn't resist the power my father had and wanted more. I was taken by the power, too. I wanted it just as badly as he did. The power drove me to kill my father."

Rhianna looked at Alexander. How could he have killed anyone? There was no way the man she loved could have killed his own father. Donavan was the evil one. Was Alexander so twisted he was only showing her one part of himself? She drew back from him. She watched as Alexander winced. "You killed your own father? But Donavan, he's the one who is possessed. How—"

"There's more, Rhianna. Remember in order to free me you had to accept all of who I am?"

"Yes, but—"

"There is no but. You have to listen to me!"

"All of this has been some kind of a joke? Do you really want me, or are you using me or something strange to awaken the magick I have inside of me? You want me to free you from this alternate dimension and then let you loose on this world so you can wreak havoc here? Is that it? What more did you do? Did you kill your mother, too?"

"Rhianna, enough! You want to know the truth!" He grabbed her shoulders and shook her, forcing her to look at him. "See the truth! See what I have become because of the evil I did."

His handsome façade melted away like candle wax, revealing a skull underneath. Unlike the jester's face, Alexander had a plain skull with blue fire burning in his eye sockets. A stab of fear went through her heart. *How could he betray me like this? I love him. Oh, God, what have I been kissing? What have I been sleeping with? He felt so real. Was it all an illusion?*

Alexander reached out a skeletal hand to her, but she backed away.

"You lied to me! All of this was to…I don't know what it was for. To use me, to scare me to death! To free you! And I fell for it. The bleeding heart. And I fell for it. God, I'm such an idiot."

"Rhianna. No! I never meant to hurt you. You know that." Alexander's voice was in her head and all around her. A jolt of pure ecstasy sliced through her, and she had to press her nails into her palms to keep from letting it carry her away. Her eyes fluttered shut as she tried not to give in, but whatever power Alexander was using on her overwhelmed her senses. Finally it passed, and she opened tear-filled eyes.

"Please stop. I don't know you, whatever you are. I can't believe I let you touch me! Leave me alone!" she shouted.

Alexander waited a moment and was about to say something when he stopped. Nightmare came alive, and he jumped up on top of the mare. He looked back at her one more time, and the horse and he made a running leap out the window, however, it did not shatter. They vanished, as if they had never been there. Rhianna sank down to the floor and stared at the window, amazed the sun could still warm her. For a few minutes, Alexander's lingering touch stayed with her, like the warmth from the sun. But it faded fast, and when she tried to sense the link between them, it was silent. She couldn't feel the energy connecting them, and that made her lonelier. It reminded her of screaming gingerbread men left to burn in her oven, the high-pitched, shrill cry she had left unanswered so long ago when she had been told about Jason's death.

Rhianna peered at the empty room and the book in the trunk. It had started all of this. Anger welled up inside of her as she gazed at the thing. Energy built inside of her as she went to grab the book, but something stopped her. If she brought it out of the room, Donavan could get it, and that would be a bad thing, her gut told her. She did not want the demon to become even more powerful. She sighed and looked at the sun. It was still high in the sky, and she was feeling weary.

Rhianna left the attic and went back into her bedroom. She sat on the edge of the bed and stared into the mirror. It reflected nothing back at her except her likeness. She got an idea and tried to move it. She tried pushing it, and it would not even move. It wasn't heavy. She lifted her music box and flung it at the glass. The music box shattered into tiny splinters.

Rhianna didn't care anymore. She felt hurt and used from letting herself be fooled. Curling up on the bed, she felt Snowball nestle into the crook of her back. His warmth was the comfort she had. *Stupid cat!*

As she stared out the window, her anger cooled. Loneliness set in and so did the heartache. *What if Alexander had been telling the truth? Endora had said I had to take the good with the bad in order to save him. I have free will. It's my choice to accept him. He never showed anything more than love and compassion for me. Even in my memories, he wanted to keep me safe from his brother.* Then it hit her. *God, what did I do? I'm such an idiot. I love him. No matter what he is or isn't. Now I've fucked it all up, and I'll never see him, just like Jason. All because of me he died. All because of me!*

Rhianna settled her head against the pillow, emotionally spent. Her sorrow, hurt, and anguish had spilled out onto the cloth of the case, and all Snowball did was purr. Nothing made sense to her anymore. Nothing.

Chapter Eleven

"Rhianna." It was her name being whispered across time and space, capturing her and bringing her back to reality. Her eyes fluttered open as she felt her hair being moved from her face. When her gaze met dark eyes, relief fluttered through her heart.

"Alexander!"

She watched him smile. "Yes, love. It's me."

She flung her arms around his neck and buried her face as renewed tears flowed from her already puffy eyes. His palm caressed the back of her head while he held her, and she cried. When Rhianna looked up, she grinned and wiped the tears away, feeling foolish at what she had said to him upstairs early. "I'm sorry. I didn't mean it. Whatever you are."

Alexander shook his head. "I know, baby. It's okay. I understand it was a shock. I'm here now. I'll never leave you again. I promise."

Rhianna backed away. Alexander was downstairs. He had told her he could only materialize in the flesh upstairs. A jolt of panic swept through her. It was dark out. She had to get out of the house before Donavan found her. She grabbed Alexander's shirt and tugged. "We have to go. Come on."

Alexander didn't move. "It's okay. We don't have to worry about my brother anymore. I took care of him."

Rhianna stopped and turned back around. Her gaze flickered to the mirror and noticed her image and nothing else. She put her hand out and touched the glass. It was cool underneath her palm. There was no strange green glow or jester leering back at her. Maybe Alexander had taken care of it. She closed her eyes and felt her power flare to life. As she turned back, she smiled slowly. Alexander would not lie to her. Maybe he had overcome his brother and now he was free.

"How are you here? I thought you could only come to me upstairs."

Alexander smiled and walked over to her, as if he were stalking her. She loved watching the way he walked. He lifted her chin, bringing her lips to his. The kiss was tender at first, and then he sucked on her bottom lip and bit down on it before letting her go. "You taste so good, baby. I want to eat you up."

"I'm an all-you-can-eat buffet. You just have to get a spoon," Rhianna whispered against his ear, going up on tiptoe to reach him. Her hand stroked his length through his pants, running over his cock as she pushed her hips into him, too.

"Oh, I'm going to do more than that tonight. You want to have a little fun?" His hand wove into her hair, and he yanked her head back in a quick, sharp tug. His tongue licked the smooth expanse of her throat, following the line of her chin, until he pressed his lips against hers. He kissed her hungrily before ripping open her shirt to reveal her breasts. He gripped them tenderly at first, weighing them as if they were a on a scale. All the while, Rhianna breathed heavily, amazed at the way Alexander was with her.

"What are you doing to me?"

"Anything I want. Can I? Do you like to be tied up? I want to see you bound. Tell me I'm your Master."

"Yes. Anything you want. You're my Master."

She felt Alexander smile against her chest as his tongue tasted her skin above her heart, and his hands played with her nipples. "I'm so happy you said that, Rhianna. Now do as I say. Strip."

Her lover backed away as she unzipped her jeans and slipped off her panties as her socks and shoes were still upstairs. The air was chillier in the bedroom than up in the attic. She stood and looked at herself in the mirror and watched as Alexander came up behind her. He kissed the side of her neck and took one hand, bringing it behind her back. Something wrapped around her wrist. He then took her other hand and tied it as well until she couldn't move them. A twinge of fear skipped through her heart. She swallowed and wanted to say something, but she didn't.

"Bend over."

"Alexander, what—"

He pushed her onto the bed. "I said bend over! You call me Master and do as I say. If not, you get punished. Understand?"

Rhianna's face was pressed into the covers. She nodded but didn't say anything. Suddenly, a jolt of pain landed on her ass. The sound of hand hitting skin echoed in the room. The pain vibrated through her, but then it was followed by a rush of pleasure.

"Do you understand? Or do I have to punish you more?"

"More," Rhianna moaned. The next slap was deposited on her other cheek. She bit her lip to keep from crying out, and once Alexander's hand landed on her ass, she was high on pain and pleasure. Another slap rolled her eyes back into her head as her fingers curled into a fist. She'd never been treated this way with sex, but she liked it. Her pussy was already dripping, and each time his hand connected to her flesh, the zing of pain and pleasure made her want his cock buried deep inside of her. She wanted to be fucked. Her breaths were coming in short bursts as his punishment continued, and without her control, her hips were bucking, and she was beyond all hope. It took all her willpower not to cry out, until finally, he stopped. Rhianna took a moment to catch her breath before she moved and rolled over. Sitting was painful, but she managed. Glancing at Alex, she saw he was sweating and breathing hard from the exertion.

He smiled and motioned for her to go up against the headboard. Then he untied her hands and tied them again to the bed frame.

"What are you doing?"

"Never question me. Understand?" he slapped her cheek so lightly she barely felt the sting.

"Yes, Master," she whispered.

He gave her a quick peck on the lips and slithered down between her legs. At the first flick of his tongue, she was lost. Her hips lifted off the bed, and she pressed her pussy into his face. Her head fell back against the headboard as she bucked in her restraints. His tongue lapped at her slowly, first cleaning her nether lips and then concentrating on nibbling on her clit. Between his teeth and tongue teasing her, Rhianna's mind was gone in a land of pleasure. She was coming so hard each time his tongue touched her, Rhianna was beyond knowing anything. Her moans had turned into pants, and she wanted to rip free of her bonds and shove his face deeper into her, but she couldn't, and it was killing her. With each lave of his tongue, he was taking her to worlds she had never gone to before. She needed to be fucked. Maybe this was the punishment, to have her hanging and so ready to be fucked.

Finally, she found her voice. "Please," she whimpered.

Alexander stopped his torture of her and slowly looked up from her pussy. His eyes flickered green. From his eyes, she saw the wicked grin and a long pointed tongue snaking up between curled-up lips.

Rationality returned like being dumped in cold water. Rhianna screamed as the jester laughed. "You taste so good. I don't know the last time I've eaten such good pussy." He licked his lips, making a smacking sound as he sucked on his fingers. Rhianna felt vulnerable and violated as she drew her legs underneath her.

"You tricked me."

The joker nodded and crawled up and stared at her. She turned her head, but he forced her to look at him.

"You said I could. You opened yourself to me. I couldn't have done it without your consent. Don't tell me you didn't enjoy it? You're disappointed it wasn't Alexander."

"Go to hell!"

"I've been there, and it's lovely this time of year. The sulfur gives it a distinct aroma. You're only mad Alexander showed you his true face."

Surprise ruptured in her mind even though she tried to keep it off her face.

"Don't look so shocked. Of course he told me. Did he tell you his sob story too? 'Poor me, I killed my father for power, and now I want to be free.' The only way he can be free is to die, and I won't let you kill him. Bitch. Let's play nice for now." Donavan's gloved hand tickled its way to her clit. Once it touched her, she was overwhelmed. A jolt of energy made her forget. Green fire filled her vision. The tongues of flame danced in her mind, grabbed her arms, and whirled her around as she was falling under his spell. She was aware she was moaning and writhing, but something else was wrong. It felt like she was falling and couldn't find a hold. Rhianna tried to breathe and couldn't. She tried to look away from the jester, but he was inside her mind with the green tongues, ready to burn her alive.

Alexander. The thought was a plea for help, a desperate cry, filled with sorrow and love. She had betrayed his trust. Rhianna knew that now and was paying the price for the betrayal. She only hoped he forgave her. Endora had said Rhianna had to accept the darkness in Alexander's soul. When he showed it to her, she had thrown it back in his face. Fear had controlled her at seeing his true appearance, but she knew that no matter what kind of a creature he was, he still had a soul or he would not have treated her as if she were a piece of gold, even when she was a child. Her mother trusted him, and she had to trust him. The green fire nearly had her, and she felt Donavan had stopped manipulating her. He said he needed her acceptance to do what he had done to her. Like Alexander had. They both needed a willing partner to get inside her brain to her body. She thought about what her mother had said about being a witch. She was not going to give up so easily. Whatever magick she had in here, she was going to use it to save Alexander and free him from the hell he was locked away in.

Something inside her opened, and she felt warmth flow over her body. In her mind's eye she saw a purple fire ignite and meet the green. Somehow she was going to win. Her will stoked the power inside of her, and she was able to look away from the jester. Suddenly, he was screaming and covering his eyes. He hid his face with his hands and fell off the side of the bed. She didn't wait any longer. She grabbed one of the bindings with her teeth and pulled. It took a few tugs until she was able to get her hand free. She looked around the bedroom and didn't see the jester. Her gaze fell on the mirror. It was glowing green. Had he retreated back to his own world? However, when she heard a low moan, she looked in the corner of the room and saw the jester holding his head.

She got off the bed slowly. "Help me, please." The whisper was filled with pain.

"I don't think so. Tell me how to free Alexander."

"Rachel? Is that you?" The jester looked up, and instead of the twisted clown face staring back at her, it was a clone to Alexander, except for the burn scar on his face. This was the real Donavan. Rhianna had not harmed him. She had hurt the demon possessing him.

"No, Donavan. Quickly, how do I free your brother?"

Donavan looked up between her and the mirror, seeing its green glow. "Oh, God," he whispered as he shook his head. A look of disgust washed over his face. "I remember everything. The demon. You hurt it. I don't know how, but you did."

Rhianna took a step forward and knelt by the injured man. She brushed a strand of hair away from his face. His burn scar was rough under her fingers. "Please. Before it comes back. How can I get to Alexander?"

"You...you have to go into the other realm and bring him out with you. Only his soul mate can do that. Can you free him? Have you accepted him? Endora tried, but—"

"I know. You killed her to keep him with you."

Donavan looked up. "What? No! The demon had me, like it had my father. I wanted to know its true power so I invited it inside of me. I thought I could handle it. It promised me so many things. I fought it at first, but it got too strong. It discovered the plot about my brother leaving with Endora. He almost made it, but I...it impersonated Alexander and led her into the mirror maze. Alexander came in before it could finish with her soul, even though it had already killed her body. He felt her loss and rushed in. He tried to use the magick Endora had taught him, along with the power the demon had bestowed on us, but the demon had grown too powerful from all the souls we had fed it, and—" He screamed. Rhianna backed away.

"He's coming back. Get me back through the mirror quick!" He tried to get up but fell down again as pain racked his body. His face went from human to the joker's. She lifted him up and made it to the mirror. Donavan stepped through, and she watched the surface ripple like water. He clutched the edge of the frame. When he was all the way through, and when he looked back, he was the demon. Rhianna tried to pry his fingers from the edge of the mirror, but they held on like a vise until she bent them back and heard them crack. The pain moved across his face, and it flickered back to Donavan. As it did, he let go and disappeared into the glass. Rhianna slid down onto the floor with her back against the bureau and let the tears fall down her cheeks, keeping vigil until the sun peeked over the horizon.

Chapter Twelve

Rhianna must have nodded off, because when she opened her eyes next, she noticed the clock said it was around noon. Her whole body ached, and she felt like she was hung over from a hard night of partying, except she remembered everything that had happened to her. Her muscles screamed at her from being locked in one position for so long. She stared at her naked form. There were no outward bruises, only the inner ones from the stupidity she felt for letting herself be tricked by the demon. She felt used and abused, but no matter how much she cried over it or stared at herself, it was doing no good. However, the more she looked at herself, the more she noticed a difference in her eyes. They seemed to have a purple hue to them. The power she had raised cracked around her like a violent storm surrounding her body. She was stronger than she had been the night before. The power stirred in her soul. It was now or never to save Alexander. The demon would never expect her coming after it in the daytime, and she had another idea as well.

She jumped in the shower, and when she came out she saw Snowball rubbing against the door. *Stupid cat. Why are you such a pain, you big old fluff ball?* He was probably hungry, and so was she. Rhianna threw together a sandwich, wolfed it down, and opened another can of tuna.

"Help yourself. I got someone to save."

Finally getting her courage together, she mounted the stairs to the attic and went up to the spare room. Nightmare was still gone, but the trunk and all its contents were not. The sun lent its warmth to the room, illuminating the stained glass Endora had made. Rhianna pulled her hair up into braid and opened up the jester costume that had belonged to Rachel, Donavan's wife. She grabbed the tintype and stared at the photo. Rhianna didn't look anything like Rachel, but with makeup, she hoped she could get to Donavan. She struggled into the dark green costume, which was too short and a little too tight, but the buttons still slipped through the holes. She grabbed the makeup tray and also picked up the book. She swallowed dryly and was amazed at the power zinging up her arms. As she looked at the pages, they were in Latin, which she couldn't read, but as she turned the pages, something fell to the floor. She put the down book and picked up the medallion that had fallen out. It was similar to the rune on the window, except it had only one symbol on it and an old leather chord attached to it. She slipped it over her head and figured it was either for protection or it opened a gateway.

She took the old tintype and picked up the book again. Its power wrapped up her arm and tried to entice her into reading some of the passages. They rearranged into English before her eyes. She shook off the desire to read the words and placed the text back into the trunk. She didn't see anything else in it to help her, so she headed back downstairs.

She applied the paints in the best mimic of the harlequin face Rachel had in the old photo. Her face was white, and she had green diamonds around her eyes. The makeup smelled old. It was heavy and cakey. Rhianna didn't think it mattered, as long as she might fit in.

"Here goes nothing," she whispered. *Not every day my agenda includes going into another dimension.* Rhianna looked at the clock, and it was almost three. Still four hours of daylight left to explore the other realm.

She sighed and thought about Alexander. As she did, the connection between them flared to life. Maybe it was because she had understood she had to accept him for who he was. Everyone had their faults. So what if he sacrificed souls to a demon to have immortal life, or he killed his father for power? She had guilt over things in her life.

It was her fault Jason had died. If it was not for her having the party, he would not have been rushing over to come and see her. She squeezed the tears from her eyes. Her love for Alexander vibrated along the bond they shared. She was so sorry she had pushed him away. It didn't matter what happened to her. If she could free him, she would be happy. With that knowledge, she opened her eyes. When she did, she saw the mirror was surrounded by the purple glow of her power. The rune around her neck burned.

Rhianna touched the glass tentatively and watched as her hand passed through it. Where it entered, it rippled, like disturbing a silent pond. Cold shot up her arm and froze it. Her instinct was to pull her hand away, forget all about this, and get the hell out of the house. But she was too involved in this now. She was in love with Alexander, no matter how strange the circumstances were, and part of her knew Donavan was not completely lost, so maybe while saving his brother, he could be freed from his torment, as well.

She took a breath and stepped all the way through the mirror. It felt like her whole body had been dunked in liquid silver, and she was fluid. Panic settled into her brain, but she kept on moving, following the connection she had with Alexander. When she opened her eyes and was able to breathe again, she found herself in a hall of mirrors. All the images reflected a perverse image of herself. They showed her with blood all over her hands, and her smile was twisted. The edges of her mouth looked like they had been slashed with a knife. Instead of her brown eyes, they were replaced with purple flame, just like the jester's. She wondered if they echoed her soul or her power. She did not know, but what she did know was she could see normally, no matter what was being reflected in the mirror.

Suddenly, her mind was bombarded with screams. The images turned into pounding fists and people pressing their faces against the glass.

"Help us! Free us!" Their cries of torment and pain filled her thoughts, and she had to cover her ears to block them out, but even

Through the Mirror 161

that didn't do anything. She closed her eyes and concentrated on her love for Alexander. It helped to dull the cacophony of voices, which began to sound like the shrieking gingerbread men she had let burn.

"I'm sorry. I can't help you. I don't know how."

All of these were the souls the brothers had fed to the demon.

"Rhianna…" There was an echo in the voice.

"Alexander." Rhianna found the strength to run and wound her way through the maze of mirrors and out the other side. As soon as she did, she was met with a night sky with no moon and no stars.

The air was heavy, like it was humid, but there was a bone chill in the air, so she couldn't get warm. All around her, a low howl, like that of a thousand ghosts, echoed in the vast darkness, but she did not see any ghostly specters. Torches and fires blazed in the camp. There were no trees, and yet phantom trees seemed to dot the landscape, and the shadows clinging to them were wispy, dark. She got the sense they were not friendly. Rotten wagons set up in an off-kilter circle lined the perimeter. In the center was a stage and benches made out of half-rotten logs. On the stage was a woman in white, along with another woman in red. Each looked like over-painted clowns. The stench of burnt popcorn filled the air. Rhianna saw creatures like the one she had seen hammering the poster to her tree. Zombies, beings who were half-dead and moving slowly as they eternally put on a show. She could see a sideshow stage, where a man with a top hat pointed to a tattered poster of a bearded woman. The man in the top hat had no face, and the pointer he used was a leg bone. Rhianna struggled to keep in her lunch. She had never seen so many twisted things in her nightmares, and yet this place seemed all too familiar, as if she had visited it before.

The only true sound she recognized was the slightly out-of-tune melody from the calliope. Steam floated out of its pipes, and it was playing itself. The whinny and pawing of horses drew her attention as they passed, hitched to a wagon, all sporting the circus's logo. *Diabolique circus. Circus of the damned. Circus of the devil* were the thoughts that ran through her head. All these souls had sacrificed something to the demon, and now they were stuck in their own hells, working for the thing they had sworn eternal allegiance to. She shook her head as her gaze scanned the expanse. Alexander's wagon was on the other side of the camp. Nightmare was tethered to it, and the blue stained-glass window in his door was a beacon.

She stepped out into the fray and hoped she would not be noticed. As she made it to the center stage, the women were being used as oversized puppets, and strings were attached at all their joints. The rope attached to them was frayed, and as Rhianna stopped to look at the puppets more closely, she saw life in their eyes. They still had their souls. She kept her eyes focused in front of her, looking for any sign of Donavan. She kept going and passed by another lost soul, sitting at a table. She was shriveled and hunched over. A tattered, old shawl covered her hair and her shoulders. Next to her was a sandwich board sporting psychic readings. Rhianna was able to see the Tarot cards on the table. When the woman sensed Rhianna's interest, she looked up. Her face was smooth except for her three eyes. Two were white. The third eye was open in the center of her forward. It was clear green and blinked at her. The woman raised a crooked finger and pointed at her. Rhianna backed away and bumped into something.

"Jester? Master?"

Rhianna whirled around, seeing she had walked into a woman. She was dressed all in black with a long, flowing lace gown. Her face was pale and gaunt but otherwise whole. Her hair was black and hung down to her waist. She was beautiful and looked a little familiar. When she saw Rhianna was not the jester, she backed away.

"Who are you?" the woman asked.

Rhianna said nothing but put a hand to finger to her lips in a shushing motion, mimicking the jester as she had first seen him. The woman looked over her shoulder and then back at Rhianna. "I asked who you are."

Rhianna stared at the woman longer and realized where she had seen her before. *This is Rachel. If she's here, then why didn't Donavan fight the demon possessing him to be with his soul mate?*

"Rachel?"

The woman looked confused. "I'm sorry, but I don't know who you are. And why are you are calling me that. M—"

"No, wait. I'm new. I'm sorry. I don't know the rules. I thought you were someone else."

The woman looked at her. "I will take you to Alexander. He will know what to do with you. The Master will be pleased there is some new blood among us. The outfit you have looks familiar. Where did you get it?" She grabbed Rhianna's arm, and Rhianna realized she was not going anywhere as she let the woman guide her forcibly to Alexander's wagon. Rhianna was dragged past a strong-man game, where someone had to hit a bell to win a prize. However, the bell was a severed head, frozen in a scream. Another was a knife-throwing booth. As she went by, she saw the knives were throwing themselves at some poor soul. Each act made Rhianna want to stop and help the poor souls as their suffering touched her heart, but she had only one purpose here. Finally, her hostess dragged her up the wagon's steps and banged on the door. It took a moment before the door opened. A skull peered out at the two of them. Rhianna hoped Alexander saw the look of desperation in her eyes and pleaded with him not to say anything.

"A new soul. The master will be pleased," Rachel announced. "I thought you might want to initiate her since you had so much fun with the last one."

"Thank you, Rachel." Alexander yanked her into the wagon and left the door open. He slammed her hard into the wall and pressed his bony face against hers. A tongue slithered in between her lips as his hands grabbed her breasts and squeezed them hard. As much as she was turned on by the gesture, she was also a little confused. He pressed against her harder, and she tried to fight him off, until she heard a moan next to her. She looked over, and there was Rachel, rubbing her own breasts.

"Can I have a taste of her, too? She looks so delicious." Rachel's tongue slithered between her lips, and her face melted away to reveal sharpened teeth and burning red eyes in a crone's wizened face. Alexander looked at her.

"This one is mine. Leave us alone."

"But I have to tell—"

"If you tell him, I will have your head. This bitch is mine until I say so. Is that clear?" The blue fire in his eyes shot out and hit Rachel square in the chest. Her demeanor changed back to normal, and she backed away, bowing.

"Yes. Please, don't—"

"I won't if you get the fuck out of my face." With a wave of his hand, Rachel was thrown onto the ground, and the door slammed. Once that happened, he turned to Rhianna, and the face she was used to flickered back into view. He looked at her and ran a hand down her cheek, which made her shiver. Once he came to the amulet, he fingered it and then kissed her tenderly.

"What are you doing here?" he asked. "It's not safe. If Donavan finds you, he will kill you and take your soul. I can't protect you here. This is his dimension. I thought you didn't want me after what you saw. Why, Rhianna?"

"I made a mistake," she whispered. "I realized I was being a fool, and no matter what you look like, what you have become, or your past, I accept you. It doesn't matter. I love all of you."

Alexander smiled and kissed her gently. "I'm sorry for the show, but I had to be believable. Rachel will eventually go to Donavan."

"Isn't she his wife? The one in the tintype? How come she is here?"

"The demon uses her as punishment for Donavan's devotion to her. She remembers nothing of her former life, and seeing her every day makes my brother's soul slip a little farther into hell. If you're here, then where is my brother? What happened to get you here? Only he knows the secret that will free me."

"I have to bring you out through the mirror. He told me. The demon almost had me, but I fought back, and Donavan was left. Somehow, I hurt it. He told me how to free you and what happened. Come on. Let's go!" Rhianna tugged on his red robe and went to open the door.

"You hurt the demon? What happened? I thought I told you to leave!"

Rhianna hung her head as she remembered what she had said and what had happened. She couldn't say anything to him. How could she tell him she had given herself to the jester, thinking it was him? How could she relive the horror of how the jester made her moan? She looked away from her soul mate, not able to meet his blue gaze. "I thought it was you. He tricked me. I didn't know until after he—"

Alexander drew her into his arms and hugged her. "It's all right. You don't have to tell me what happened. I can figure it out. I swear. I won't ever leave you again. What you said stung, and I overreacted. I assumed you had accepted me already, and you would see what I truly was. I'm sorry. Forgive me?"

How could he be asking for her forgiveness when she had said and done horrible things?

"Because I love you, Rhianna. You've given me back my soul. And I owe you so much more than what I can give you. You have done nothing to be ashamed of. Understand?"

Rhianna nodded. "Alexander, Donavan is still there. He's not been lost. He fought against the demon twice to save me. Isn't there any way we can save him, too?"

"If I only knew a way."

"What about in the book?"

His expression dropped. "Please tell me it is safe in the attic."

"It is. I didn't bring it. It has so much power, though. It was like it called me to open it and read from the pages. I didn't, though. I knew it was evil."

"Good. I'm glad you found the power inside of you to get you here. Your mother was right. You're strong, and your compassion for my brother is a godsend and maybe enough to free him. I don't know."

"Alexander, please, come on. Let's go."

Alexander looked around the wagon and then nodded. A sigh of relief flooded her system. They were going to get out of this nightmare and get back to reality. She had found him, and that was all that mattered now. "Play along."

He grabbed her arm. He opened the door and shoved her outside. She tripped on the steps and landed hard in the dirt on her hands and knees. A sharp sting moved up her knee and her hands. Alexander lifted her up roughly and shoved her in front of him. "That will teach you, bitch. No one ever denies me. I don't know what your deal is, but there's only one place for you."

Rhianna noticed Rachel was peering from behind her wagon with a smug smile on her face and glee in her red eyes. She felt bad for the lost soul, since she would never know the life she had once upon a time with Donavan, and the demon was using her to keep her in line. Rhianna got up, noticed the tear in the suit, and saw red welling to the surface. She let herself be led by Alexander and hung her head without saying a word.

They made it across the carnival lot as he brought her to stand in front of the mirror maze. A sign above it called it *The Hall of Lost Souls*. She shivered as she looked back at Alexander and he nodded. He pushed her through the door until they were out of sight before he took her hand and kissed it.

Chapter Thirteen

"I didn't mean to hurt you, but—"

She leaned in and kissed him. "It's okay. I understand."

He nodded and intertwined his fingers with hers. Rhianna smiled, and he let her lead him. As soon as they entered the hall, the cacophony of the trapped souls split her mind. Their agony and suffering made her fall to her knees and cry out as she felt like she was drowning in their sorrow. All of them wanted to be freed. All of them had their lives stolen from them.

"Rhianna," she heard Alexander say into her ear. "You can block them out. Think of me. Follow our connection."

But she couldn't. She was lost in their torment and madness. Suddenly, her world was filled with green light, like when she was losing herself to the jester. It was like he was in her mind and knew all her secrets, except this time, he was there leering at her, and it was not pleasurable. Her head was splitting apart, like thousands of miniature dwarves were pounding with railroad spikes inside her thoughts. She grabbed her head and screamed. If it didn't stop, she would be joining the thousands in the mirrors. The jester knew she was there and what was going on.

"You're on my turf now, bitch! Did you think you could have him without me knowing about it?"

"Leave me alone!" she shouted.

She opened her eyes as she felt a hand grip her arm. Instead of Alexander being there, it was the jester. She screamed and tried to get away, but the grip on her arm was steadfast and not letting her go.

"Rhianna, it's me. Not him. He's fucking with you. It's what the demon does to get his rocks off. Focus on my voice. Focus on us. Use your power, and come back to me. Don't let him take you away."

His lips moved, and after a moment, she swallowed and let her panic subside. Her own power rose inside of her, and it helped to dampen the voices. However, the jester was still inside her thoughts. She felt for the bond between her and Alexander and found it like a life rope as it led her back to him. She had to pull on it to make herself remember who was in front of her. Once she did, the image of the joker shattered, and Alexander stood before her once again. She tried to stay calm, but when she looked around at all the mirrors, the joker's face stared back at her. Alexander looked at them, too.

"He knows I'm trying to escape with you. Listen to me. You have to get out of here. Go to the end of hall and take a right. You'll see the mirror you came here in. Go through it, and don't look back. As soon as you step through it, destroy the mirror. It will close the gateway between the worlds." Alexander kissed her, wiping the tears away, smearing the green diamonds on her eyes.

"No, I won't let you go. I can't lose you. Please!"

"Rhianna, there is no time. I'm the only one who can keep him at bay. You're the most important one here. You still have a life to lead and a soul."

"But I came here to save you. I—"

"And you already have, love. You've given me hope and strength to find a way to fight the demon and hopefully free Donavan. Hope and love are lights here that burn brighter than anything else. He can't take those away from me. I'll always be with you. Remember, I'll always watch over you. Now go. Please! Nightmare will be there waiting for you. She'll be with you when I can't be. Go. He's almost here."

Rhianna locked her lips to her soul mate and felt her heart break. It was not her fault Jason had died. He loved her and always had, just like Alexander. They both wanted the best for her. Alexander pulled away and pushed her behind him. He nodded. The blue energy between his fingers pulsated, forming into a ball. A tear slipped from her cheek, and she didn't wait to see what was going to happen. She did as she was told and ran to the end of the corridor. There she stopped and peeked out from around the corner. Behind her, her bedroom reflected in the mirror. She swallowed as the jester come into the mirror maze.

"Did you really think you could get away? You're mine! I made you into what you are! I gave you the power."

"You made me into a monster and twisted everything I ever cared about. You stole my brother from me and made me kill my father."

The jester chucked. As he did, it shook the mirrors. "Please. You wanted the power more than Donavan did. You were going to rule by my side. You never had the balls enough to give me your beloved Endora. Human love? What is it compared to the power I gave you?"

"You forced Donavan to kill Rachel and the baby. Then you stole her soul to remind him of her every day. What you gave my brother wasn't power but a living hell. And you never turned me like you wanted to. Go back to the hell you came from. You don't have a complete grip on my soul anymore, and that burns you up even more." Alexander raised his hand and threw the bolt of blue energy at the jester, which seemed to be absorbed into him. The joker drew himself up and then shook his head.

"Alexander, Alexander, did the bitch tell you how I made her howl? She tastes wonderful. I know you've tasted her pussy, and it is so good. She was moaning for me to fuck her and slap her silly."

Alexander's reflection tensed. She bit her lip and tried to stay quiet. The demon was egging him on. She wanted to butt in and say something, but Alexander had already thought she had gone back to her own world. The joker brought his hand back and threw a bolt back at Alexander. It hit him square in the chest and knocked him on his back.

"Alexander." Rhianna couldn't stay in hiding any longer. She rushed to his side and picked him up in her arms. The illusion of his fleshy appearance faded away, and she was holding nothing more than a skeleton in a robe.

"My, my, she comes out of the hiding. You look fetching in the outfit. I'm sure Donavan would approve. Poor Rachel looked wonderful in it, too. I think she looks better now though. Don't you?" The demon laughed.

Rhianna cradled Alexander in her arms as she wanted nothing more than to get him back on the other side of the mirror. Tears stained her cheeks and fell onto the skull of Alexander. She stared at the jester and felt her own power rising, but she was not going to attack the jester yet. "Donavan, I know you're in there. Please help us! If you do, it can give you back your soul. Let go of the guilt you have for Rachel. Free your soul, and the demon will leave you!"

The jester's face wavered, and she could see the twin underneath the façade. "Take Alexander and go. I'm doomed."

"No. You're not. You've fought back before. Do it again. Fight until we can find away to free you. Please!" Rhianna begged Donavan.

In her arms, Alexander stirred. He got up slowly, and when he did, Rhianna noticed he was no longer a skull face. He was whole and fleshly. He stared at his hands. "Donavan, his hold can weaken. Rhianna did this to me. Her love made this happen. Look. The curse is almost lifted. Come with us. Please, brother."

The joker's face fell away. "I can't. He has too much of my soul. What I did to Rachel! How can I live with that?"

"Brother, please!"

Donavan shook his head. As he did, he pulled out something from around his neck and handed it to Rhianna. "Take this. With it we were able to come through the mirror. Alexander, go with her. I have no place in the world out there."

Through the Mirror

Alexander got up and gave Rhianna a hug. "Do you understand why I can't go with you?" She saw tears in his eyes as the decision between her and his brother was splitting him in two. She nodded.

"I understand. He's your family. You can't abandon him."

"If there is any other way. I swear I'll find a way to get back to you, my love."

"I love you."

"I love you, too. Go. Please."

Rhianna nodded and ran a hand along his cheek. She got up, and her knee was killing her from her fall. The souls in the mirror had quieted, and she looked behind her to see her soul mate picking up his brother and leading him out of the mirror maze. She wanted so much to go after him and pull him along, back to her world, but it would do no good. He had made up his mind, and he was not going to come with her. The hurt and the love she felt at that moment were unbearable, and yet she understood his decision. His love for his brother was one thing that gave him hope, just as her love gave him back his soul. His brother needed some of that hope.

"Goodbye," she whispered.

As she did, Alexander turned and met her gaze. Rhianna clutched the other amulet Donavan had given her. She was going to make sure nothing ever came through the mirror again. Racing down the hall, she knew if she didn't go now, she never would. She focused on the mirror showing her room. In the distance, she could see it was nearly dawn. If that was the case, she wondered if the gateway would close, since the jester could only cross over at night. She was not sure, since she had opened the doorway in the first place, but she didn't want to take any chances.

Before she was about to reach the gateway, something jumped out in front of her. The thing looked like the jester, but more twisted. His teeth were longer, sharper. His skin was grey and his costume in tatters.

"Did you really think you could get away from me?" His voice was gravely.

"Donavan, what did you do with Alexander?" she asked.

"Silly bitch. I don't have to be attached to Donavan all the time. It seems he found a little backbone."

"Oh, God!" Rhianna realized this was the true demon, which had possessed the other twin and had stolen all those other souls. She clutched the amulet harder in her hand. He was not going to get it, no matter what she had to do.

"I will be your god. Now look at me!"

The demonic voice forced its way into her mind, ripping it apart. She fell to her knees and cried out.

"Humans are so easy to manipulate. Your minds are like cheese. I can cut them up easily. I can make the pain go away, Rhianna. You have to give me the amulet."

Rhianna clutched it in her hand even tighter. "Never."

"I thought you would say that." The demon traced a finger over her breasts and up along the line of her throat. Once it touched her skin, it felt like she was being burned. Her screams were echoed by the souls in the mirrors.

"I can make the pain go away," it whispered in her ear.

A chill went through her as the pain subsided some. She closed her eyes and focused inward on the power she had deep inside her. She felt it spark to life. The fire rose and engulfed her as she let herself be immersed. She was not going to let the demon win. He was not going to have her soul or Donavan's. The purple flames seared her flesh in cold heat and moved through her being like she was attached to an electrical box. She had never experienced anything like it. When she opened her eyes, she met the demon with a purple stare.

"I don't need you to do anything!" The power sparked between her fingers, and it seemed to fill the room and bounce off the mirrors, as well. She opened her hand and watched as the energy poured from her and hit the demon in the chest, burning a hole in its green costume. A look of shock and pain moved over the demon's face. He was not expecting her to counter his power and defend herself.

As the energy poured out of her, a strange kind of knowledge filled the inside of her. Rhianna knew she had always been a witch, and this was her destiny to destroy this kind of evil. It was almost like she heard her mother's voice, whispering to her of all the things she could do. Her mother had been a water witch. She was a fire witch. She could ignite the fires of the soul, of love, of rage, and manipulate the energy around her. Doors were opening inside her mind Rhianna never knew existed. The more she focused on the demon, the stronger she got. The demon screamed in agony, and as he did, she noticed he was starting to fracture like a broken mirror. As he started to break, so did the mirrors all around her. The glass burst outward, and she had to protect her head from the explosions. As the glass broke, the trapped souls escaped.

"Thank you," they whispered as they disappeared, until finally, like the mirrors, the demon shattered, as well. Rhianna looked behind her to notice the room was collapsing in on itself. Since the demon was gone, it seemed the dimension was unstable.

Rhianna didn't have any time to go back and get Alexander. A tear slid down her cheek, and she dived through the mirror. Quickly, she turned back around and saw the face of the jester screaming as the mirror cracked and fell over, scattering on the floor in a million pieces going everywhere. Rhianna was glad it was over, but it also meant she had lost Alexander forever.

Epilogue

Rhianna stared at the boxes. After she had returned from her fight with the demon and losing Alexander, it had taken her a few months of waiting for the jester to appear in the house again or any sign of Alexander, but there was none. The attic room remained empty except for the trunk. Nightmare had not returned as her soul mate had promised, so she was left with Snowball, who had pranced around the house like he owned it. However, Rhianna knew she could no longer stay there. Too much had happened. What little belongings she had left were in boxes, and the house had sold. The only things she was taking with her from the house were the stained-glass window and the trunk. She was not going to let the book fall into the wrong hands. She would be its keeper until she could figure out what to do with the thing. She wore the amulet Donavan had given her and put the other one back in the trunk.

For months, she expected to see the jester's face, leering at her from the bathroom window, or his reflection in the glass, but he was only present in her dreams along with the music of the calliope. The power she had discovered inside of her was growing every day, and she was learning she could summon fire at a thought and have it float in her hand. There were other things she could do, like summon her cat when he was outside. She had even put her hand on a wood carving she had of an eagle, and she had seen it come to life.

Rhianna was not afraid of the power. She was lonely, like half of herself was missing. Her love and loss for Alexander grew every day. She prayed she might see a glimpse of his reflection, but there was nothing. Nights on end she had followed the connection between them, hoping for an answer, until finally she had given up trying.

Outside, the sun was setting, and the leaves on the tree rattled. The chill of fall was in the air. She rubbed her hands over her arms to try and stay warm and looked into the empty field. It went on for miles, and she wondered when it would finally fall into the hands of some developer. She had seen nothing in the field once the gateway was closed. Even the flyer on the tree had disappeared. It seemed the Circus Diabolique was gone for good.

"Come on, Snowball. It's time to get out of Crow's Creek once and for all."

The cat looked at her once. "Meow." He seemed to agree with her.

She grabbed the wrapped bundle on the bed, which was the stained-glass window from the attic. Everything else was marked for the movers to come and get. Part of her itched to sit at a computer and get on with her life, and yet a part of her would always be here, stuck inside the broken shards of a mirror. She had gotten most of the pieces, but there were a few she was not able to find.

Outside, she locked the door one last time and looked at the sold sign driven into the gravel. *Hopefully, it's truly over.* As she backed away, she thought she saw a figure in her bedroom. Fear shot through her, but she shook her head and felt energy spark between her fingers. She was not going to be afraid, and there was nothing there. Swallowing, Rhianna tuned her back and loaded her bundle into the car, along with the cat carrier. As she did, she heard a horse whinny in the field next to her. It was probably a rider going along the trails.

Rhianna turned around, and her heart dropped. Standing by the tree was a black, riderless horse. She slammed her door shut and walked over to the horse.

"Nightmare?"

The horse nodded and stomped her foot. She patted her flank and rested her head against the mare. She was solid and real. Maybe, just maybe? Rhianna wiped the tears away. "Is Alexander alive? Do you know?"

"Does she know if I am alive?"

Rhianna saw a dark head, and a man emerged from behind the horse. "Alexander?"

The same smile she loved spread on his features, and he circled the mare. "Yes, Rhianna. It's me."

He took her in his arms and kissed her long and hard. Her hands wrapped around his neck, and the connection between them sparked to life. His energy was a blue flame engulfing her, and hers fired back. Together, they ignited a fire, rivaling to burn her soul, until she pulled away.

"How did you escape?" she asked him.

He pulled her tight and held her. "When you destroyed the demon, the realm collapsed. Donavan and I made it back to his wagon. He had a mirror there. I always had the power to manipulate reflections. It was how I could watch over you as a child. I begged my brother to come with me, but he refused. He said he had to stay with Rachel, that he owed her that much. I went through the mirror and ended up back in my father's mansion, or what was his mansion, and it took me this long to find you. God, Rhianna, I swear never to leave you again."

She was so glad he was back. Her life was complete now. "What about Nightmare? What is she?"

Alexander patted the horse. "She is exactly that. A nightmare born of people's wildest dreams and fantasies. She was a creation I made back when I was learning the magick from the book. I conjured her from my deepest, darkest fears and tamed her. And she has been mine ever since. I can summon her wherever I go."

The horse stamped her foot again, as if agreeing with Alexander. Rhianna patted her and saw the red in the horse's eyes. She thought about it and shrugged. Her world had been turned upside down and filled with events she could not explain. Now she was part of a strange reality. It didn't faze her. Her soul mate had returned, and she was complete. Time had tempered her into a new person, and whatever the future held, she knew Alexander was going to be with her, no matter what happened.

THE END

Siren Publishing Ménage & More

Crymsyn Hart

CIRCUS DIABOLIQUE

Lost Souls

LOST SOULS

CRYMSYN HART
Copyright © 2010

Chapter One

Selena stared at the empty house with a box in her hand. Everything she had wanted to salvage was in it. Hardly anything remained of Trevor, her husband. They had been happy when they looked at the big old house at the end of the cul de sac with plenty of open space all around it. The woods and fields next to the house were a plus. The location reminded her of the place she had grown up.

She had fallen in love with the house, seeing so much potential for the family they had planned. Trevor saw the potential office in the attic, where he could work on the novel he perpetually hacked away at once or twice a month. Selena remembered arguing with him that he would never finish the book because he always had three or four other projects going at the same time. He never completed any of them so she had learned quite a lot about home repair in the past three years of their marriage because it took so much prodding for her husband, who was a carpenter, to get them done.

Selena shifted the weight of the box, realizing now they would never get the deck on the back of the house and Trevor would never finish his book. Tears burned her eyes while she stared at their dream home.

Just after they had bought the house, Trevor had been working on a job when one of the heavy beams he was helping lift hit him on the head, killing him instantly. It was a closed casket funeral. Selena had demanded to see him, but the doctors wouldn't let her due to the severity of the injury. Later at the funeral home, she had stolen a glimpse of him to say good-bye. The mortician had tried to reconstruct his skull, but it was still misshapen. Selena wished she never looked.

The funeral was long and she was a zombie for the next three months. Her friends even stopped coming around to make sure she was okay. By then, she had to tell herself it was okay to get up every morning and function because she was still alive. She still had to get by no matter how much the ache in her soul ate away at her.

Selena contemplated putting their new house back on the market, but she knew how much her husband loved the place and decided to take a leap of faith. Maybe a fresh start was what she needed. She gave up the rented paradise with its lime green and pink walls, sold most of their belongings, and started her drive across the state to Crow's Creek where she was a new resident.

Now Selena slipped the key into the old lock and it went in with ease. She held her breath. Part of her wondered if Trevor was playing a joke on her the way he used to do, and when she opened the door he would be standing there, naked. A smile tugged on her lips thinking of the many times she came home, weary and feeling like hell, to find him completely nude, leaning on the doorway with a drink in one hand and a box of chocolate in the other. The gesture was one of the things she loved about him.

Everyone adored Trevor. He had so many girlfriends when they first met, Selena was surprised he had chosen her out of the lot in college. But he told her she was something special. Once they met, he got rid of all his girlfriends. Selena even befriended many of them, including Phoebe, who had dated Trevor for the first two years of college until she discovered she was gay.

The door opened soundlessly on well-oiled hinges. The movers delivered her belongings more than a week ago. Bubble wrap was still on the futon, but she collapsed onto it, not caring about the small explosion filling her ears. The plastic wrapping was somewhat comfortable, too. Now that her journey was done, the weight of all the months came crashing down around her. Before she knew it, her eyes closed from exhaustion and she slept.

* * * *

"Please, help me!"
Selena opened her eyes to the whisper.
"Trevor?" she asked, not realizing she had said his name out loud. She listened, but didn't hear anything more. Shaking her head, she decided it was time to get up. Her body was stiff. It was dark out and the front door was still open. A flash of fear moved through her. Had someone gotten into the house and was playing a trick on her? She swallowed dryly, looking around for some kind of a weapon. The house was silent. The night had made it damp and cool. A breeze floated through the house and the draft caused the door to slam shut.

She screamed at the sudden bang. Realizing how silly she was, Selena started laughing with her hand over her racing heart. *Get a grip, Selena. There's no one there. I bet there's no crime in this small town. You've been through a lot and no need to let yourself get impressionable when the only thing in the house might be a stray cricket.*

"Please, help me."
Selena did a one eighty. The voice was not her imagination. Someone was in the house, and it sounded like a man. His voice sounded faint coming from upstairs. *Maybe he came in and got hurt while I was asleep.*

Selena hadn't explored that part of the house yet since she intended to sleep on the futon and not even venture upstairs unless she had to pee. The thought of being alone in the bed caused her soul to ache. During her drive, she had made up her mind she was going to sleep downstairs until she got used to the house and being alone. Alone and lost—that was how she felt at that moment. If Trevor was there, he would have gone upstairs and taken care of the situation.

Quietly, she tried the light switch at the end of the stairway. After flicking it a few times, she remembered she hadn't had the power turned on yet. She didn't have a flashlight handy, so she pulled out her cell phone from her jeans pocket. The illumination from the phone gave her enough light to see. She bit her lip and stared up the stairs. *No way am I going up there without something.*

She tiptoed into the kitchen and grabbed one of her knives, and clutching the handle in her free hand she went to face the voice. When her foot hit the first wooden step, it creaked and echoed throughout the house. Selena heard something drop and roll across the floor. Next came the sound of jingling bells. Halfway up the stairs, her heart jumped between her throat and her stomach. Her grip tightened on the knife. Her flesh broke out in goose bumps. She was never one for horror movies, but now she was living out the scene of one.

Trevor, if you can hear me, I'm going to kill you for dying.

At the top of the stairs, Selena peered around the doorway. There was nothing in the first bedroom except warped floorboards. She even checked the shadows to be sure they were empty. She went into the room and stared out the window. Blurry shapes moved in the field below. When she blinked, they were gone. Her cell phone beeped, signaling it was running low on batteries.

She closed the phone and then decided to tackle the master bedroom. Selena listened and heard soft tapping on glass coming from the other room. In the hall, everything was dark so she opened her cell phone again. *Damn, the battery. I'll charge it again in the morning.*

When she got into the master bedroom, she noticed the large full length mirror Trevor had made for her for their last anniversary. She saw one in an antique shop and really wanted it. Phoebe was with her and tried to coax Selena into buying the glass, but she didn't want to spend the money. Phoebe told Trevor about the mirror and he replicated it in his workshop. When Selena arrived home one night, it was sitting in their bedroom with a great red bow on it. Trevor was in the bed, naked, with champagne, two glasses, restraints on the bedposts, and a red bow around his hard cock. She smiled at the image and the love making they had after that. He tied her to the bed to make her "pay" for her new gift. It had been one of the best nights of her life.

When her eyes moved over the mirror, she saw the empty bed. The light in her cell phone was about dead so she turned it off and sat on the bare mattress. She ran her hand over the place where her husband used to sleep. The fear faded away. There was no one in the house with her. She eased her grip on the weapon and let it rest on the bed. Whatever it was, whoever it was, could be left over from her fading dream she had about Trevor. The move and being awake in the middle of the night were playing with her mind.

"Please, help me," whispered a man. This time the voice was in the same room with her.

Selena turned around slowly, and grasped for the knife. The fear, which she thought was gone, doubled in its intensity. In the mirror was a man surrounded by a neon green glow, reaching out to her. He had dark hair, tan skin, and dark green eyes. Half of his face was covered by his hair. He was dressed in a white and green harlequin outfit from another century. Hypnotized, she went to the mirror. The guy was handsome. Something about him tugged on her heart. He seemed familiar to her, like Trevor had been when she first met him.

She didn't believe in the supernatural or things that went bump in the night. Granted, she believed in angels and beings who watched over her, but nothing to make her worry. Her mirror had never done this at the other house.

"Help me!" The plea came again from his lips. The look in his eyes was one of pure agony. He was trapped, and lost like she was.

"How can I help you?" she asked the man in the mirror.

"Free me from this never ending hell. The original mirror was shattered. Help me before he comes back."

Selena stared into the mirror, noticing that it didn't reflect her or the clothes strewn about the room behind her. He seemed to be in a cramped space. "Before who comes back? Where are you?"

"No time! He's herrree—" the word was drawn out into a garbled groan. The man covered his face and bent down. A pang of worry went through Selena. *What is going on?* Somehow this man was hurt and needed her help. She inched closer to the mirror, reaching out to touch the glass. The knife clattered to the floor.

When her hand was inches from the surface, the man jumped and uncovered his face. He pressed it up against the glass, trying to get through. However, he was no longer the image Selena had first seen. Instead of the handsome stranger, in his stead was a Jester with a white painted face, jagged brown teeth, no hair, and glowing green fire filled his eyes. His suit was now dirty and torn. Bony fingers stuck out through holes in his white gloves. He belonged in a living dead circus. A scream escaped her lips while she backed away from the mirror.

"You can't have him, bitch! He's mine. MINE!" the entity yelled. He stepped away from his side of the mirror and made a running leap, trying to crash through it. Selena instinctively covered her face with her arms and cowered on the floor. However, no spray of glass hit her, only a thud, and then the sound of pounding on heavy glass.

When she peeked through her arms, the Jester was banging on the mirror. He couldn't get through. Relief washed over Selena while she looked back at the Jester. His lips were pulled up in a perpetual smile revealing all of his teeth. She got the impression he was seething.

"What do you want?" she asked.

He rotated his head all the way around cracking his neck, peering at her. Some force pressed against her mind, trying to break into her thoughts. Her head began to swim as she watched the fire in his eye sockets dance and grow brighter. Choppy images flashed through her mind but she could barely make them out.

"No. You can't have her!" A scream rang in her mind and in her ears, and the images vanished. When she blinked, the reflection of the Jester flickered and the man returned. He clutched his head, staring intently at her. One side of his face was horribly scarred, probably from a fire.

"Run. Get out of here now! Leave the house, please!" His voice contained so much agony it touched her heart.

"But I want to help you," she found herself saying.

"No one can help me. I'm damned. I should never have asked. Please go." He laid his palm flat on the glass. Selena copied his gesture, but instead of the glass she felt his flesh. The green glow from around him enveloped her hand, zinging up her arm. A look of disbelief crossed his face. Selena desperately yearned to stroke his skin and see if it was rough or smooth. She thought the burn scar would make him seem less handsome, but it enhanced his features.

"It's not possible," he muttered.

His fingers closed on hers, breaking the surface of the glass. His flesh was warm and another zap went through her while they touched. The shock flushed her cheeks and reached her thighs. "What are you?"

He pulled his hand away, leaving Selena empty again. "I can't believe it, but if it's true he will try to have you. Leave this place before it's too late. The boundary is the woods. He cannot move past there." Without another word, his face contorted in pain again. A scream came from his lips. When he turned back to her, his face was half his and half the Jester's. The Jester was winning. The Jester pushed against the glass and it sounded like it was going to crack. Selena yanked her hand away. The amused smile disappeared and his features contorted into an expression of pure hatred.

"You will pay!" the thing said. Then the Jester was gone. A sudden wind blew up, whirling papers around her. Selena looked up.

Flyers fell from an empty ceiling. Terror encompassed her. She backed out of the bedroom, running down the stairs and out the door. She didn't bother to lock it, but got back into the car and stared at the house, not believing what had happened to her. For a long time she didn't move and wondered if the Jester was somehow going to get out of the mirror. She studied the windows of the house and from her bedroom window she thought she saw the Jester's face staring down at her. When dawn finally eased over the horizon, she drifted off to sleep with the off key melody of Circus Calliope playing in her head and the maniacal laughter of the Jester purring next to her ear.

Chapter Two

Selena opened her eyes and shivered from the chill in the early summer air. She felt a crick in her neck from sleeping scrunched up in the car. It wasn't every day she raced from her house for safety, or saw handsome men in mirrors for that matter. She blinked, wiping the sleep from her eyes while she listened to the birds chirping outside. *It was all a bad dream. That's all it was. I fell asleep in the car, and it was all a strange, messed up dream.*

However, part of her knew she was deluding herself because when she pulled her cell phone out of her pocket, the battery was completely dead. Sighing, she grabbed her car charger from the glove compartment and plugged the phone in. When the little red light came on, she was relieved. At least something was normal and worked the way it was supposed to. Getting out of the car, she stepped into the gravel driveway and looked up at the bedroom window. There was no one there. Even if she had seen something last night, it was all a hallucination brought on by hours of driving. To prove the point, she marched across the driveway and went back into the living room. When she passed the foyer, she noticed a note sitting on a table with an extra set of keys.

Strange. I don't remember that being here last night. Then again, last night I freaked out about my own reflection. Trevor's death is still hitting me hard. Only I would dream up a handsome ghost in a mirror who was possessed by a Jester. A Jester from a circus? I hate the circus. She shook her head, pocketed the keys, and read the note. It was from the former owner.

The note said if she encountered anything odd about the house, to give the previous owner a call and let her know. Cold washed over Selena. She shoved the note in her jeans and took the stairs two at a time. When she got into the master bedroom, she found the mirror only reflecting herself and no strange creatures or men. The hardwood floor was spotless. The mattress was bare. There was nothing out of place; no shower of flyers had rained down on her last night. Laughter burst from her lips as she sat down on the bed and the tension left her body. It had all been her imagination.

Selena stayed in the room for a few more minutes and decided she had wasted enough time being scared. It was time to unpack and get settled in.

"Hello? Anyone home?"

Selena froze, not even daring to breathe. She looked toward her mirror and didn't see anything.

"Selena, you here?"

A sigh of relief melted her. She jumped off the bed and raced downstairs. The voice was Phoebe. In the foyer, she practically jumped into her friend's arms and gave her a big hug. She needed to be sure the other woman was real.

"Thank God," Selena whispered.

Phoebe's arms went around her automatically and then let her go. Selena was so happy to see her because she had not gotten a chance to say goodbye. Phoebe had been away on business for a couple of months traveling in Japan and China. Selena stepped back and examined her friend. Her dark hair was free from its normal French Twist. Her normal attire of a severe gray suit, black pumps, and briefcase were left behind. Her almond shaped eyes had a dash of blue on their lids to accentuate their gray blue color. Phoebe's father was a traditional all American guy and her mother was strictly traditional Japanese, but it was her Asian heritage that had sculpted her the most, except for her height. She was almost six feet tall. Selena barely made it up to her chin. When they first met, when Trevor and she were dating, Selena wondered how she was going to compete for Trevor's affection when he was dating such an exotic beauty. When she found out Phoebe was gay, they hit it off. Now when they went out for drinks, Phoebe had to fight the men off no matter if they were in a gay bar or not, the straight ones always found her.

"I love what you've down with your hair," her friend commented while she took in the aura of the place. After a moment, she decided it was okay and plopped herself down on the still bubble wrapped futon.

Selena's sat next to her while her hand went to her mousey brown hair. She had put red highlights in it before she left. The stylist said it brought out her own hazel eyes and contrasted against her medium skin tone. "Thanks. I almost forgot I had it done. Trevor would have…well…"

Phoebe put an arm around her. "He would have loved it. I know, hon."

Selena couldn't help it, but started crying in her friend's arms. Of all the people she felt close to after her husband's death, Phoebe was the only one who had seen her through the worst. Now and again she would drop by with a chocolate cheesecake and they would spend the night watching campy eighties movies and devouring the cheesecake until Selena didn't want to look at another one again. Finally, feeling foolish, she wiped her eyes and smiled. "I'm sorry. It's been a strange night."

"Don't be sorry. You have nothing to be sorry about. You and Trevor were soul mates. It hurts when you loose one of those. Now, why was last night strange? Did you find monsters in your closet?"

Selena laughed. "Not exactly." Selena told Phoebe about what she experienced, but her friend didn't react.

"Sounds like a crazy dream. I'm sure my mother would have found some significance in it, but you found one handsome dream hunk. Not sure about the crazy Jester though."

"Cute. What about you? What are you doing here?"

"I could use a vacation and my best friend needed someone to help unpack all her stuff. But looking at the place, I didn't realize how much you had actually sold. Sweetie, are you doing okay?"

Before Phoebe had asked the question, Selena would have wondered the same thing, but now that she thought about it she realized that strangely she was okay. Her heart did not hurt so much. *That's odd. I haven't felt at ease since before Trevor's death. I wonder what triggered it. Maybe getting settled in the new house has made everything all better. Or gotten me on the road to being better?*

"I think the worst of the storm has finally passed. I'll never completely get over loosing Trevor, but all of this and you being here makes me focus on something other than not having him here.."

A rare smile enlightened Phoebe's face. "Good. I'm glad to hear it. So where do we begin? Let's get down and dirty."

* * * *

Between the two of them, they unpacked and cleaned up the downstairs in no time. The house was dusty. They removed the bubble wrap from the futon and it was much more comfortable to sit on, and not so noisy. The one box Phoebe left was the one Selena had brought in with her, the one with just the few things left from Trevor. She put that upstairs on the bed. Selena's gaze settled on the contents of the box. She kept two of his favorite shirts. She drew one out and lifted it to her nose, inhaling his scent. Under those were a couple of photo albums of pictures he took of them while on vacation and whenever he wanted to be silly. Selena smiled when she flipped through the images. At the very bottom were his watch, wedding ring, and a pocket size tape measure he always carried. She hugged the shirts and then placed everything back in the box.

Glancing outside, the sun was sinking, taking the light with it. She was grateful for Phoebe for buying a generator because she had no power and the power company wouldn't be out for a couple of days. While Phoebe explored the basement, she discovered Selena had a gas heater so Selena could take a long soak in the bathtub. That was the next thing on her agenda to soothe her aching muscles. Phoebe was downstairs waiting on their pizza to be delivered.

In the old fashioned claw foot tub, she let the scalding water and lavender bubble bath take her away. Her head fell back against the lip of the tub. Her mind drifted. The scent of lavender was replaced by cotton candy and popcorn. Her ears filled with the strange and yet eerie music of the calliope she had heard last night. Then she felt hands on her shoulders, massaging away her tension. She jumped, but the hands held her steady. An overwhelming sense of serenity washed over her. Whoever this was was not going to hurt her. She let the stranger carry her away to a more peaceful place. The hands traveled lower on her shoulders, over her chest, stopping at the top of her breasts. Lips gently kissed the side of her neck. Hot breath tickled her ear. Selena waited for more.

"Only if you allow it. Do you want me?"

Selena recognized the voice from the man in the mirror. Part of her was afraid of what was happening because she had never experienced anything like it. Another part was so lonely from not having Trevor around that she welcomed it. The man's hands trailed along her collarbone as he waited for her to answer his question. The softness of his hands caressed her jaw, and he used the water to draw designs on her chest. Everywhere he touched left a warm impression. Desire sparked to life inside of her where she never thought it could again. Did she want him? Oh yes.

"Then say it. Tell me you want me!"

He was reading her thoughts. A bit of fear went though her. *How much does he already know about me? Does he know I haven't been with anyone since my husband? Does he—*

"I only know what you want me to know. I need your permission to do anything to you. It's part of the rules that bind me. I won't hurt you, I promise. The Jester isn't here. It's only me."

"Kiss me," she whispered.

Soft lips met hers. His tongue parted them while he leaned over her. She arched up out of the tub to meet him better. His fingers entwined with hers. Once they did, she was hit with the same spark she had experienced before except it was stronger and made her swallow a moan as he released her lips.

"What's your name?"

"Donavan."

"How come I can't see you?"

"Think of this as a dream. It's the only way I can come to you without being outside of the mirror and arousing the demon's suspicions. I can only be half here because your mind is already halfway between our two worlds. I can give you pleasure, Selena, if you allow me to."

"Yes."

"Good." His hands slipped beneath the water and cupped her breasts. The light flicker of his fingertips on her nipples hardened them instantly. He pinched and massaged them, played with them lightly until her toes were curling, but she slipped her hand over his and pressed it over her breasts.

"Harder."

"Anything you want."

At her command, pain erupted from her nipples as he squeezed them. Her toes seized up. Selena bit back a scream of pleasure. Donavan eased up a little, but she shook her head no. Selena loved the pain. She had never experienced the ecstasy of pain until Trevor had shown her, introducing it to her slowly. First with nipple clamps, then spankings, whips, paddles, wax, anything he could think of to make her understand the true meaning of being alive in her flesh. From the first taste of it, she couldn't get enough. Gone were the days when she wanted a guy to be gentle with her. She liked it hard and rough. The more painful the better because it made her hot. Even now, her pussy throbbed from the experience Donavan was giving her.

He twirled and pinched her nipples harder and longer each time, alternating between them so the sensation would return and she could come down from the high. Finally she was so hot and wet it didn't matter that she was in the tub, she needed to shower all over again. Her toes gripped the outside edge of the tub as her legs spread wide and she waited for him to take her. She needed him to take her.

As if on cue, Donavan's fingers slithered under the water and caressed her clit, then two fingers slipped deep inside her pussy.

"Oh, God!" Selena groaned. The muscles in her thighs contracted. His thumb massaged her hard bud in slow circles while his lips worked the line of her throat. She wished she could see him to look him in the eye. She yearned to see the expression on his face, wondering if he was enjoying her reactions. When she did open her eyes all she saw was blackness. It seemed the world had fallen away. She was lying in the tub and there was nothing else around her. It was frightening.

He worked his magic on her with his lips by biting one of her nipples. Selena arched her back and let her eyes flutter shut. It was easier knowing she could sense him and still feel him. The idea of him being a phantom lover was daunting since she needed him inside of her.

"I want that too, Selena. But it would be too risky and attract the Jester's attention," Donavan whispered in her ear. His fingers applied pressure inside her pussy. She pushed against him while he created a rhythm of pumping in and out of her slowly. That combined with his other manipulations was pushing her over the edge. Her toes hurt from being curled for so long that they were starting to cramp. The more Donavan was kissing, biting, licking her and the faster he moved his hands the more lost she became. Her hips rocked against his fingers. His teeth nipped the side of her neck as if he were a vampire. Each burst of pain from his mouth left her craving more.

"How...can...I...oh, Donavan. Faster."

His thumb rubbed her clit lightning quick and her stomach was in knots. She was surprised her body remembered how to have an orgasm and he was building her to a whopper of one. Donavan's lips locked onto hers. Their tongues caressed one another while with one swift stoke she came so hard she almost blacked out. All she saw behind her eyes was green while she became aware of her body again. However, he didn't stop her with one orgasm. He kept stroking her, carrying her higher so her entire body was electrified. His kisses could no longer hide her moans and Selena gave into sheer abandon.

She was disappointed when he finally brought her back down. He kissed her and caressed her until she was putty in the water. Where his mouth touched her still turned her on. His touch had amplified the sensations in her pussy and clit. Even when the bubbles brushed against her, she was still coming. Finally, Donavan's arms wrapped around her shoulders and he held her, letting the waves of desire settle.

"Thank you, Selena."

"Why are you thanking me?"

"Because you made me understand something my brother said to me."

"What was that?"

There was silence. The air thickened and she felt someone watching her. "Donavan?" The scent of popcorn she had smelled earlier turned stale. The jingle of bells was close. Opening her eyes, she was still surrounded in a black void, which now seemed to be tinged green. Slipping her toes and legs back into the tub, the water was ice cold now. She looked around, but could barely see anything. The jingling bells sounded next to the tub. She slipped her hands into the water, too. Her instincts told her to stay right where she was.

"Donavan? Dona—"

It happened so quick she swallowed a mouthful of water as she went under. She tried to come back up for air, but there was a hand on her head. When she looked up, she didn't see Donavan above her.

Instead, she saw the leering, upturned grin of the Jester. Panic shot through her when she tried to surface for air. Her arms and legs flailed in the water, but his grip was too strong. Her lungs burned for more oxygen. Selena grabbed a hold of his hand and tried to push him off of her but it was no use. Her struggles were futile. She was wasting oxygen fighting to stay alive. Darkness started to appear on the edge of her vision. Her limbs were growing heavy. She tried to pull up one more time. *Donavan, help me. Where are you?*

She reached out to no one in the blackness and someone grabbed her hand. Selena opened her eyes and was able to come above the water. Her lungs drank in the air. She wiped the water out of her eyes. When she looked over, Phoebe was staring at her with a concerned look on her face.

"Are you okay? I heard you flailing around. If I had known you were that tired I would have suggested you take a shower. You have to be careful, Selena. Falling asleep in the tub. It sounded liked you were having one hell of a nightmare."

Selena stared at her friend. Phoebe wouldn't believe her if she told her what had happened with Donavan let alone the Jester. How could she explain mind blowing sex, well, one-sided sex, with a ghost, or not really a ghost since she could feel him? Hell, her nipples still hurt and her muscles were sore from the experience. She had not fallen asleep.

It really happened, which means the other night really happened too, when I saw the Jester in the mirror and Donavan fighting him as if he was possessed. He's asked me to free him. How can I do that? Where do I even start? Is it possible to free him without letting the demon out?

"Selena?"

"What? Yes. I'm fine. You were right. I'm more tired than I thought. Guess that teaches me never to take a bath again. What were you doing, anyway?" Selena noticed Phoebe had her hair up and was all dusty. She had something in her hand.

"You caught me. I was setting up your bedroom. I hope you don't mind. Oh, I found this." Phoebe handed her friend a folded up flyer. Selena wrapped herself in a towel and winced at the contact with her flesh. After a moment, she took the flyer. It was an advertisement for a traveling sideshow. There were two jesters on either side of the page. One balanced on a ball while juggling swords and the other was doing some sort of acrobatics. The paper had a clean fresh smell to it, and the ink was still wet. It read:

CIRCUS DIABOLIQUE
Enter a realm of nightmarish wonders to indulge in your darkest dreams.
The marvels will mystify, haunt, and entrance you.

Her hand began to shake when she stared at the jesters. Their leering faces taunted her. The one on the ball winked and seemed to be aiming at her with one of the swords.

He's mine, bitch! A guttural voice whispered in her ear.

"Where did you find this?"

"It was on the bed. You know, it's strange because I didn't see it on your bed when I went in there. It was like it appeared out of nowhere. Selena, I'm not one to believe in weird shit, that's my mom, but something is going on here, isn't it? You just didn't fall asleep in the tub, did you?" Phoebe asked.

Selena stared at the flyer and crumpled it up. The flyers raining from the ceiling had really happened. She glanced at her friend. "I don't know, but something's not right with this house."

"Maybe your house is haunted by the dead owner and they want you out, like *Poltergeist*. Hopefully you won't get sucked up into the television set."

"It's not the old owner and the little girl got sucked into her closet. It's someone else, something else. Oh, God—" Realization came to her as she remembered the note she had found and shoved into her jeans. It had said to call if anything strange started happening at the house. What had the old owner meant by that? At first Selena assumed she meant termites or heck, even a skunk living in the attic, not a demonic Jester and a man who knew how to caress her in all the right places but seemed to be a ghost. She rushed into the bedroom and grabbed her jeans from the night before, still balled up on the floor. Inside the pocket was the number.

"Can I use your phone? Mine is still out in the car."

"Sure. It's downstairs."

Selena raced down the stairs and found the phone in Phoebe's purse. She began to punch in the numbers with shaking fingers. Finally, she was able to press send. She stared at the display waiting for it to connect. When it did, it rang and rang until voicemail picked up. *What am I going to say? Hey, thanks for the note. Love the house, oh, and by the way, I have a crazy demonic Jester living in my mirror who tried to drown me. That would go over really well.* She ended the call and tried to figure out what was going on. Maybe she didn't need the help of the owner. *Worst off, the owner might think I was nuts if I told her what I had seen. No, I'll call her if something else happens.*

"So, did you get a hold of whomever you were calling?"

Selena looked up. "No. I'm sorry. This is crazy."

"Hey, do you hear that?" Phoebe asked.

The house was quiet without the hum of electricity and the generator was not turned on yet. The only sounds she heard were the crickets out in the field. "No, I—" Then she did hear something. It sounded like the rumble of voices in a crowd, then the movement of horses and the snapping of whips, along with the music of a circus calliope that she would have heard if she were on a merry-go-round. Walking to the window, she stared out into the field. Coming down the road were the green outlines of horse drawn wagons, a whole line of them.

Both women watched in awe while the line continued into the field. Before their eyes, there were shapes of tents and transparent people walking around. Voices echoed in the night all around the house. The ghostly circus took on a life of its own around the two women. Smells of cotton candy, popcorn, and other sticky treats scented the air. Selena watched the spirits set up camp.

"Let's go out and see!" Phoebe exclaimed.

Selena glanced at her friend and saw the look of childish glee on her face. Phoebe was lost, swaying with the melody of the calliope. Selena touched her friend's shoulder and she turned to her. "I don't think that is a good idea. I have a feeling we're safer in here."

"Well, of course you can't go like that, silly. Go upstairs and put something on. Hurry up, Selena. The next show starts in a few minutes."

"How do you know that?"

"Can't you hear the ringmaster? He's right over there!" Phoebe pointed to the middle of the field, but Selena didn't hear anything. The music and the voices had all blurred together. Selena heard the bang of the door. When she spun around it was open. In the doorway were a bunch of green balloons. Phoebe turned quickly, letting out a small shout of joy, and ran to the balloons. Selena grabbed her hand before she touched them. Her friend gave her a dirty look, but Selena didn't want her going out alone.

"How about I go up and put on some clothes? Then we can both check it out."

Phoebe nodded. Selena hurried up the stairs and threw on her clothes from yesterday. She shoved the phone and the number into her pocket and went back downstairs. When she did, Phoebe was already outside holding the balloons. Her fingers were entwined with a pale skinned woman wearing a black dress. Selena guessed she looked normal enough except she doubted it was one of the new nosey neighbors that lived a mile down the road, and the slight green sheen around her gave it away. Selena didn't want to spook the spook so she touched Phoebe's hand, but both women stopped.

"Phoebe, I thought you were going to wait for me."

When her friend turned, her face was blank. The other woman gave her a wicked grin. "Your friend is in here with us," she hissed.

Selena took a step toward the woman, but she gripped Phoebe, putting her hand around Phoebe's throat. The woman's face melted into that of an old crone with bleach white hair and candy apple red eyes. Her nails became sharp points against Phoebe's skin. Selena's gaze slid to the field while the atmosphere was thickening. The ghostly carnival had solidified some and was watching the show. "Look, give me back Phoebe. I don't know what any of this is about. I just bought the house. Do you want me to leave? Is that it?"

The woman smelled Phoebe the way a vampire would, taking in the aroma of her blood. Her tongue stretched out longer than it should and tasted her friend. The spirit licked her lips and turned her red gaze back to Selena.

"She's ours now. We don't care about the house. We want our master back, bitch. You trapped him in the other realm, now release him with your magic!"

"What are you taking about? Magic?" The other ghosts were more solid than before. Most of them appeared to be zombies with rotting flesh peeling off their bones. One ghost was missing half its face, revealing part of its cheekbone and a row of intact white teeth. Another had a left eye missing and was dressed in tatters. There were others in various stages of decay. Some were nothing more than skeletons dressed in rags. They were getting closer to her.

"You, witch, stole our master away from us and locked him in the other realm. Free him now or her soul is his."

Tears streamed down Selena's face while she studied the creatures around her. She had no idea what was going on. All of this was getting out of hand. Within a couple of days, her life had turned into something out of a horror movie. This did not happen to people. She needed help. She needed Trevor. She was lost without him. Why hadn't she admitted it to herself before? Then she had met Donavan and felt like she had with Trevor, but now he was lost to her, too. "Please, I don't know what you're talking about."

The hag growled. "Fuck it! Take her!"

Fear sliced Selena. She wanted to help Phoebe, but didn't know how. The only way to assist her friend now was to escape these ghosts and figure out a way to free her. Selena turned toward the house, but found the way already blocked. The horde of undead surrounded her from all sides. She bolted from them. Her feet carried her down the gravel road. The field was filling with freaks and everything sounded real. The wagons, the pure smell of cotton candy, and popcorn along with the aroma of burnt wood from the fire. Selena tripped and fell on the ground, slicing open her leg. She looked behind her. They were following, slinking over the dirt road. Defeat washed over her. Everything she and Trevor had worked for was gone. Pain shot up her leg. She tried to get up, but tripped again. Her hope was failing. She began to crawl away from them, but their cold presence was close. She could feel their ghostly hands reaching out, trying to touch her and invade her soul. She closed her eyes.

"Selena..." She heard a voice on the wind. It was Donavan.

She opened her eyes and looked around. She noticed a form standing down the road a few hundred yards, which seemed like a mile. His image faded in and out. She remembered what he said about the barrier. The Jester could not cross over where the field met the woods, so maybe the other ghosts couldn't either. Hands were enclosing her ankle. Her leg was sticky and her jeans stained red. A surge of hope gave her renewed strength. Maybe she had a chance.

She got up with the pain racing up her leg and tried to run. All she could do was limp, but she got closer to the barrier and further away from the ghosts. The music of the calliope was fainter the closer she got to the woods. The house, Phoebe, and all the others fell behind her. Donavan's form flickered and stared at her in the night, the glow around him was green, too. She got to him and reached out. He reached back, but his hand passed through hers. She stood on the line of the forest and the field, watching as the ghosts still pursued her. She took another step and crossed the line. The air was crisper and cooler. It was easier to breathe. Selena looked up toward the horizon. The first rays of sunlight were cresting over the forest.

"Thank you."

He smiled, but his fingers could not pass over the barrier. He was trapped, too.

"What do I do?"

"Find my brother. He can help."

"How?"

Donavan's form wavered with a forlorn expression on his face. "I'm sorry. It's all I can do." He tried to brush her face with his fingers. Selena felt the caress in her heart even though it didn't touch her flesh. She saw the love for her in his eyes.

"I'll find a way to save you and find your brother."

He smiled. Selena looked at the green vapor and realized he was melding with it. The emerald mist banked at the barrier, curled upward, and stopped. The zombies had disappeared, leaving Phoebe all alone by the house. Selena's instinct was to turn back around and go to her. When she thought about stepping over the line, the hag sprang up. Selena jumped back. The hag clawed at the air and screamed.

"We will get you, bitch! He can't save you!"

The hag smiled a wicked grin and stepped back into the mist, leaving only her red eyes. "We will have your soul…just you wait."

Chapter Three

For sometime Selena cried, bathing in the dawn light, too afraid to go back into the house to see if there were any more ghosts waiting for her. After wiping her eyes, she looked at her leg. The wound was deeper then she thought and still seeping with bits of gravel in it. She needed to get to a hospital or somewhere where she could clean it out. However, her keys were in the house and she didn't know if she could make it to the neighbors. She was stranded. Then she noticed a vibration in her pocket and realized it was Phoebe's cell phone. Out of habit, she opened the phone.

"Hello," she sniffled.

"Did someone try to call me from this number?" a woman asked on the other end.

Selena swallowed and stared at the digital display. She recognized the number as the one she dialed earlier. A glimmer of hope warmed her heart.

"Yes."

"Did you?"

"Yes. I called. Please, I need help."

"What happened?" the woman's concern in her voice was genuine. "Was it Donavan? Did he hurt you?"

Relief flooded through her. This woman could help. Maybe she had even been the same one the hag mentioned about being a witch. *What happened before I bought the place? The realtor never said anything about it being haunted.* Selena had even met the old owner at the closing. She had seemed normal and didn't mention the house was possessed by some freaky-Jester-demon or that a haunted sideshow was going on in the field next to the house, either. Why was she asking her about Donavan?

"Are you there?"

"Yes. Sorry. It wasn't Donavan. He was trying to help. It was the Jester and this crazy woman, hag thing. Look, I'm hurt and I'm afraid to go back into the house. Please, what do I do? They took Phoebe."

Selena heard the whisperings of a male and female voice on the other end. Finally, the woman came back on. "You'll be safe in the house during the day. The Jester and the other ghosts can't come out during the day. We'll be there in a few hours. There's a hotel on the outskirts of town. Be there around seven. We'll meet you in the café next to it. Can you do that, Selena?"

"I guess so." She thought about it, wondering what had happened to Donavan. She stared at the rising sun and realized she had been sitting outside for a few hours. If she could make it back to the house, she could get cleaned up. "How do you know my name?"

"We met at the closing, right? I'm Rhianna. Look, we're on our way. Please meet us and get out before sundown. I'll explain everything then, okay?"

"Fine." Selena closed the phone, deciding it was time to go face her fears. She couldn't fall back into the same kind of slump she was in when Trevor was killed. Phoebe's life depended on her finding out how to save her from the ghosts. Trevor would want her to continue. Selena shoved the phone back into her jeans and tried to get up. She tried to put weight on her leg. Once she did, it hurt like hell, but she could hold herself up. Gritting her teeth, she made her way back over the line and then stopped, waiting for something to come out of the field and claim her. The only thing that greeted her was the cawing of crows.

She needed food and water. Slowly but surely she made her way down the driveway, inching closer to the house. Once she got to her car, she saw a balloon floating by it. It was neon green with a white string. It bobbed and hovered above the ground. Curiosity told her to investigate it, but she knew better and moved past it, slowly waiting for it to pop or something to jump out at her because that was what happened in the movies. When she went by the floating orb, it followed her until she got to the house. There it drifted in the doorway, but didn't cross the threshold. It turned around and on the other side was an image of the Jester. His white face leered at her as if he was watching her. She waited for it to pop or to hear the jingling of bells, but she heard nothing. Selena felt a little safer in the house, but not much.

"W-what do you want?" Selena asked the balloon.

It banged against the doorway and was not able to enter. At her question, she heard bells jingling in the house. A disembodied voice echoed through the room.

"I want your soul! Now I have your friend's. She's rather tasty. HAHAHAHAA! If you want her, come and get her!" The balloon popped, sending confetti into the room and nearly stopped Selena's heart. Fear gripped her and made her move into overdrive. If Rhianna said to be out of there by sunset, then she was getting out of there now. She could deal with her leg the way it was a little longer.

She ran, or hopped, up the stairs, trying not to shake. She went into the bedroom and grabbed her bag from the closet. There she started throwing in some of the clothes she already had on the hanger. She bumped her calf, sending pain shooting up her leg, and she had to sit down. Frustration enveloped her and made her scream. She threw her bag across the room. When she did, she noticed the mirror. There was no one in it, just her reflection. She wondered if Donavan was anywhere. Part of her needed him. After the other night in the tub with his hands all over her, she hadn't thought she could ever feel like that again. Part of her missed Trevor, but he would never return and this complete stranger, a ghost in a mirror had brought her to the brink of ecstasy. Now part of her yearned for his hands to be on her again.

How had he gotten himself caught up with the Jester? Why was he stuck in a mirror and where was his brother? What does all of this have to do with me and the mirror?

Selena sat down on the bed and stared at the sun. The tree outside tapped on the window, making her shiver. She watched a crow perch in the boughs and stare at her with beady black eyes.

"Selena."

She heard a voice in her room. She looked around. There was no one, but then she realized it was Donavan. Turning back toward the mirror, she saw him standing and watching her. Her heart soared at the sight of him. She wanted to rush into his arms and have him protect her from the evils of the world, but she didn't know how to get him out of the mirror.

"Donavan, where's Phoebe?" He was not wearing the Jester's uniform that he had on before. He wore black pants and a green tunic over then. The outfit showed off his perfectly sculpted body, letting her know he was built in all the right places. His dark hair was pulled away from his face showing the deformed side and the angelic one. Dark green eyes studied her and she yearned to discover how he liked to be touched and fondled.

"I don't know where your friend is. I'm sorry. I came to see if you were okay."

Selena chuckled. *Am I okay?* That was funny. The look on Donavan's face showed he was serious about her well being and he wasn't joking around. "I'm sorry, but no, I'm not okay. All this is a little much for me. Jesters, ghosts in mirrors, haunted carnivals. This isn't something I experience everyday. My life has turned into a nightmare these past few days. I regret ever coming here."

Donavan sighed. "I see. I'll leave you be then."

He turned and began to fade out and she realized how she must have sounded. "Donavan, wait. I didn't mean you. Please come back," she called into the now empty mirror. She waited and he didn't return. Defeated, Selena sunk down on the floor with her back against the dresser. She didn't care if the brass knobs dug into her back. He was the only good thing about her experience in the haunted mansion. Selena rested her hand on the glass. The cool surface felt good on her skin. The ache in her leg had subsided a bit. Getting it looked at was the last thing on her mind. Her thoughts were drifting to Trevor and the times they had been together. Whenever she had been sad, he would make her remember how to live again. She had always loved how he would take control of her and show her the pleasure of being able to rely on someone utterly.

He taught her the art of pain. Pain made her feel alive. It had made her feel the world opening up inside of her all by the manipulations of her lover. God, she needed Trevor. After he died, she never thought she would experience that state again. The pleasure mixed with pain made her know she was not lost anymore and that her soul had been claimed.

"Shh, don't cry, Selena."

She opened her eyes. Donavan had returned. His hand was over hers on the other side of the mirror, and Selena saw the energy between them sparking green against their palms through the glass. It charged up her arm and made her shiver deep inside.

"What's happening?"

"You're my soul mate, Selena. Only my soul mate can free me from this hell. My brother was right."

"What about the Jester? I thought he possessed you."

"Only at night. I've become separated from him ever since my brother escaped this place. The demon does not control me entirely, the way he used to, so I am able to come to you now. If you let me, I can do so much more. Do you want me, Selena?" His voice was soft and seductive.

"Yes. I want you." When the words left her lips, she watched the surface of the glass become liquid. His hand slipped between her fingers and she was able to know he was real and not a figment of her imagination or some dark creation of the Jester. Donavan stepped through the mirror and appeared on the other side. He enfolded Selena into his arms and kissed her. His tongue met hers as he tasted her mouth and his hands cupped her ass. She tried to stand, but the wound in her leg throbbed again and she couldn't hold up her weight. She cried out, but Donavan held her up.

"You're hurt." He scooped her up and laid her on the bed. He propped her up with a few pillows and then began pulling away the torn fabric of her jeans. She tried not to flinch when he looked at the gash. "You were lucky not to have broken your leg. This wound is pretty bad. I can heal it for you, if you wish."

"You're a doctor? Great. Stitch me up!"

Donavan laughed. "No, I'm not a doctor." He closed his eyes and lifted his hands so his palms were even with one another with a small space in between them. A ball of green light formed between his hands. A wave of fear rolled through her. He knew magic. Maybe he was just using her to free himself and he truly was the Jester.

"Please, don't hurt me."

Donavan opened his eyes, smiled, took the energy between his hands, and lowered it to the wound. A tingle and burning sensation ran up her leg, while green light infused the slice. He moved his hand over the wound, his forehead knotted in concentration. The light wavered some.

Trust me, Selena. If you struggle against me, it drains my already weakened magic. I won't hurt you. You know that. Please, know this is me and not the Jester playing a trick on you.

She sensed the fierce concentration he was using on her and what he said was true. There was no trace of the Jester in his power. The demon was not with him when the sun was up. She relaxed and let him work his magic on her and in no time, the wound began to close and the blood receded as if she was never injured.

Finally, the green light of his power faded and he slumped against the footboard of the bed. Selena ran her hand over the skin and found the spot to be completely solid. Not even a scar remained. She looked at her savior and her heart swelled at the sight of him. She never thought anyone would replace Trevor in her heart and Donavan already had. She missed her husband, but he would be glad she found someone to be happy with, even though the circumstances behind their meeting were a little unusual.

Selena leaned over on the bed and reached out to feel the scarred side of Donavan's face. Before her fingers touched his cheek, he snatched her wrist. He opened his eyes and drew her into him. The energy ignited between their bodies, burning her up inside. Her nipples were pert against her T-shirt. She desired to tease his entire body and feel the softness of his dick between her lips. She went on her knees, leaned in even more, and claimed his lips. He pulled away from her and got off the bed.

"Strip," he demanded.

Selena took off her clothes and let the cool air caress her naked flesh. Something cool and soft slithered around her wrist. When she tried to move away, Donavan grabbed her other wrist and she felt the same kind of feeling embrace the other hand. When she brought her hands down, they were tied in a thick green cord.

Blood rushed to her cheeks. She could barely look at Donavan. Questions formed in her mind. How did he know?

"I know because I saw it in your thoughts, Selena. God, you're so beautiful and so ripe." He grabbed the cord and his lips met hers in a fierce kiss until he released her. He walked around her and then ran something soft along the curve of her shoulder. "You brought me here, Selena, but I can only do things to you if you let me. I can read your desires, but I can't act on them unless you give me permission. I know you want me, but do you want me to bring you the same pleasure your husband did?"

Donavan grabbed a handful of her ass and pinched it. Her knees buckled from the joy of the pleasure. Images raced through her mind of what Trevor had done to her, the spankings, the whippings, the hours of being tied up and him tickling her until she was in a pool of her own wanting. Donavan licked her neck and nipped her ear. His hand came around and pinched her other nipple.

"I need you to say it. I can fuck you, punish you, or neither. Do I have your permission?"

Selena heard the pent up passion in his voice and answered, "Yes."

Donavan snapped his fingers. A hook appeared suspended on a thick green cord hanging from the ceiling. He lifted her over head by unseen hands and she was suspended. Pain erupted on the left mound of her ass. The sensation dulled from the cool air hitting her skin and she shivered from the experience. Another hit her right mound. Once the paddle left her flesh, her skin was warm and prickled from the blood rushing to it. Her thighs clenched together as she jumped forward from the momentum and the yearning for more. He didn't use a lot of force, but the quick slaps on her ass made her wet and shiver with anticipation.

Before she met Trevor, Selena never imagined she could be awakened to the desires of this form of pleasure. She had lovers before who were all vanilla and liked straight sex. Their idea of kinky was using flavored body lotion. Never in a million years would any of them have the balls to tie her up. Trevor had first suggested it and she went along with it. He blindfolded her to heighten her experience. He used a riding crop on her first. The stiff bristles tickled her nipples while he whipped it across them, but the sting of pleasure and euphoria the pain gave her was like nothing she had ever experience before.

The paddle stopped and immediately she couldn't see anything. Donavan had blindfolded her. She tried to move her hands when a slight hint of panic moved through her brain, but Donavan leaned in and kissed her quickly, easing her fears. "Whatever you think of, I'll do. You wished for the crop and you will get it."

He brushed the bristles across her breasts. Her nipples grew harder at the contact. The cold handle trailed down her belly and touched her moist slit. Selena gasped. It wasn't enough. She needed more. The crack of the whip split the air. A jump of excitement slithered through her skin at the anticipation of the slice of pain.

"God, Selena. Your appetite is insatiable," Donavan whispered against her ear. The agony of the whip caressed the expanse of her back. Selena strained forward when the sting electrified her body. She bit her lip, but a moan escaped her anyway. Her pussy was wet and she craved more.

"Tell me you want it," Donavan demanded.

"No," Selena whispered.

He hit her with another cut of the whip. This time the tail of it rested on her neck. It was soft and not so harsh. With the blindfold on, she was a creature of whatever sensation he gave her. She was at his mercy, just the way she liked it. Trevor had been an artist and always left his mark, but never split her skin. Donavan flicked the whip diagonally along her back. With one more swing she would come. Her muscles were so tight and she was so wet. All she needed was one more flick.

"Please!" she begged. "More."

"No, Selena. You are mine to do with as I please." Instead of the whip, Selena felt something cold trickling along her breasts. She moaned and quaked at the new sensation. Donavan traced the ice over the lash marks to cool them. Each time the cubes touched her flesh, Selena jumped at the alternating sensations. The longer and slower he trailed the ice down her back, following the curve of her skin, he would then trail his tongue where the ice had been, lapping up the water droplets. She had no idea where the ice had come from, but she was beyond caring. Her entire body was his. Not even Trevor had gone this far with her. He had always stopped at a few licks of the whip, a few slaps of the paddle. He had never brought her this far outside of herself where even the slightest touch was maddening. Her whole body was a pool of desire, but maybe Donavan knew this and was using it against her.

The path of ice glided down between the mounds of her buttocks. Then she felt her tormentor insert the ice cube deep inside her hot, moist depths. "Oh, God." The words came out on a groan of pleasure and agony. Her muscles contracted around the ice cube and his finger. His other hand brushed her clit in slow, excruciating circles. She panted, trying to stay sane from the arousal devouring her body. She needed more. She needed him inside of her.

"Please!" Her anguished plea escaped her lips while the cold dripped down between her legs along with her warm juices. Donavan moved his fingers faster on her clit. Her hips bucked forward without her consent because he had control of her body now. Another cold cube slid into her, but it he couldn't get it all the way into her. She was too tight and her muscles were shivering from the orgasms inflicted upon her. If she moved, the air tickled her. The soft cord against her skin rubbed her and added fire to it all. She needed Donavan deep inside of her to satisfy the growing craving.

"God, you're so tight, Selena. I love that." He licked the side of her neck while his hands traveled up the inside of her arms to the cords. She felt him tug on the bonds and then she was free. He caught her, lifting her up and placing her on the bed.

She still couldn't see because of the blindfold, but felt him spread her legs and wrap the cord around her ankles. This time he left her hands free. His tongue traced the inside of her thigh while his fingers lightly scratched the other side until he got to her pussy. There, his tongue lapped at her nether regions, burying inside her.

Selena completely lost it. Her moans had become grunts. She grabbed the sheets to remind herself she was still attached to her body. Her lover laved her, slowly nibbling her clit. Each time she was sent into another roller coaster of ecstasy until her heart was going a mile a minute and she thought she was going to black out. Minutes seemed to pass like hours for her as he tortured her with pleasure.

Finally, giving her what she longed for, he entered her slick depths. Donavan was bigger than Trevor, but he fit inside of her better. His strokes were slow at first, but the tension between them built fast. Selena desperately wanted to wrap her legs around him, but they were still tied. His lips met hers. Their kisses were no longer tender, but needy and full of anticipation. Selena wrapped her arms around his neck while he pumped into her. One hand rested on her hip and the other touched the back of her neck. Energy she flared down her spine in short bursts in time with her heart.

"Fuck me, Donavan. Please, fuck me. Don't stop."

"Oh, baby. I couldn't if I wanted to. You're so good to fuck."

Donavan increased his rhythm. Their pelvises touched each time he dove inside of her. Her nails dug trails along his back.

"God, Donavan." When she reached her height, she saw the green energy flowing between them behind her eyes. Her mind opened to his otherworldliness. She craved more of him. At that moment, the bonds around her ankles disappeared and she was able to wrap her legs around him.

"Selena, I love you," he whispered in her ear and released inside of her. She cried out from the orgasm ripping her apart until they both collapsed on the bed.

For a moment, they rested, locked together. Finally, Donavan removed the blindfold from Selena. When he did, he brushed the hair away from her face and smiled at her. To her it was amazing to see the difference in him just by looking at him. One side of his face was so badly burned and the other was angelic without a mark. She smiled back and traced the lines of his scars. He curled his face into her palm, captured it, and then kissed it. Their noses were inches from one another. She never had such an intimate and vulnerable moment with Trevor. Donavan was showing her part of his soul and she cherished that.

"What happened to you?"

Donavan glanced outside and then back at her. "My story can wait for another time. You should go soon. The sun will be setting in less than an hour and I don't want to be on this side of the mirror when the demon emerges. I fear what he will do to you. Already I can feel him encroaching on my thoughts. He knows I'm here with you and hates that you have the power to free me when he is still trapped in the other realm."

Selena looked at the bedside clock and her heart plummeted. They had been together for hours and it seemed like no time had passed at all. She nestled into his arms, feeling how well his body fit against hers. Everything about her was so tired and so relaxed she could just fall asleep. It seemed Donavan sapped all the strength from her limbs and put a spell on her. She tried to move, knowing the danger, but she couldn't.

"Selena, love, you have to get up and leave before the sun sets." Donavan ran a hand over her stomach and brushed it over her hardened nipple. A shiver of lust went through her. Slowly, he untangled himself from her and she noticed a tattoo on the back of his shoulder. It was a Jester. The leering face gave her a small jolt of energy to rouse her.

"Why do you have the tattoo?"

The expression on his face hardened somewhat and was a little paler than it was even a few minutes ago. Selena glanced at the window and saw that the sun was on its descent. She had to get up, but it was so hard to move.

"It binds me to the demon. It was his twisted idea to brand me with it to remind me of the role I would always play."

"You mean the Jester? Is that what you used to do in the side show?"

Donavan nodded. He crossed the room to Selena and cupped her face between his hands. His green gaze stared deeply into hers. "My brother and I summoned the demon up from a text that my father had. It contained dark spells to banish and to call up beings from hell. I used to entertain in the sideshow of the circus as a Jester. My brother, Alexander, was ringmaster. We ran it together. It was the perfect way to gather souls. My brother came up with the idea since the demon had picked him for its favorite at first. To gain power, Alexander killed our father. Over the years, my brother grew to hate what the demon had made us."

"What did he make you?"

Donavan kissed her. "I have to go, and you have to meet Alexander. He is close. I can sense him. Please leave now while you still have time."

Selena tried to get up, but found that she couldn't. All she wanted to do was fall back to sleep. "I promise, but I can't keep my eyes open right now."

Donavan nodded. He caressed her cheek and walked to the mirror. "I'll keep him away from here as long as I can, but you must leave. I'm sorry that my magic has sapped your strength. It must be a side effect of the magic. Sleep for now, my love." He placed his hand on the surface of the mirror and it turned liquid when he stepped through the opening. When he was all the way through, he turned and stared at her. He put his hand on the glass and this time it did not come back through. He nodded toward the sun and she nodded back, understanding his warning. She tried to rise again, but was unable to. The only thing she could do was let the darkness take her into oblivion.

Chapter Four

Selena opened her eyes and stared at the bedside clock. She had slept for another three hours. It was full dark now. The house was silent. She glanced at the mirror and saw nothing in it save her own reflection. She listened intently and didn't hear anything off in the house. She was supposed to meet Rhianna and Alexander, but they could wait a little longer. Her entire being hummed from the aftermath of her love making with Donavan and she needed to take a shower. *A little bit longer in the house can't hurt. At least long enough to get cleaned up and then go.*

She got out of bed, still feeling drained, but able to move this time around. She gathered her clothes and her purse to leave directly after she dried off and placed them on the hamper. She let water wash over her, but it did little to satisfy the growing lust she had for Donavan. With the water droplets caressing her flesh, her mind wandered to the experience she had with the man only a few hours ago. His hand and actions had tattooed themselves to her flesh. Just thinking about him made her hot. Without thinking, her fingers trailed to her nether regions, settling on her clit. Her eyes closed and she stood back against the cool tile wall to try to calm the tidal wave of sensations washing over her. Moving the node in circles, the tension mounted inside of her. Her muscles clenched. Behind her closed eyes, she saw the green energy, which had sparked between her and Donavan. She licked her lips and found herself panting, imagining Donavan doing the actual fondling.

I only wish I was. She heard his voice next to her. She opened her eyes to be sure but he had not magically appeared even though she desperately wanted him to.

Baby, where are you? Selena thought.

He appeared in her mind and she felt him caress her breast the way he had the other night when she was in the bathtub. His hands replaced hers, he moved her clit slowly, and then she felt his mouth working on her. Her hands gripped the shower bar above her while his tongue flicked lightning quick over her hard node. Shivers of ecstasy coursed through her. Her breathing came in small gasps. He was fucking her with his tongue in long luscious licks.

More, baby, please. I'm ready.

She felt a pause in him. The green energy zinged through her. Selena barely noticed the water had grown cold. She was so hot she couldn't contain her moans. At that moment, she didn't care what he did to her, she just needed him. Then he started up again. His fingers slipped inside of her. One. Two. And then three. He curled them inside her pussy. His teeth nibbled at her. Her hands gripped the bar tighter when she pushed her pussy into his face. Even though it was a ghostly sensation, she felt him through their connection.

Do you like it? Do you enjoy being eaten?

Yes. Yes! I need you in the flesh like earlier. Come to me, please.

I was waiting for you to say that, but aren't you afraid of the Jester? I can only keep him away for so long.

I trust you. Please, I need you.

The jingle of bells and laughter filtered through the bathroom. Suddenly, Donavan's manipulations grew rough, but she didn't care. She needed him.

You taste so good. His fingers moved inside of her more. Donavan's power descended over her. She tried to open her eyes, but her body was not responding to her commands. The green energy surrounding her became a vice. Instead of being alone in the shower, she sensed someone else was with her. Donavan had crossed over and come to her. Hands kneaded her breasts hard. Selena was amazed at the passion moving through her. Her hips buckled at the sensations.

You want more. Tell me you do. I can give you more if you let me. You reached out and I answered your call. Are you afraid of me? Afraid I'll consume you?

Selena wasn't sure what Donavan was talking about. How could she be afraid of him? He was rough with her before and this was nothing new. *I love it. You know I want it. Give me all you have. I can take it. Please!*

Please what? Lips touched the back of her neck. She didn't want it to stop. She wanted to be fucked.

Do you want me? Tell me and I'll give you what you crave.

Selena didn't dare open her eyes in case she broke the mood and Donavan would retreat back into the mirror. She was proud of him for keeping the Jester at bay. It only meant that he was stronger than the demon. Hands clutched her ass. Something hard touched the inside of her thigh. It was colder than the water. A tongue licked the side of her face. Fingers rubbed against her faster. She moaned. God, she wanted him. Trevor had opened her up to a whole new kind of sexual appetite she had never thought would be sated and now Donavan had brought her to another level.

I came here to satisfy both our needs, Selena. You get one free pass and this is it. Tell me quickly before the Jester comes. He's near. I can smell your lust and see it in your thoughts. I can fuck you as you ask, but I need your permission.

"Fuck me. Hard," she screamed.

I thought you would never ask.

Donavan worked her clit. She pushed her ass into him, gripping the bar so hard she didn't know it if would break. After a moment, his dick slid into her. *Oh, fuck.* It felt so good and calmed the raging sensations. She needed him. Needed all of it. Without another word, he thrust himself all the way into her.

Does this feel good, Selena? Is this what you wanted? Donavan purred in her mind.

Yes. God help me, yes.

You're such a good lay. It's been a long time since I've had such a great piece of ass. You know what you want and we make such beautiful music together.

He moved deeper inside of her, sending chills to calm the waves of ecstatic torment flowing through her. She tried to hold in the moans, but couldn't. His fingers ran trails along her stomach and the inside of her thighs, making indentations and pressing her hard enough to leave bruises. With her eyes closed, she could see the green energy glowing strong around her. That energy buzzed between them and only grew stronger from their lovemaking.

One hand rested over her heart and the other settled below her belly button. Pulses of energy moved through her, matching the rhythm as he fucked her. Each one brought her to new heights. Donavan showed her where she had the power to do whatever she wanted. She could have any man she desired. All her lusts could be sated. Donavan was offering her the world and all she needed to do was reach out and grab it.

He rocked into her. Selena was beyond moaning and grinding her hips. Her body was his. He continued to pump inside of her, filling her mind with power. The high was so wonderful she didn't want him to stop. Donavan knew her soul, could read the lust and perversions she wanted to do and have done to her. Everything in her yearned to be used and abused and she could have it all.

Her pussy quivered at each thrust. Her soul craved what Donavan was offering. The power wasn't so bad. He was giving her the choice to join him completely. His spell over her was complete, owning her body and soul. She wanted him to fuck her and be at her disposal to fill her naughty fantasies. They were both there and she could feel him under her skin.

Oh, Selena. I could offer you so much more than what you ever imagined. Do you want that? Do you want me to fill you up? Do you want me to give you the ride of your life?

Fuck me. Just fuck me. I need it. Oh, God. I need it.

Donavan smiled and slowed his rhythm. Her body was beginning to hurt from all the stress it had experienced. His hands were still above her heart, but he was loading her with energy that burned through her soul. It was a roller coaster ride of sensation she didn't know existed until Donavan had broken it wide open earlier.

Tell me what you want. He rolled his dick around in her pussy so she moaned out in pleasure while the biggest and hardest orgasm she had took hold of her. She rode the waves that kept bringing her higher. What did she want? She wouldn't have to be alone ever again. Donavan would be there with her always if that was what she desired. She just had to give in to him. His hands moved lower and rubbed her clit again as he stayed buried deep inside of her. He wasn't letting her go. It seemed he was fucking her to death and she was letting him, loving every minute of it. How could she say no to the man that she loved?

Yes, Selena. You want me. You've always wanted me. This is your destiny. I'll never leave you. I swear it. You can have me all to yourself. Will you have me? Will you let me fuck you forever?

His free hand moved over her heart again. She wanted it all. "Yes. I don't care. Do it. Take me please. I'm yours."

Oh, baby, you don't know how much I wanted you to say that. His tongue worked on her faster and she was lost. She saw the green energy surrounding her. Donavan was so deep inside of her now, body and soul, that nothing could separate them. *One more thing, Selena. Turn around. Open your eyes. I need you to look at me.*

"But...can't stop...please!" Selena stammered.

We won't stop, baby. I'm more than flesh and blood now and can do whatever I want to your mortal body. More than you ever dreamed. Trust me.

Selena nodded. She trusted him. Why would she not trust him? Slowly, she turned around. She opened her eyes and realized the water had somehow turned off. Maybe the Jester had done it. As she turned, she stared into the handsome features of her beloved. For a moment she thought his image wavered. A jolt of fear moved through her, but it was overcome with the ecstasy he gave her. There was nothing to worry about. Her fear of the Jester was overtaking her reason. The allure of the Donavan's eyes tugged on her soul.

Yes, just a little more, love. One more push and you can have whatever you want. I'll be there for you always. You don't have to worry about loosing me. I'll never be unfaithful to you. You can have me all to yourself.

His words echoed in her mind. Selena tried to keep her composure, but it was so hard. His tongue darted over her lips, while his hands caught both of her wrists and held them above her head while she bucked against him. He supported her weight now. She was beyond caring what he did to her, she just longed to be taken.

Selena, no. Don't give in to him. If you do, you'll lose me forever. She heard Donavan's voice in her thoughts, but how could that be because Donavan was here with her? The voice must have been the Jester trying to trick her. It was so far away she could barely make it out. He kept pleading with her not to give in. Donavan was already so much inside of her that she didn't know if she could stop. It felt so good. His power was so cold and she was so hot.

Don't listen to him. He's trying to trick you. It's only the Jester. , Listen only to me, come for me, baby. Just one more time. Can't you do that for me? Donavan redoubled his efforts on her body. Selena was slipping into his delicious power even more. Her body was building toward an orgasm that was near earthquake proportions setting to rock her body. Donavan had unending stamina and was fucking her harder, riding her so she couldn't get away. The green flames in his eyes had expanded and flared in her soul. The fire was a cold fire, full of lust. Part of her consciousness was filled with so much power she didn't know where the universe ended and she began.

Donavan's voice was retreating fast. *Please, Selena. I love you. Don't give in.*

A current of love surged along the connection she shared with Donavan. At that moment, the image before her wavered. She saw a pale white pace and glowing flames for eyes. She shut her eyes against the image and focused on Donavan. This was something the Jester was doing to her. Selena remembered her love had freed Donavan from the clutches of the Jester and she latched onto their connection by seeing the images Donavan showed her. Eons of taking souls to feed the beast, of losing his wife and child. How he got the burn because he had tried to save his wife, Rachel. Something awakened inside of her. This wasn't right.

Don't listen to him. You know you want it. Look into my eyes. You're so close. We can both taste it. If you stop now, you'll never know what I can truly give you.

Selena let her head fall back against the wall. Donavan's mouth was on her breasts. God, it felt so good, but she couldn't completely give up. "No, this isn't right," she whispered.

He rammed into her harder than he had before and his hands were around her throat. *You're so close that I can gobble you all up in one bite. There's nothing else that you can do, you're already mine.*

"Get away from her!"

Selena looked over at the sudden intrusion. There was a woman in her bathroom she had only met once before at the closing of her house, Rhianna. A blue glow surrounded her.

Selena's gaze switched to the man before her. It wasn't Donavan, but the Jester. The demon grinned and waved its fingers at her. The Jester's eyes narrowed and his smile widened. All the sensations he was playing on her ceased. He still gripped her arms in his and she was burning from the inside out.

My, my, the witch is back. I didn't expect that. Where is my darling Alexander? I'm sure he's not far behind. You can't have this one. She already gave herself to me just like you did. The Jester's long pointed tongue wagged at Rhianna. She then formed a ball of blue energy in her hand.

"She might have given herself to you, but what wiles did you use to fool her? Either way she did not pledge herself to you. Let her go or I'll make you!"

Dark laughter filled the bathroom that shook Selena's soul. *I'm not afraid of you!*

Rhianna's eyes narrowed. She murmured something and the ball in her hand grew bigger. She flung it at the demon, hitting him square in the chest. The Jester let his gaze slide down to the hole, and his face began to crack and crumble. His hand around Selena's wrist released, followed by the rest of him. Selena tried to squirm away as the Jester's remains turned to ash and the stench of burnt popcorn filled the bathroom.

Frigid water came on full blast. However, Selena wasn't shivering from the water. Rhianna turned off the water and the ashes were washed down the drain. She reached for Selena, but now that the Jester was gone, Selena found she was dizzy. Darkness wavered on the edge of her vision. The woman said something to her, but the words sounded garbled. Selena reached out, but her consciousness snuffed out and she plunged into oblivion.

Chapter Five

Selena opened her eyes only to discover she was no longer in the bathroom, but lying on a foreign bed. She was wrapped in a towel and her robe. Part of her felt empty, where the Jester had sucked out part of her soul. Even though he was gone, she could still sense him, still see the green flames burning in the back of her mind.

She sat up slowly and saw she was in a hotel room. Her clothes sat on the bed across from her. Selena pulled on the jeans and T-shirt. When she looked at herself in the mirror a bolt of shock went through her. Her face was gaunt and her cheeks were hollow. Her blue eyes were tinged green and her hair had gone bone white. When she smiled, her teeth were a little sharper. To confirm it, she ran her tongue over them and almost cut herself. Anger welled up inside of her and she balled her fist and smashed the mirror, but her hand never hit the glass even though it shattered onto the bureau. Her fingers were covered with green light like that of the Jester. She swallowed hard and when she relaxed, the energy dissipated. Selena wondered what it meant. She closed her eyes and tried to get it together.

"Are you okay? I heard something break." Rhianna in on Selena and saw the mirror along with the fading green light from her hand. Their eyes met. Selena realized they shared adjoining rooms in the hotel and the door was open.

"Can you explain any of this?" Selena walked into Rhianna's room and saw a man staring out the hotel window. When he turned around, she gasped. He could have been Donavan's twin except his face was not scarred and his eyes were blue and not green. She blushed when she thought about all the things Donavan had done to her. Obviously, this was not him, but his brother, Alexander. Donavan had not told her he was an identical twin. It might have been better if he did, then she would not have been so shocked at seeing the man standing in front of her.

Looking at the two in the room, she could plainly see a blue energy around them. This was getting way too complicated and creepy for her. Selena had just entered the Twilight Zone and wondered if she was going to have any sense of sanity anytime soon. She needed answers. She needed to free Donavan from wherever he was trapped and get Phoebe before the demon did anything to her. But the big concern was killing the demon. Whatever the old owner, Rhianna, did had hurt it and sent it back to its own hellish dimension.

"When was the last time you saw my brother?"

Selena looked up and saw Alexander was staring at her. His power surrounded her and brushed against her mind. She sensed he was trying to see if she was lying or how much of her was influenced by the Jester.

"I...I..." she stammered and tried to catch her breath, but all she could hear was the Jester laughing in her mind. She covered her ears with hands and cried out. "Make it stop!"

Alexander put a hand on her shoulder. The evil presence vanished. Alexander's cool power washed over her. He led her to the bed to sit down. Rhianna handed her a glass of water, which she took with shaky hands. She took a sip and was then able to answer his questions.

"I saw him this morning."

"And he was normal? The demon wasn't bound to him?"

Selena shook her head. "No. I pulled him out of the mirror in my bedroom and we, um, you know..." She gestured and felt her cheeks turn red. Her gaze fell to the floor as she could not look directly at Alexander and tell him the things she had done with his brother, or the things his brother had done to her. However, in her mind, she wanted Alexander to do those things to her also.

"It's okay. I can understand how alluring the Rosin men can be," Rhianna chimed in. "The mirror. Did you find it in the attic?"

"Attic? No. My husband—late husband—made it for me. It was one of the only things I kept from after...sorry, it's still hard." Selena smiled and felt her teeth shift slightly back to normal, even though they were still pointy. It was strange. *I wonder what the dentist will say next time I go.*

"What happened with my brother? Why was the demon in the shower with you? Why were you giving yourself over to it? How did you free my brother? Can you call him?" Alexander started questioning Selena.

Rhianna shot him a look and poked him in the stomach with her elbow. Selena thought it was funny, but it did get him to purse his lips and take a big sigh. The energy around him evened out. He relaxed and ran a hand though his hair.

"I'm sorry. I don't mean to be so pressing, but it's important you tell me everything you know. I want—we want to help you. It's just, the last time I saw my brother I thought would be the last time I ever saw him. He was trapped in the same world I was in and I didn't think he could get out. I tried to get to him, but it was too late. I had to leave or I would have been lost, too. As it was it took me so long to find Rhianna again."

She heard the concern in his voice for Donavan. It made her feel good he truly was interested in helping him. She calmed herself and started her tale from the beginning, from after they bought the house, to when Trevor died, to when she moved in and how strange things started happening the same night when she heard Donavan's voice in the mirror. She even described how she pulled him from the mirror just hours earlier, how the demon was still attached to him at night, and what had happened in the bathroom. Rhianna and Alexander listened and did not interrupt her this time.

When she was done, Selena listened to the story of how Rhianna met Alexander and how she had stepped through the mirror to bring him back. Selena wondered if she would have to do the same thing. She might have to for Phoebe. Rhianna explained how Alexander had appeared to her in her own mirror, how she had rescued him from the demon, learned she was a witch, and that they had hurt the demon.

"I'm sorry to hear about your friend," Alexander said. "Whatever damage we did to the Jester has had a lasting effect. That's a good thing, but it worries me about Donavan. You said he's only tied to him at night and it seems through his futile attempt at converting you, you have gained some of his powers."

"Will I stay like this?" Selena asked Alexander.

"I'm not sure. The Jester completely took over my brother for centuries because he gave into the guilt of Rachel's death, his first wife. My brother looked somewhat like you do now, but you did not give up your soul to the demon. It's apparent he's influenced you, hence you are still connected to him and have some of his power. Will you be able to keep out his evil? Can you fight him?"

"I'm not sure. I hear him in my thoughts. You're the only thing keeping him out."

"Selena, do you love Donavan?" Rhianna asked.

Selena stared at Rhianna. It was a question she had posed to herself recently and had not really been able to answer. She loved the feel of his hands on her body, of him buried inside of her. They fit together so well. When she had heard the loss in Donavan's voice and thought she would never see him again, she knew she felt something for him. He had said he loved her. That statement was what had made her hold on so she would not give herself up completely to the evil growing inside of her. Yes, she loved him more than she had loved Trevor, if that was possible, and it was.

"Yes. I love him. He's part of me. It was like that with Trevor, too. But this is deeper, like we're cut from the same mold. Is that wrong? I've felt so lost these past few months since Trevor was killed. I felt so responsible for his death. I know it was an accident, but he was working so hard so we could buy the house, you know, and putting money away so we could start a family. Look where it got him."

"Guilt is a hard emotion to wipe away from the soul. It was what Donavan wallowed in and he gave himself over to the demon. Even I was prey to it until I met Rhianna and understood that she was my soul mate. It was how I was able to come through the mirror. When my brother and I first summoned the demon from the book, we made a pact with it for power and immortality. I retained the power even after I escaped the realm. Rhianna discovered her magic. Now you're tied to my brother and the Jester, too. Together, I am sure there's a way we can defeat him."

"Great. How do we do that?"

"I'm not sure. I have to talk to my brother. Which means we have to go back to the house where we found you."

"I don't ever want to go back there."

"Why do you think I sold it?" Rhianna chuckled.

"So, you sold it knowing this could happen? Gee, thanks for telling me! At least you could have given me more of a warning instead of a note that said, 'Call me if anything seems a little weird.' This is pretty fucking weird, okay?" Selena started screaming at Rhianna. She should've told her if the house was possessed when they first bought it. Wasn't it against the law to sell a haunted house and not tell the new owners? *Maybe not in her world!* Selena thought.

"Look, I never asked for this. For all I know the house killed my husband or some shit! I'm not going back to the house!" Selena felt the energy crackling around her, and when she looked at her hands, they were lined with fuzzy green energy.

The power consuming her made her feel all powerful. The voice of the Jester filled her thoughts. He was a dark tide and had taken over. He whispered for her to kill Alexander and Rhianna. If she did that, she could have Donavan with no strings attached. All he wanted was souls. If she gave him souls, he would leave her in peace. She was the perfect emissary for him. She could bring him what he needed to be strong. His power caressed the inside of her. She shuddered and drank it in. A heavy ball of green energy appeared in her hand. The corners of her mouth twisted up into a smile. She brought her hand back and was about to throw it when she realized what she was doing.

She stopped herself in mid throw, but the energy ball veered off and went straight for Rhianna. Alexander dived in front of her and caught the ball, absorbing it into himself.

Selena swallowed and started. "I'm sorry. I can't do this. I can't!" She rushed out of the hotel room door and into her car. Rage burned through her and cracked around her in a neon green haze. She was mad at herself. She didn't care where she was going, just away from Crow's Creek. The further away the better.

Chapter Six

Selena didn't know how long she drove. Time was a blur and seemed nonexistent. Her emotions spurred her onward to get away from her new life. Finally, she stopped her car, got out and stretched. She barely knew where she was she was so tired. Her body felt worn out. Her feet took her to a spot where she sat down, curled up and went to sleep.

"Selena!"

Selena opened her eyes. She winced at the bright sun flooding her kitchen window. She looked around, wondering what she was doing sitting at the Formica table she hated so much. It had belonged to Trevor's mother. When they first got married, he had stolen the kitchen set from her basement so they could have something to eat at. She ran her hands over the speckled tabletop and caught the nicks in it from the many times they had played target practice with the table. She had hated it so much. When Trevor died, she put it out on the side of the road hoping a bus would hit it. No such luck it seemed.

She scanned the rest of the kitchen and it was exactly the same. The wooden spoon and fork were still on the wall. Trevor thought it would be kitschy to have them out, she thought it was stupid and something her parents would have on the wall, but she let it go. He was so insistent and he let her have her collection of gargoyles and dragons in the house peeking out from everywhere, so she was happy with the trade off. Now her knickknacks were in boxes waiting to go up to the attic. She hadn't been able to take them out since they had reminded her too much of Trevor.

Selena had some of her happiest memories in the kitchen. It was cramped with the table and had a small breakfast bar, which went into the dining room. She blushed to think how many times she and Trevor had made love on the bar. If houses could talk, theirs would have a couple of series to tell with all that went on between them.

"Selena."

She looked across the table. Warm brown eyes met hers and a smile that lit up the room more than the sun. Trevor had started to thin a little on the top of his head from wearing a baseball cap all the time and she jokingly complained about it, but he didn't stop, considering he worked out in the sun a lot. Working with his hands had sculpted his muscles and body so that he was a perfect specimen of a man with a golden tan and a beautiful demeanor. He always knew how to make her feel better no matter how foul a mood she was in.

"Am I dreaming?"

Trevor smiled. He ran a finger down her nose and hit it. It was his little pet way of telling her he loved her. He felt real enough.

"You're kinda dreaming. Your body is asleep and your mind is here with me."

Selena pulled back from him. He could be the Jester trying to mess with her mind. She got up from the chair and grabbed a knife from the holder. "I told you I don't want any part of you. Get the hell away from me!"

Trevor's smile didn't falter. He held out his hands for her, letting her know he was not a threat. "Selena, I'm not the Jester. It's me. It's Trevor. Please, put the knife down. I'm only here for a little bit. It's all I'm allowed." He walked toward her and gripped her hand. She let him have the knife and take her into his arms as she began crying. It really was him. She tightened around him, not wanting to let him go.

"Sweetie, I still need to breathe," Trevor chuckled.

"God, Trevor, it's really you." Selena wiped the tears from her eyes. He was real, at least for now, and she was grateful for the slight reprieve from the hell her life had become.

"Yes, it's me. You asked for a place that would make you happy before all of the craziness in your life started. Well, here we are. Are you happy?"

"I'm so sorry you died. I didn't know what to do. What was I supposed to do?"

Trevor kissed her lightly on the lips. His mouth still felt the same and his gesture was like a prayer had been answered. She wanted to slip into his arms, crawl back under the covers, and make love to him. It was all she wanted and she couldn't have that with him again. Did he mind what she had become? Did he blame her?

"No, Selena. I don't blame you for anything. Sometimes things are meant to happen. Everything we are is meant to happen. I loved you. I still love you, but this is something you were destined to do. I'll always be watching over you, I promise. Just don't let this thing beat you. I know it's hard and the evil is inside of you, but don't let it win. Remember our love. Remember the love you have for Donavan. Together, all your power can kill it. Evil, which was summoned ages ago, does not belong in this world." He cupped her cheek and ran his hand along the curve of her neck.

"Trevor, what does all of this mean? Why me?"

Trevor wrapped his hands around her waist. Selena closed her eyes and enjoyed the sensation. He was so warm and felt so alive. Why did he have to die? Was it true what he said, that she was fated to meet Donavan? That her life was meant to change the way it had? Was he so sure she could fight the evil that had taken root inside of her? She wasn't. She was afraid to face it. What if the Jester won and everything Alexander and Rhianna had worked for was lost? What if they were killed? What if Donavan was killed?

"I'm scared, Trevor. I never thought my life would turn out this way. Can't I stay here with you?"

He squeezed her a little tighter. Selena looked over at the window, seeing the sun was a little brighter and the Formica table was starting to blur. "I'd love you to stay with me, but it's not your place. You have to go back. Listen to your heart, Selena. It will tell you what you have to do. When you think you are at your weakest, just remember what I said and what you have in your soul. You're stronger than you think you are."

"Don't leave me!"

"I have no choice."

The room was fading now and she could barely feel him against her. Trevor had told her how to overcome the evil inside of her. If she followed his advice she would be able to save Donavan and Phoebe. To do that, she had to go back to the house and face her fears. She had to own up to everything.

"I love you."

"You too..." His voice echoed in the light. It was so bright she had to cover her eyes. When she did, she realized she had opened her eyes and the sun was shining directly in her face.

Selena looked around. She was in a graveyard. Her back was against something cold and smooth. It was a tombstone of black marble. She traced the carved letters with her fingers, feeling their angles. She stared at Trevor's name, feeling the finality of his passing. Trevor was never coming back. She had known that before, since she had been at the funeral, but now she was left with a sense of hope. It was time for her to let him go completely. She had to worry about rescuing her best friend and the man she loved. She would always love Trevor, but he was in a better place and she had to live her life. Maybe moving into the house had been the right thing to do.

She got up, stretching out her stiff muscles. Selena didn't know how long she had been there, but it was long enough that everything hurt and the sun was starting to climb into the sky. She took in a deep breath and scanned the surroundings of the graveyard. Forms hovered near some of the stones scattered throughout the cemetery. When she looked back at Trevor's, there was nothing there. These were spirits in some form, which was new and interesting at the same time. What other kinds of powers had she gotten from the Jester? Selena felt bad for these lost souls and realized for a long time now she had been one of them. Of course, she wasn't dead. Even with Trevor, she had been lost. He had anchored her for a while, but now she had found her place in the world. She was the one who would make the decisions about her life and who ran it.

A sense of resolve and strength awakened in her. It was still shaky since she was not used to the feeling, but she was going to cultivate it and not loose it to a crazy demon. Now she had to worry about saving Donavan. She was really the only one who could reach him in the other realm and not even his brother could pull him out. Selena ran her hand over the black marble, feeling the life in the stone. At that moment, she understood how everything was connected.

The Jester had given her more of his power than he expected. Whatever power he had imparted to her she was going to use to kick some demon butt. Selena smiled at the thought and stared at the sun. It was going to take her several hours to get back to the house. She had driven in a fog last night, so mad and scared she didn't realize where she was going. It must have been fate that led her here or Trevor had pulled her toward him, but it was the last time he would have to do that. She kissed her fingers and placed them on the stone.

"Good-bye."

Chapter Seven

Her gaze kept going between the sun and the speedometer on the car. She was pushing her car to the max and flying down the highway doing ninety. She normally played it safe, but time was against her. It was at least a six hour drive and she had gotten caught in traffic, not to mention it was nearly impossible to find a gas station on the highway. Everyplace she went was closed or out of gas. It was just her luck until finally on fumes that she was able to fill up.

She had tried every radio station on the way, but all she could get was country and gospel, and she was not in a praying kind of mood. Her mind was set on seeing the demon defeated, but as the hours grew later and darkness loomed her thoughts turned darker, too. Selena had begun plotting how easily she could play the nice, concerned, helpless victim and then kill Alexander and Rhianna so she could have their power, too.

Of course, she knew this was not her thinking, but the Jester. The smell of burnt popcorn was faint in her car, but she could still smell it along with the sickly sweet aroma of cotton candy. It stuck to the back her mouth. The Jester was trying to hack into her thoughts and control her, but she was not going to let him do it. She pressed her foot to the floor, not caring if she got a ticket. She had to get to the house before sun down. She only hoped Alexander and Rhianna were there waiting for her.

When she pulled up the gravel road the sun balanced on the horizon and twilight was only a few streaks away from claiming the sky. A green haze had settled over the field like pre-dawn fog.

Rhianna's Jeep was in the driveway next to the house. The front door was open and Selena could see movement in the bedroom upstairs. She pulled up closer to the house, got out of the car, and ran up the stairs. She got into the bedroom and found the bed had been turned and pushed against the wall. The carpet was rolled up and the mirror now stood all alone in the center of the room in a circle of candles. Alexander sat before it, staring deep into the reflection, waiting to see what would happen. Rhianna was behind him.

They both looked up when she entered.

"I didn't think you'd be coming back," Alexander stated. His focus remained on the mirror while Rhianna watched the sun.

A splinter of anger tinged Selena's emotions. The heat of her new power rose up in her. She even heard it crackling in the air. However, she closed her eyes and squelched her feelings. Alexander was testing her to see if she had changed her mind. She swallowed and did what Trevor said; she thought about the love she had for him and for Donavan. It was about saving him now and Phoebe, not about her. When she opened her eyes, Alexander nodded.

"Good. You're getting a handle on the power. You understand it is fueled by rage and strong emotion. The demon feeds on the rage, guilt, any dark emotion we have. Hold on to what you love and you can conquer the darkness."

"I'll try. What are you doing? Or what's the plan?"

Her gaze skimmed to the windows. Outside the sun was about gone and night had taken hold. The green haze solidified into buildings and people as it drifted through the grass. It was creeping closer to the house. The sound of a calliope echoed through the house sending shivers up Selena's spine. After this, she did not want to go to another circus in her life.

"I feel the same way," Rhianna chimed in. "If I ever hear that sound again, I'll scream. It grates on your nerves to hear the same off key melody over and over again."

"Yes, it does."

The door downstairs slammed against the wall. Selena jumped. The atmosphere grew heavy. The little hairs on her arms stood up. She heard bells in the background. Whatever was outside was coming inside. The other ghosts were not playing around this time. They were playing for keeps.

"Can they get in here?" Selena asked.

"No. Do you see the symbol above the door and on the floor? It prevents them from entering and the Jester from getting out."

"But I thought you didn't want the Jester to get out. I thought you wanted to get Donavan out of the other realm."

"We want both. Our plan is to separate the Jester and Donavan here. If the Jester can remain on this side of the mirror, we can destroy him once and for all. All the souls he has trapped will be free," Rhianna explained.

"First, I need you to summon Donavan." Alexander motioned for her to sit inside the circle of candles.

Selena nodded. She sat cross legged on the floor, stared into the mirror, and studied her own image. Her eyes seemed greener than they had the other night and she was still pale, but her face had filled out more. Her hair was bleach white and she had a sense it was not going to go back to its original color no matter what she did. Maybe it could hold a dye job if she tried. She would worry about it later. Selena looked over at Alexander.

"Just call out to him?"

"Whatever it is you do to call him to you."

Selena thought about Donavan. How he smelled. How he felt. How he sounded. It wasn't too hard considering his mirror image was seated right behind her. But there were differences, like his eyes. Donavan's hands knew her body and where to tickle her, but most of all she followed the connection between the two of them. It burned hotter and stronger now that she understood a little about the power inside of her. She let the floodgates open on her emotions and poured it into finding him, pulling him to her. When she opened her eyes, she was staring into his.

"Hi," Selena said.

He smiled at her, but his eyes went to his brother behind her. "Alexander, it's good to see you."

"You too, big brother. You ready to end this?"

"More than you'll ever know. If it wasn't for you I wouldn't have gotten this far. And if it wasn't for Selena I never would have had the freedom I do now." He took in her new appearance. She looked away, ashamed at what she had given in to to become the way she looked now. However, she felt a wave of such love and endearment from Donavan that it brought tears to her eyes. Within their silent communication there was also an understanding.

"Selena, when I tell you, I want you to pull Donavan through the mirror. No matter what you do, don't break the circle of candles. It will keep you and him safe," Alexander instructed.

Selena looked into the mirror and nodded. Alexander was the more experienced one so she was going to do what he said. She put her hand on the glass and watched Donavan do the same. The energy sparked between them. Behind them she watched Rhianna pull out a book and hand it to Alexander. She sensed it was filled with power.

"Alexander, what are you doing? You know what can happen from reading that. Remember what happened to Father? What happened to us?!"

"I know, Donavan, but there's no other way to summon the demon in its true form. The spell will pull it from your soul and manifest it here. Once that happens, you will be free. Then we can use it to destroy the Jester."

"If you let the Jester roam free, his minions will be free to descend on the house. If he can get past the barrier, do you know what havoc he will wreck? I can't let you do it. Selena, pull me through the mirror. Do it now," Donavan demanded.

Selena looked between him and Alexander. She started to send the current of energy along their connection when she heard the faint jingle of bells. Swiftly she shut down her power before the glass was completely liquid and she could take hold of Donavan's hands. "You're not Donavan. What did you do with him?"

Lightning cracked in the sky outside. Calliope music and the din of voices were clearer than they ever have been. The stench of rotting food and burning wood and flesh filled the room. Rhianna coughed behind her. A gust of wind blew through the room. Selena stared back into the mirror and there before her was the true Jester.

His eyes were completely hollow except for green flames. His teeth were pointed and browner than she remembered. His lips were frozen in a perpetual grin and seemed to curl into his cheeks, revealing all of his teeth. Once white gloves were torn showing knobby, bony fingers. His harlequin suite was green on one side and white on the opposite. Marble sized jingle bells made up the buttons of his suit. They were tarnished and rusted. He even had on matching slippers that curled on the ends with bells. The suite was torn, showing patches of white and decaying skin. Strands of stringy hair clung to his scalp. He was everything she had seen in her worst nightmares. Silently, she cursed herself to think she had given up part of herself to that thing. Now she was altered because of it.

You're a smart one, Selena. And such a great fuck. I saw all the naughty things you did with your dead husband. How sweet. We could have had so much fun. We still can. Just kill them for me.

"Go to hell!"

I've been there, love, and it smells like roses this time of year. Dear, Alexander, so predictable, trying to save your brother. You won't find him. You see, since Selena, my luscious kitten here, decided to give me part of her soul I got strong enough to detach from your pathetic brother. He was getting on my nerves. So what do you say? Want to go at it a few rounds? Deep laughter filled the bedroom. The demon disappeared from the mirror. The gust of wind came blasting out the glass. Selena dived down and covered her face to protect herself.

Chapter Eight

When she uncovered her head, one single candle was spared the onslaught of the phantom wind. She picked it up and looked at the damage the room sustained. The mirror was completely devoid of glass. Her heart sank when she saw the treasure Trevor had made for her. There was no way for her to pull Donavan from the other realm.

"Rhianna?" Selena whispered.

She didn't hear anything and then there was a giggle in the background. When she stood up, she saw Phoebe. Relief washed over her, but when she got closer she realized what was standing in front of her was no longer her friend. The woman she knew was gone. Phoebe's dark hair was chopped off. There were slashed scars on her face. Her eyes were tinged red and so were her lips. She was dressed in a white baby doll dress with a red corset that was too tight and pushed her tits out so it gave her the appearance she had some. On her cheeks were perfect red circles of blush.

"Phoebe, what happened to you?"

"What? You don't like the new look, Selena? Come on, I figured I would try it for you." Her friend moved closer to her and she caught the scent of decay. Selena backed away. Her foot hit something. When she looked down it was Rhianna's hand. She was buried under the bed. Selena looked back at Phoebe, but she was already gone. Hands closed around her shoulders and hot rank breath filled her ear.

"Come on, chicky. I know you want me! I've wanted you for a long time. Trevor and I used to argue over you for a long time. I wanted to fuck the both of you, but he wouldn't let me near you. He said you were all his. He was so selfish, don't you think?"

"Where's Donavan? How come you were able to get in here? They said—"

"What? That the big evil monsters couldn't get through the doorway because of the itty bitty protection symbols? Tsk tsk. Bad sorcerer. Bad witch," Phoebe said to her.

Selena hopped over the remains of the bed and looked out the window. What she saw mortified her. "Oh, my God!" Selena turned back around to face her friend.

"Surprise! Don't you like it?" Phoebe clapped her hands and jumped up and down.

"The Jester didn't just cross over. He crossed everything over. The whole carnival is here."

"How did you get so smart?" Phoebe tapped Selena on the nose. She tried to react, but her friend was gone again. Rage burned through Selena. She figured that Alexander and Rhianna had not presumed the demon would be powerful enough to break through the mirror again or bring his carnival over. They had assumed he could come over on some spell they read in that book. The book? Where was it? Selena had sensed the power in it. Both brothers said that was how the demon was summoned in the first place, by reading from the book. If the Jester had it then it was bad. She had to find the book, Alexander and then Donavan. First she had to get by her friend.

Selena looked around the room and realized there was no one. She tried to move the remains of the bed off Rhianna and was able to move a few things. Selena checked Rhianna's pulse. She seemed to be okay since there was no blood and she was breathing. It just appeared she was knocked out.

Selena had to venture into the carnival alone. She made her way to the door, still holding the candle, which was near the end of its wick.

When she got to the door, Phoebe was there staring at her with her eyes burning red. Fear moved through her and she felt the power inside of her spark to life around her hands.

"You're not going any where, love." Phoebe stepped into the room. Selena moved her hand back, but Phoebe caught it and shook her head. The smile on her lips curled into a devilish grin. "Shame. Trying to hurt your best friend. Why don't you give us a kiss and we can make up? I so want to gobble you up." Phoebe began pulling Selena into her and pursed her lips.

I'm so sorry. A jolt passed between them when their lips touched. Phoebe stopped and Selena dropped the candle so it snuffed out. However, the glow of the green carnival outside made her see Phoebe's eyes go from red to green. The expression on her face froze and she stopped, splitting apart into a thousand pieces. Selena raced down the hallway and downstairs. When she got to the door, she saw floating balloons like a lining on a walkway. Next to the tree by the field was a large banner suspended in the air. It read:

Circus Diabolique

The melody of the calliope blared, reminding her of a carousel. Horses were tethered to old fashioned wagons. Stages were set up along the sides of the circus and there was a large center stage, too. There was nothing going on in the center stage, but everyone was gathered around the stage awaiting a show to begin. Selena wondered what kind of show that was going to be. Quietly, she made her way between the balloons, expecting them to pop as she walked by, but they never did. It was hot outside and the smell of cotton candy choked her. Everything in her told her she was never going to look at the circus the same way again.

She passed underneath the banner and into the well-trodden field. Fear amped up her power. Donavan was close by, she only hoped he was okay. The demon said he had plans for her lover. Even Alexander was in danger. Both of them had known the demon longer than she had ever dreamed up. Alexander told her about the pact the two brothers had made with the demon. Souls for immortality and power.

They had delivered souls for years under the guise of a carnival, trapping them in the hall of mirrors, but when Selena looked around, she did not see the hall of mirrors. Rhianna said she had destroyed it when she had hurt the demon before and evidently the demon was not able to recreate it. Maybe that was a good thing. At least the souls trapped there had been released, but as Selena got closer and saw the hundreds still sitting and waiting on at the stage she knew all of these were still lost. Whatever it took, she would free them.

"Hurry, hurry, hurry. The show is about to begin. Come and see an amazing and horrifying site. For one night only see the death defying skills of the amazing Rosin twins."

Selena recognized the voice of the demon. It was amplified bouncing off the trees and drawing her attention. Selena held her breath while she wound her way through the carnival. Not all of its inhabitants were at the show. There was a skeleton dressed in a top hat and tails with a whip, flicking it at a woman who appeared to be half crocodile and half woman. Selena didn't see where the separation ended so she guessed it was the real thing. When she saw the lash marks on her back and the anguish on her face, she knew this was one of the souls who had given themselves over to the Jester to become a freak in his dark side show.

Meandering along, there was another wagon covered with shrunken heads, dried roots, finger and toe bones. A hunched over woman sat outside with a tattered green shawl covering her hair and shoulders. Next to her was a sandwich board sporting a palm with an eye in the middle of it and a crystal ball. On the table was a spread of tarot cards. When the old woman sensed Selena's interest, she looked up. Her face was smooth except for her two eyes, which were white and another, a third one, which was open. It was clear green and it blinked at her. Selena held in a shiver of disgust and kept on walking. The old women turned her head and pointed a finger at her.

As Selena made her way further into the dark circus, she came upon the calliope. It was set up on a wagon all by itself. Steam wafted out of its long pipes and the crank was slowly turning on its own. The music was off key and eerie.

As Selena continued to walk, she heard the screams of another lost soul. She looked over and saw a woman pinned to a twirling wheel with knives in her wrists and ankles. One of the Jesters' zombies was throwing more daggers at her while the wheel spun.

Selena finally came to the outskirts of the small stage. All the inhabitants on the benches turned and stared at her. Their expressions were empty and yet filled with wanting, waiting for her to go up on stage. Her eyes scanned the lot and her heart went out to them. The ghastly sight ignited her power. She swallowed and stared at the Jester.

She understood why Alexander and Donavan wanted to be free of the torment they had put themselves under. Selena would help free them and herself from the Jester. Looking at the seated audience, she understood the meaning of the sideshow. Dark carnival. Diabolic circus. Circus of the damned and the lost. She had almost been one of these souls.

My, my, my. We have a volunteer from the audience. Why don't you come up and join us? The Jester's smile widened. Hollow applause filled the air. She stared at the demon.

He was dressed in a white top hat and green tails over his harlequin suit. He was the parody of a circus ringmaster. Next to him on stage was Alexander. His head was down and his body slumped over. He was dressed in a red robe, and yet he was perfectly still. Even in the stillness, Selena sensed his power was building. Next to him Donavan was dressed in a black tunic and green tights. His arms were spread out and his wrists were limp. His head rested on his shoulder, showing the burned side of his face. His left wrist was moving. His eyes were closed. The brothers appeared to be living puppets waiting for someone to pull their strings.

Selena got to the stage. A hand was offered to her from the hag who had taken Phoebe. She looked normal, dressed in a black lacey high collared dress. Her brown hair was unbound around her shoulders and her eyes burned red. This was Rachel, Donavan's first wife, or at least her soul. She stared at the hand and then back at the Jester who waited patiently.

"You don't want to keep the audience waiting, do you?" Rachel purred. "Be a good little girl and come up on stage so everyone can see you!"

Selena took her hand and played along. The audience clapped again while Rachel brought her between the two brothers and had her stand next to the Jester. Selena spied the book off to the side of the stage. If she could get her hands on it maybe she could send the demon back to hell.

The Jester ran his bony fingers over her shoulder and she saw her clothing change into a diamond checkered green and white outfit that was identical to his. It was form fitting and low cut, showing the tops of her breasts. The only difference was she had a skirt to go over the tights. She even had the curly belled shoes to match. Her hair was curled in tight ringlets and fastened on top of her head with a comb.

We can't have you be part of the show if you're not dressed for the part, now can we? The Jester handed her a mirror. Selena gasped when she saw her reflection.

Her face was pale and gaunt. Her eyes were bright green like his and she could almost see the fire in them. Her lips were painted blood red to stand out against her white face. Her teeth were longer and sharper. Her fingernails were painted the same color as her eyes. Before she could do anything, the demon clasped her around the waist. She dropped the mirror and found his lips locked on hers. Instant orgasm and passion filled her soul. She tried to fight his grip, but there was nothing she could do. Everything about her wanted to be thrown against the stage and be fucked in front of the audience, in front of the man she loved.

Wouldn't that be a lovely sight, to see Donavan squirm? Her lips twisted in an evil smile while kissing the Jester harder.

Oh, Selena. Join me and we can rule the world. The Jester was winding around her brain, trying to strangle her will.

What do you want in return?

The Jester purred in her mind like a satisfied lion. *I'll let you keep your soul and your body, pretty one. I just want to fuck you. You're so delicious and your mind is almost as twisted as mine. I love it.*

I thought you wanted to kill me. Phoebe almost did me in. Besides, you're a demon. I thought demons couldn't love.

She felt the Jester's thoughts burn in anger. *She was not my creation. It seems Rachel is a little jealous. I've punished her, but if you desire we can easily take care of her.*

A scream filled the air. Selena looked up from the Jester's lips. Rachel was screaming in pain and horror from the green and black flames surrounding her. She pressed herself against the demon harder, showing her appreciation. His fingers dug into her ass while she wrapped one leg around his waist, pressing herself against the bulge in his suit. His will lessened some, but his power was still surging through her, making her moan against him. *Oh, God!*

Yes. I can be that for you, Selena. Give yourself to me and I'll give you anything you want.

Her mind slid to Donavan. Since she was fusing with the Jester she could feel Donavan's will. He was aware even though he was trapped. Fury and rage rolled through him as he knew what she was doing with the Jester. A sadness so profound also consumed him from her actions and Rachel's death. Alexander was struggling against the demon too, and he was winning because the Jester was distracted.

I'll stay with you. Let them go. If you want souls, I'll bring you souls. Each time I fuck someone you can have them. You can enter me and consume them through me. Then I'll be all yours. Selena ran her hand along his thick cock, slow and then fast, through the fabric. Her body craved for him to drive his shaft deep inside of her, but she had to hold onto her will. She had to play her cards right.

The Jester's nails dug furrows in her back, shredding the cloth. She didn't cry out, but moaned when his tongue licked the side of her neck. She closed her eyes, letting her power grow inside of her. The demon was playing with her thoughts, using her body for its own gratification as he manipulated her into another orgasm. She screamed, this time not able to contain herself.

Scream louder for me when I fuck you and I'll give you anything. You're such a whore. You know that, don't you? You know you want me to fuck the life from you, don't you?

"Yes!" It was true because part of her wanted that desperately. She needed the pain to make her remember she was alive. She was trying to remember Donavan and hoped he would understand. She felt along their connection and through him that he understood, and he was battling the demon's will too, and he was winning. Her distractions were working.

"You promised to let them go," she whispered aloud while the demon was sucking on her ear. His hands came around her front, tearing her suit so her breasts sprang free. He gripped them hard and stared deep into her eyes.

Give yourself to me first and I'll let them go free of my will.

"Swear it," she managed to say when the Jester held her body in a constant state of arousal. He had toned down his power, but every caress of air, of his fingers, was murder and she needed to be filled soon.

I'm not stupid, Selena. Did you really think I was going to fall for your little trick? Oh, you're good. And I will *have you replace Rachel. I'll let you keep your soul and you'll be my fuck toy. I'll make you enjoy it. Every tickle, every caress, you'll beg me for more and Donavan will be watching. What do you think of that?*

He pushed his will against hers, but this time she remembered what Trevor had said. Don't give into the evil. It was the only way to be free of the demon. Selena met the demon with her own power. It might have originated from him, but by claiming love and light she had turned it into her own. She pushed back against the Jester. He released her from the hold on her body, but he was not letting up on the onslaught of her will. He redoubled his efforts and Selena was cracking under the pressure of it. The pain in her head was magnifying and she tried to hold on, but he was beating her down mentally. She could feel the cracks in her power falling, failing. She was already on her knees and clutching her head.

You are no match for me. You really think I would swear to give up my two most valued prizes? I was willing to give you a chance, and you destroyed that. Do you know how many people I actually let keep their souls? Do you, bitch? Now you'll be like the rest of them and I'll eat you up. Once I'm free of this place I'll take the carnival on the road. I hear there are more magnificent circuses in this century. Imagine the souls I can get from just one of them. In time, I will be more powerful than your god and you'll wish you had been at my side. Time's up, Selena.

The demon drew the full force of his will down on her. However, the death blow she expected did not come. Instead, she felt a wall in her mind. When she looked up, she saw Alexander and Donavan staring at the Jester. She could see their combined power had wrapped around her to keep her safe. The demon looked at the twins and smiled. He pulled back his hand and threw a ball of red energy at them. Alexander dodged it, but did not break his hold.

Selena spied the book and made a dodge for it. When she was about to grab it, a hand got a hold of it before she did. When she looked up, it was Rhianna. She looked a little pale, but she smiled. She opened the book.

The demon must have sensed it because he spun around and stared at the both of them. The witch didn't look at him, but began reciting from the page. It didn't seem to affect the Jester, only pissed him off more. Selena looked at Donavan and saw the effort he was putting forth at trying to fight the demon so Rhianna could read a spell.

Selena looked out into the audience and was amazed to see the outskirts of the carnival did not seem so substantial anymore.

"It's working."

Not for long, The Jester turned his gaze on the both of them. The green flames in his eyes expanded and shot out at them. Selena jumped in front of Rhianna and felt the heat sear her flesh. She screamed in pain as the flames licked at her hair and her face, but even before they were any bigger they were gone. A blue bolt of energy hit the Jester in the back, causing him to stagger and stop the onslaught on her.

Rhianna kept re-reading the spell. The carnival had now receded to the outside of the stage. Even some of the inhabitants on the benches seemed to disappear. The demon was loosing his power even if he didn't want to admit it, but so were the brothers and so was Rhianna. Selena looked at the twins and sensed they were weary. She knew she had to act. She took a step forward and grabbed a hold of the demon's arms. He spun around and growled at her. She pulled him into her and planted her lips on his. He was overtaken by shock.

You have the power to kill them all. I want that kind of power. Take my soul, take whatever you want. She rubbed her hand along his dick and knew she had his attention.

Oh, Selena. You are such a whore. Batting for both teams. We will have so much fun. Stand aside and let daddy work then.

Selena kept rubbing him. Her gaze met Donavan's. He nodded, sensing what she was doing.

"Focus all of your power on Selena. Give it to her now!" he yelled to Alexander and Rhianna.

All of a sudden, Selena felt a blast of wind take her. Green and blue energies swirled and met inside of her. She grabbed the Jester's skull between her hands. She closed her eyes, feeling the rush of power pour out of her and into the Jester. The other three were chanting around her and she was not sure if she heard them in her head or in her mind, it was just the sheer high of the power. It curled her toes like no orgasm she ever had. She understood in that one second how the power could have been so seductive, why Alexander and Donavan had sold their souls for it, why anyone would sell their souls for it. Even though she wanted to bask in it, she knew she couldn't. The link she shared with Donavan was vibrating not only with the combined power of his brother and the witch, but with love. Selena grabbed a hold of that love and pushed it into the Jester through their close contact.

The demon was trying to get away, but this time she was the one who had an ironclad grip. His cries of pain sliced through her mind but she didn't let him go. She continued to kiss him and mold her body to his. He wanted to fuck her, but she showed him images of what true love was. It wasn't all about having sex. It was about trust, being together, understanding, loyalty, devotion, and feelings there were no words for. She poured all of this into him and he was not able to handle it. Finally, the demon shoved her away. When she looked up the other three had surrounded him. She joined in the circle and picked up the rhythm of the chant. The power lent to her had seared it into her consciousness along with other knowledge waiting for her to discover.

The Jester looked at her and put his hand to his head. A crack formed in the stage. The Jester was out of power. He was out of time. The demon was going back to his own dimension. Selena saw a white light appear in the night sky and shine directly on the Jester. A bolt of lightning hit the demon square in the chest. Suddenly, the light was gone and the demon was going up in white and blue flames. His screams filled Selena's ears and part of her was dying, too. However, she did not stop the chanting. She continued. She locked her eyes with Donavan and smiled. He returned the gesture. They kept on chanting until the fire died down and there was nothing left of the demon except a blackened bell button from his harlequin suit.

Chapter Nine

Selena stared at the twin and saw Donavan's face was completely healed. There was no mark from when he went into the fire years ago to save Rachel. She crossed the small space between them and ran her hand along his cheek. He smiled and kissed it in return.

"You're healed."

"Yup. Now he can't brag about being the handsomest of the both of us." Alexander patted his brother on the back.

Selena looked between the two of them and realized the only way to tell them apart now was from the color of their eyes. Donavan's were still green. Selena looked down at her hands and noticed her nails were still sharper, but when she ran her tongue over her teeth they had returned to normal. So had the color of her skin. She wondered about her hair.

"You are beautiful no matter what you look like." Donavan wrapped his arms around her waist and lifted her off her feet. He brought her down to meet her lips and gave her a long drawn out kiss. "I've been waiting to do that since the other night. We had fun, didn't we?"

Selena caught the gleam in his eyes and looked down, remembering all the wonderful things he had done to her. Her body needed to be reminded what it was like, but this time she had a few ideas of her own. She returned his gesture with a devilish smile. Her hand traced his crotch while she felt his cock respond to her caress.

"Maybe I don't want to play your games any more."

"You don't want me anymore?" The hurt in his voice made her heart skip a beat. He sounded so vulnerable.

She kissed him back harder, desperately. "I didn't say that. I want to play my own games this time, silly."

Donavan laughed. "Well, I guess I'll have to learn to play nice."

"Come on you two. Can we go back to the house, please?" Rhianna asked.

"Is it safe? I mean is the Jester really gone?" Selena asked.

She saw Donavan look at Alexander who took a moment and then nodded. "He is gone. The house and the land are clean. It's been over a hundred years and finally the land is pure again. Just like us, right brother?"

Selena saw Donavan eye the book Rhianna held. He unwound it from her grasp and took the book. "I think it's time we get rid of this once and for all. What do you say, Alexander? This way the demon can stay gone and no one will ever be able to summon it again."

His brother nodded. Both brothers formed balls of energy in their hands and together they threw it at the book. One minute it was there, and the next it was gone.

Peace and serenity washed over Selena and a sense of finality came into her being. It was over. She didn't have to worry about being haunted anymore. Trevor was at peace and her love for him would never die. Donavan had come into her heart, but did not replace that of her first husband. He only expanded on it. When she looked over at Rhianna, she saw the same peace come over her, too. Selena wondered what her encounter with the demon had been like. Maybe they could swap stories after time had gone by. It seemed they all were free.

Love encompassed her heart when she looked over at Donavan. She had come a long way from not being lost anymore and so had he. He had lived two centuries in another dimension to come to her and finally beat the demons in his soul. None of them were lost anymore. They had just been found.

"I want to go take a shower and, um, put some more clothes on. I don't think I ever want to hear anything about another circus in my life. Donavan, you want to join me?"

A wide smile spread across his features. "Do you really have to ask that?" He pulled off his shirt and draped it over her shoulders to cover up her exposed breasts. She licked her lips at the expanse of his chest. She had many wonderful ideas on what she was going to do with him. Her eyes trailed over Alexander and Rhianna. It was strange because she could feel the lust coming off of the both of them, too. It seemed a brush with death made anyone horny, or at least them.

She had an idea and whispered it in Donavan's ear. He pulled away from her for a second, almost shocked she had suggested it, but a delicious smile lit his features and he nodded. He looked over at Alexander and conveyed the thought to his brother. Selena figured he was the more conservative of the two. Alexander then nibbled Rhianna's ear. When he pulled away, Selena saw the suggestion move across her mind when she thought about it. The tension in the air was thick from wanting, but after a moment the witch moved to Selena and let her hand slide underneath the torn material and touch her breast. Selena's nipple hardened instantly.

"All you had to do was ask, Selena, but I think I'll watch. Alexander has been eyeing you since he first saw you in the shower at the hotel. I know Donavan won't mind sharing. They've done it before." Rhianna kissed her lightly. "But I think we all need to take a shower before anything happens. Don't you think so?"

Selena nodded and leaned into Donavan. Rhianna backed away and entwined her fingers with Alexander. The couple followed Alexander and Rhianna back into the house. Selena stopped at the door and noticed a single green balloon hovered by the doorway. She looked over at Donavan, who nodded. She reached out and touched the balloon. It popped in a burst of confetti and bells. She let out a small yip and flung herself into his arms. He smoothed her hair.

"It's just the demon's last word to make us jump. He has no more influence over us, I swear. I don't feel his weight on my soul anymore. And I have you to thank for that. Selena, I love you."

"Donavan, I did things with—"

He put a finger to her lips and shushed her. "It doesn't matter what happened or what you did. It's in the past. We all did things in our past we wish we never did, but we did them and we move on. I did horrible things. Maybe one day I will tell you what I actually did when I was possessed. But for now, I have other needs. And you did promise me." He leaned in and kissed her deeply. She blushed, crossed the threshold of the house, and when she did, she saw Phoebe lying on the floor.

"Oh my God, Phoebe. I thought she was dead." Selena glanced back to Donavan. He knelt by her and checked for a pulse.

"She'll be okay. The Jester's power didn't have an ironclad grip on her. When he destroyed Rachel, your friend's soul was released. Alexander, help me with her."

The other brother helped lift Phoebe up and they placed her on the futon. Selena went by her friend's side and ran a hand over her face, feeling relief flood her system. She had saved her after all. "What's the matter with her?"

"She'll sleep for the night and wake up feeling like she had an awful hangover, but she'll be okay," Alexander reassured her.

Selena brushed the hair away from her friend's face and kissed her lightly on the forehead. "Sleep well." She stood up knowing her friend would be okay and stared at Donavan who had lust in his eyes. She stuck her tongue out at him and made her way up to the shower. As she did, she stopped and stared at her reflection. Her eyes were still the same color they were. Her hair was bone white, but everything else about her was the same. She slipped out of the suit and promised herself she was going to burn it. She undid her hair and saw it was held up with an ivory comb carved with a C and a D intertwined together. Circus Diabolique. She put the comb in the basket and slipped under the water, letting it wash away the grime and dirt.

Once she was done, she wrapped a towel around herself to find the other three waiting in the bedroom for her. Alexander and Donavan were on the bed and Rhianna sat in a chair in the corner watching. It appeared nothing had ever happened. The only thing wrong with the picture was the mirror was gone. Her bed hadn't been that big before. It was a full and now it was appeared to be a king size. Donovan saw her look of confusion and laughed.

He got up and crossed to her. "Isn't magic wonderful?" He pressed his lips to hers and tugged at her towel. Selena slid her gaze to Rhianna who gave her a smile and nodded, giving her permission for this to happen. Alexander leaned his head back against the wall waiting. Selena grabbed Donavan's hand.

"Ladies first." She pushed him away and disrobed in front of Rhianna.

Selena set her knee on the bed between Alexander's legs. She leaned in and kissed the other man. His lips were soft, inviting, and eager to meet hers. Alexander was the mirror image of Donavan, but that didn't mean that they tasted the same or that they liked to be touched in the same manner. Her finger trailed up the inside of Alexander's legs. She felt a shiver of excitement move through him as her mouth moved from his lips and captured one of his nipples. She bit down gently. Her lover responded in kind and slid his fingers down to Selena's clit. She let out a moan of pleasure and pulled away from Alexander. Selena kissed the side of his neck and let her power flood through him. He arched his back and groaned. Selena felt the echo of it ripple through her too because of their connection. Next she ran her hand along his shaft in slow steady motions. Rhianna moaned in the background also feeling Alexander's pleasure through the shared link.

Selena felt Donavan's lips on her flesh, leaving hot trails of kisses and the hardness of his cock pushed into the small of her back. His hands wrapped around her waist and tickled up to her breasts, which he held gently thumbing her nipples. Alexander's rhythm increased on her clit. She arched her back and found herself pushing into Donavan.

"God, Alexander," Selena whispered. She opened her eyes to see blue energy encompassing the both of them. She could feel the buzz of it hovering on the outside of her mind. Alexander's passion was rocking her, too. Selena pumped her hand up and down, slow and then fast. Donavan wrapped his hands over Selena's breasts, squeezing the nipples hard, the way she liked it. She let her head fall back against Donavan's chest. Alexander's manipulations brought her higher and higher and when Donavan rubbed her nipples everything in her quaked. She turned her face to Donavan. His lips sucked on hers and his tongue probed her mouth. His kiss was hungry for her and yet gentle. She opened her eyes and saw the spark of green fire igniting in his.

He released her lips. Selena leaned in and kissed Alexander, letting her tongue explore his mouth. His hips bucked forward. Donavan was hard against her back, too. The power joining all of them was intense, burning her mind and theirs also. Selena felt Alexander's and his brother's needs. Donavan sent a jolt of energy crawling up her back sending Selena into an instant orgasm.

"Oh, fuck," she moaned. "More. Please more."

The power was overwhelming and kept cycling through them all, and Selena wasn't sure after awhile where she began or ended. It was like having their minds meld together.

Alexander's teeth nipped at her lips.

Selena, now. Please now. Donavan begged her in his mind. He wanted to feel his dick plunging inside of her. Alexander freed her lips while Donavan parted her legs from behind. Alexander bit down on Selena's lips, drawing blood, but the pain sent her into another orgasm as Donavan slid his cock deep inside her pussy. She broke the kiss then and focused on setting a rhythm with Donavan. His hands grabbed her hips hard to control their pace. Selena hung her head down and took Alexander's cock into her mouth. Every time Donavan pushed into her, she went down on Alexander's dick, taking more of it into her mouth and swirling her tongue around the shaft.

Selena tried to keep herself focused on just Donavan, but it was hard because the pleasure gripping her was so intense. Donavan was creating a rhythm that was hard to keep up with, banging into her so every time his dick buried inside her pussy, she wanted another pounding. Through their combined power they were wrapping their bonds closer. Their instincts were weaving together. Selena tasted the first drops of pre-cum on her tongue from Alexander. Selena sensed something magical was going to come out of this, but she didn't know what.

"Selena, take all of me, baby," Alexander mumbled.

Selena increased her pace on his cock, pulling him in and out of her mouth. Donavan gripped her hips harder. Inside her mind, Selena saw their combined energies building to a climax. All at once, she felt and saw it collapse. Donavan released inside of her and she came, while Alexander ejaculated and she swallowed his sweet seed.

After a few moments, Donavan removed himself and let her catch her breath. When she looked up, he was smiling. Rhianna sauntered over from the chair and pulled the covers down. She patted the other side of the bed and winked at Selena. Selena looked at both Alexander and Donavan who had devilish grins on their faces. Selena punched Donavan lightly in the chest, knowing the brothers were saying something about the two women. He didn't respond, but pushed her gently toward the bed. After a moment, she slipped in between the covers and Rhianna ran her hand over Selena's breast. Donavan crawled into the bed behind Selena. She could feel he was already hard again.

"I think we might have created a monster," Alexander said to Donavan.

Donavan kissed Selena's neck. "Naw. I think we unleashed one. What do you say brother, you up for another round?"

Alexander's fingers played with Rhianna's nipple.

"Only if the ladies are."

"I never thought you'd ask," the witch asked.

"Guys, I don't know about you, but if it doesn't involve carnivals, circuses, zombies, or jesters, I'm up for just about anything."

All four of them paused and bust into laughter. This was the start of something she was never going to forget. No matter what happened between them, she would always have Donavan. She stretched out her new found power and touched his mind.

I love you.

He smiled in her thoughts while his fingers traced her shoulder blade. *I love you, too. Now and forever.*

Selena nodded as she felt Rhianna's mouth on her breast. Yes, now and forever. That was the way love was supposed to be. And she had it. She wasn't lost anymore, on the contrary, she had been found.

THE END

WWW.RAVYNHART.COM

ABOUT THE AUTHOR

Crymsyn Hart's worlds are filled with luscious vampires, gorgeous gods, quirky witches, and brooding shifters.

Crymsyn is a psychic who, for many years, worked in Boston while attending Emerson College. She graduated with a degree in Creative Writing. When she gets bored, she sneaks away to local cemeteries and coffee shops to find peace and quiet. Crymsyn shares her life with a small zoo including two playful puppies and her hubby, Mark.

Siren Publishing, Inc.
www.SirenPublishing.com